UNWANTED
TRILOGY

BOOK ONE

The Unwanted

DANIEL L. CARTER

OAKTARA

WATERFORD, VIRGINIA

The Unwanted

Published in the U.S. by:
OakTara Publishers
P.O. Box 8
Waterford, VA 20197

Visit OakTara **at**
www.oaktara.com

Cover design by Muses9 Design
Cover images © iStockphoto.com/cloaked man, Alexey05; plaque,
Yargin; wood, poiremolle; black background, Günay Mutlu

Author photo © 2010 by Daniel L. Carter

ISBN: 978-1-60290-223-7

TO MY WIFE, MARGO,
AND TO JESUS CHRIST

Both of whom are the loves of my life.

I would have given up on writing a long time ago
if it had not been for them.

Acknowledgments

I'd like to thank a couple folks who have had a big impact on me:

Randy Johnson, who gave me the encouragement to keep writing and taught me a lot about the publishing business.

Pastor Wayne Hedlund, who was blunt enough to tell me the truth about my writing, helping me grow and learn.

OakTara, for having the faith to publish my story. I am truly grateful.

One

Nightclub

Nick slipped two one-hundred-dollar bills into the doorman's hand as he cautiously entered. The nightclub crowd was in full party mode. Men and women engaging each other rhythmically on the dance floor, along with the thumping bass of the live band, made it difficult for Nick to concentrate. Purposefully he adjusted his three-thousand-dollar suit and took a deep breath to calm himself. His jacket felt tight around his shoulders; he wished he'd taken more time with the tailor. But he pushed those thoughts aside. He had to stay focused on the meeting he was having tonight. It was too important to screw up.

He made his way toward the bar, ignoring the women smiling in his direction. He thought it would have been nice if this was a social meeting, but it wasn't. Fun and socializing were not options tonight.

With a wave of his arm Nick got the bartender's attention and asked, "I'm looking for a Damon Hannah."

"Who's asking?"

With one fluid motion Nick slid a one-hundred-dollar bill toward the bartender. Nick locked glances with the man and didn't say anything. Pointing to the back of the club, the bartender took the money and walked away. Nick could see the booths in the back. Again he adjusted his suit, only to be met with the sensation of someone running their hand through his hair.

"Where you goin', you dark hunk of meat?"

He turned around and looked into the face of a beautiful young woman who was very drunk.

"Nice watch, handsome. Vacheron Constantin, right?"

Any other time this would have been a welcome diversion, but not tonight.

"Yes, thanks for noticing. I'm sorry, miss, but I can't stay and talk." He politely pulled the woman's hand out of his hair and walked away.

"Jerk."

Ignoring the woman's comment, Nick weaved through the crowd and headed to the back of the club. He could see Damon sitting in a private booth with two large bodyguards standing nearby. Taking another deep breath, Nick approached. Just as he expected, the larger of the two muscle-bound guards stepped in front of him. Nick knew he was no slouch at 6' 2", but he felt small as he looked up into the man's face.

"I think you're lost, pal."

Nick smiled politely at the bodyguard. "Tell your boss Mr. Prospero is here."

"It's all right. Let him through," Damon ordered. "Please sit down, Mr. Prospero. I have to ask, are you a Poe fan?"

Nick cautiously sat across from Damon. "Not really, but I hear you are. I thought you would appreciate it."

"Nice. Do you know the story of Prince Prospero?" Damon's crooked smile made Nick feel like he was some sort of prey.

"Not really."

"The story tells of a prince who thought he could escape death and ignore his own sickness. He believed the Red Death couldn't touch him. In the end he died." Damon took a sip from his wine glass. Nick wasn't sure if he should say something in response, but Damon continued. "The moral being that pride comes before a fall. I hope you're not such a person."

Nick was glad to let Damon do all the talking. It gave him a chance to size up who he was dealing with. Damon wore a nice suit adorned with expensive chains and several diamond-studded rings that he clearly liked to flaunt. His pale complexion and wrinkles were most likely due to working at night and taking too many drugs. Even though Damon spoke like an educated man, his mannerisms told Nick he was a low-level soldier and not the one in charge.

2

"That's a lesson we can all learn from, Mr. Hannah."

Damon chuckled at his response and said to his bodyguards, "Mr. Hannah. I like this guy already. He knows how to show respect. So how can I help you, Mr. Prospero?"

Nick wasn't sure if there was a hint of sarcasm in Damon's question.

"I believe you are in the market for some high-end medical equipment, or so I was led to believe."

"Go on. I'm listening."

Nick reached slowly for the list inside his jacket so as not to alarm the bodyguards. He slowly slid the list across the table to Damon. This was going to be a complicated transaction, and he didn't want to start trouble. Yet.

"I also have in my possession an ABI PRISM 310 Genetic Analyzer. Interested?" Nick waited to see what kind of reaction he would get.

Damon tapped his PDA with his pointer and leaned back in the booth. It was hard to see Damon's face in the shadows. *Who is Damon selling to? Why does he want DNA equipment?* For now Nick could speculate, and Damon was his only connection to those answers.

After several seconds Damon leaned forward. "I believe we can do business, Mr. Prospero. I'd need to see that all of the equipment is working before we can talk price."

Something was wrong. Everything was going entirely too easy. Nick expected questions about where he acquired the equipment, and the lack of mistrust was setting off internal alarms. Any street thug would have patted him down for weapons before he was allowed to sit down and talk. Also, the lack of female companionship was a sure sign that Damon was all about business tonight. Nick knew there was no genuine intention of purchasing any of the equipment, but that left one question unanswered: *What does Damon have planned?*

"Perfect, Mr. Hannah," Nick said. "If you'd like, I can take you to my warehouse, where you can examine the merchandise."

"Let's go."

The deadness in Damon's eyes as he rose from the booth answered Nick's question. It was a look he had seen before—*murder.* He hurried to follow behind Damon as the two bodyguards took up the rear.

"My car is just around the corner out the front. We..." Nick tried to stop and redirect Damon, but he was met with a stiff shove in his back followed by one of the bodyguard's hands latching onto his right shoulder. He knew this was not a good sign. Damon led the way through the crowds and headed toward the back exit hallway. Nick's life was on the line. If he were going to survive the night, he would need to do something—and quickly. Sweat poured down Nick's face as his heart rate accelerated in his chest. He tried to wipe his brow, but another large hand clamped onto his left forearm.

Nick's breathing was becoming more rapid. Immediately he forced himself to take deeper breaths. He couldn't afford to panic or be distracted. What he needed was an advantage, and finally it came.

As Damon led the way down the back hallway past the restrooms, the second bodyguard stepped in front of him. It was now or never. Nick watched as the bodyguard in front of him turned his attention toward Damon. He attacked. With all his weight on one leg Nick kicked backwards with his other foot and hit its target. His escort's right kneecap bent unnaturally. Nick could feel the give of the bone from his kick as the bodyguard yelled out in pain and released him.

Immediately he spun around and landed a right fist across the now-kneeling bodyguard's jaw and sent him to the floor, unconscious. The other bodyguard grabbed for his pistol. Again Nick attacked. Without forethought he jabbed his right hand into his attacker's throat. The man dropped his gun and gasped for air. Nick had to finish him off before Damon turned around. He kicked the bodyguard in the groin and double-fisted the man's back, forcing him motionless to the floor.

Trying to focus on what to do next, Nick looked up to see Damon finally turn and face him. There was a brief shocked expression, but it was gone in a blink of an eye. Damon reached for his gun underneath his black blazer just as a young brunette came out of the ladies' room. Nick leaped forward and tackled the woman back through the ladies' room entrance. Bullets buzzed past his head. The woman screamed. It seemed to happen all in slow motion, but Nick forced himself to his feet. He could hear the screams of the nightclub members replacing the now-silent band.

Nick stood just inside the ladies' room, cursing himself for not grabbing one of the bodyguards' pistols. After a few seconds he cautiously peered into the hallway. The exit door was latched. Beyond it a motorcycle sputtered, stalled, then sputtered again. Correcting his earlier mistake, Nick grabbed the gun from the nearest bodyguard and ran toward the back exit. He slammed open the door with the gun pointed in the direction of the motorcycle engine, but he was too late. Damon raced down the alleyway on a blood-red motorcycle.

Tires screeched as a black van halted behind him. He jumped into the passenger side. "Where were you?"

The driver, Allen, glanced over. "We couldn't hear you over the noise. You knew that was going to happen, Nick. Or should I call you 'Prospero'?"

Nick pulled off his Armani jacket. "I was nearly shot! Do you have a bead on him?"

"Sorry. Yes. He's heading eastbound on West Kinzie Street just past North Clark."

Nick sometimes wondered about his team member, Allen Young. They were good friends, and Allen seemed steady, but Nick often found his humor inappropriate; this was one of those times. Nick used the van radio and called all local units to pursue the subject as he put his gun holster on. The motorcycle wove in and out of traffic as Damon ran a red light and nearly caused an accident. They couldn't lose him. They had spent months setting up this sting, and Damon was their only lead. Yet Damon moved further away.

Nick spoke again into the radio. "Suspect is heading northbound on North Rush Street," he said and turned on their pursuit light in the front windshield, hoping for something to go their way. They made the turn to follow the motorcycle. The police had blocked off East Grand Street as their lights flashed two blocks away. Oddly, Damon stopped in the middle of traffic and was looking back at them. Allen floored the gas once again as Damon spun his tire and headed east on East Illinois Avenue away from the roadblock. Was Damon taunting them? Whatever he was doing, it gave them a chance to catch up.

Nick grinned as two Chicago police cars joined the chase behind them. After four blocks of pursuit, Damon began to slow down. Damon didn't have much further to run as they approached Lake Michigan. Nick called all units to block off the exits of the pier immediately. They had him trapped. The road ended at a circle that led to East Navy Pier Street, which was a dead end overlooking the lake.

"Hurry, Allen, before he finds a way out."

Allen shot him an agitated look. Nick didn't care. They couldn't let Damon escape. Allen turned, following Damon into a parking garage. With great agility Damon slid the motorcycle on its side underneath the entrance railing, then propped himself back up without stopping his momentum. Allen broke through the entrance railing and followed Damon. He was trapped. Nick watched as Damon sped upward to the roof. There was no way out now. Nick's mouth dropped at what he saw. On the far end of the roof the motorcycle lay on its side. Damon strapped into a glider and leapt from the building.

Jumping out of the van, Nick watched from the roof edge. Damon glided out over Lake Michigan, along with any hope of capturing him. Clearly he had planned this from the beginning. Nick shouted out in frustration, "You've got to be kidding me!"

"Sorry, Nick." Allen put his hand on his shoulder. "He's probably going to land somewhere out in the middle of the lake, where a boat is waiting for him. I should call in the Coast Guard and have them begin searching."

Nick replied, "Yeah, do that," but he knew by the time they got in touch with the Coast Guard, Damon would be long gone.

An explosion shattered the night sky behind them. Smoke and flames shot in every direction. Allen and Nick ducked down instinctively. Nick's stomach ached as he watched the smoke from the explosion begin to blow over Chicago.

"Not again," he whispered.

Nick replayed the evening in his head as they drove to the explosion site. Something had tipped Damon off that he was an FBI agent. He didn't want to consider just yet that it may be a "someone," but tonight made him feel even more uncomfortable. Damon wanted them on that roof to witness the explosion. That much was certain. The more Nick thought about it, the more upset he became. Whoever was behind this was playing games with him and the Bureau.

Nick watched from a distance for a couple of hours as fireman fought back the flames coming from the building. The scene was chaos. Crowds of onlookers and every news crew in the city stood at the barricades fighting to get a better look.

"We've discovered several bodies so far in the fire," the police chief reported.

Just like the other two times. Nick asked, "How many of them were babies?"

Shooting a stunned look at Nick, the police chief replied, "At least three so far. How did—"

"Keep searching. There'll be five, Chief, and at least ten or more adults. Always."

Nick let out a sigh and walked away before anything more could be said. He was disgusted with himself. He felt like a failure. This was the third mass murder in just over twenty months, and they were still in the dark as to who was behind it. Their only lead was somewhere over the middle of Lake Michigan.

He ordered Allen to get forensics on the scene as soon as possible. He wasn't looking forward to reporting the day's events. On his way back to the hotel Nick played the night over and over in his head. Crimes like this gave him nightmares.

Two

Escape

July 17, 2007
Poughkeepsie, NY
Fourteen months after the Chicago murders

Once again Janet Renard found herself hitting the hard pavement and, for a moment, breathing eluded her. Several deafening explosions rocked the ground underneath her as section by section the building behind her spewed out debris in every direction. Finally Janet inhaled sharply, then coughed from the thick smoke in the air. The almost-paralyzing pain in her ribs made it even more difficult for her to take another breath, but survival outweighed her physical state. *The Jeep™.* The Jeep™ was only a few feet away. *But the pain. No, forget the pain. Get to the Jeep™!*

Ignoring her pain, Janet jumped into the driver's seat and slammed the door shut. Another explosion from the building caused her to instinctively scream as debris crashed against the window. Screeching the tires, she pulled away as fast as she could. She watched in her rearview mirrors as several more explosions rocked the facility. Like a dam bursting, she wept. She tried to stop, but the torrent of emotions was beyond control.

The crying of the five infants lying helpless in the backseat only added to the hysteria. Before she even knew where they were or how they had gotten there she parked the car in the back of a nearby McDonald's. She needed to check on the children, but the pain in her side made her examine herself first. Now that the adrenaline had worn off, she became aware of her injuries.

There were several cuts on her hands and arms and a couple of

8

gashes that probably should have stitches. Sharp knife pains on the left side of her chest told her she had at least one broken rib, probably more. Using the mirror on the back of the sun visor, she examined her face. One very deep cut over her left eye had been bleeding but was now clotted. She'd have a scar for life, but at least she was alive. Her long strawberry hair hung limply, and she was covered in gray soot from the building. She tried to wipe the tear streaks from her filthy cheeks. Another wave of emotions involuntarily consumed her. She pushed up the visor and sobbed once again.

Why me? Why is this happening? It had been two years since her husband had died, and all she'd wanted to do was run away from the pain. Now she was running again, but this time it included five innocent children, and their lives were at stake.

A hand grabbed her shoulder. Janet screamed. The babies cried louder as she looked at the backseat. Her friend Michele had regained consciousness. Holding her head in both hands, Michele asked, "How did we get here? Oh, my head."

"We need to check them for injuries," Janet said as she gently got out of the Jeep™.

Michele helped her hold the babies and examine each of them. Both she and Michele were surprised that the only injuries the infants had were minor cuts and bruises. Michele, on the other hand, had two broken fingers on her left hand and most likely cracked ribs and a concussion. Janet knew she had better keep an eye on Michele just in case things got more serious.

With a shaky voice Janet said, "We need to go to the police right away."

Michele pointed at the bottom of the dashboard. "I don't think that's such a good idea."

Janet followed Michele's finger. A police badge lay in the ashtray. The realization that they were sitting in a stolen police vehicle dashed all hope Janet had left. They couldn't go to the police or the FBI, given what they had overheard earlier, and they didn't have either of their purses with them. To add to the dread, Janet didn't know if anyone would be coming after them or not, so going back to either of their apartments didn't seem like a smart idea.

9

Michele interrupted her thoughts. "We need to ditch this Jeep™ right away."

Janet's mind took a moment to catch up to her friend. Reluctantly she said, "I know where we can hide."

"I have a cousin in Newburgh who can take care of the car and get us some cash. Where did you have in mind?"

Janet hesitated again. "My uncle has a place where we can stay, but we're going to need supplies for a couple of days for these babies." She didn't want to tell Michele that, besides the memory of her dead husband, her Uncle Leigh was the reason she had moved away from Oklahoma. Now her past was catching up.

"Won't they check your uncle's place?" Michele asked.

"We won't be staying at his house. Don't worry. No one will find us where we'll be." But Janet was unable to let Michele's comment go without an inquiry. "What does your cousin do?"

"He runs a chop shop on South Street." Michele grinned, despite the pain. "And don't look at me like that. It's not like we've got a lot of options. Besides, we can easily get a few hundred for this fine piece of machinery—and a replacement."

Janet shook her head, but Michele's idea was their only option. She suggested they take turns going to the restroom with the babies and cleaning up their wounds before heading over to Newburgh. The day ahead of them was going to be rough; traveling with five infants and not knowing if someone was after them made it even more stressful. In the back of Janet's mind she knew if they could get to her uncle, they would be safe. Or, at least, she hoped they would.

Three

Mistake

T he sight was getting old to Nick. He stood with Allen several yards from the burned-down building as the fireman finished putting away their equipment. Nick was disgusted. If his team had gotten on the scene just a few hours earlier, they may have been able to prevent this from happening again. It felt personal. A part of him always felt responsible for each of the victims' deaths. And the children—why children? He knew he needed to stay objective; that was the job, and he did it better than most. But pride was on the line with this case—along with something more he couldn't express.

Having grown up a single child of an Irish mother and an Algerian father, Nick had been forced to overcome prejudices and fears that most of his coworkers had never faced. Being a light-skinned black man meant facing prejudices on both social fronts, black and white. He had no crowd to belong to. He took a deep breath. That was part of what made him a stronger person and propelled him to overcome obstacles. Because of this motivation, he had landed the team leader position with the FBI before he reached thirty. Nothing was going to stand in his way of solving this case.

A picture of his ex-wife Rebecca's face flashed through his thoughts. His heart raced slightly. There was a downside to his motivation. Having to always succeed had cost him dearly. Why he put her through the torture of being married to him was still a puzzle. It only lasted a little over two years, and quitting was not something that came easily to him. In the end she left him—no, he gave her no choice. The job always came first, and after Rebecca miscarried, their relationship became nonexistent.

The feelings of losing their child once again rose to the surface of his emotional barriers. It was his fault. The stress of their marriage falling apart had been too much for Rebecca. Although she had never verbalized it, he knew she blamed him. Why not? He did, too.

A revelation struck him. That's what was bothering him about these murders—the children. It wouldn't take away the guilt, but maybe he could atone for it.

Allen leaned close to Nick and said quietly, "If I didn't know any better, I'd say they knew we were coming...again."

Nick snapped out of his thoughts and replayed Allen's words in his head. It was the first time either of them had verbalized what was becoming obvious. There was a leak within the Bureau. Nick knew they must have been very close this time, because the crime scene looked much different than the other two. First, the parking lot was full of vehicles.

There weren't any cars or trucks at the other crime scenes— nothing to tell them who was involved or might be a potential witness, making it more difficult to identify the victims. Whoever was responsible for these killings was in a big hurry to leave, which boded well for catching this psychopath. Also, both previous buildings had a concentrated, controlled fire centered on the victims. This one was different. Not all of the bodies were burned as severely as the others. Something prevented them from being consumed by the flames, leaving more evidence.

Nick watched as Sam made her way from the wreckage. Agent Samantha Coles was part of Nick's team and one of the smartest women he had ever known. She was only twenty-eight, but her demeanor gave the impression of someone much older. Nick couldn't understand how she could be married with two children and still do the job she was doing. The job had already cost him his wife and kid.

"What'd you find out?"

Samantha asked, "Do you want the good news or the bad news first?"

12

Optimistically he answered, "There's good news this time? Great, give me the good."

"We found twenty-four bodies so far, but none were children."

Nick gave a sigh of relief. "What else?"

She smiled. "We also found several pieces of medical equipment intact, multiple fingerprints throughout the wreckage, and those—" Samantha gestured toward the parked vehicles covered in ash and debris.

Nick pushed the issue. "That's it?"

"So far."

"All right. What's the bad news?"

"Like I said, there are twenty-four bodies so far. We've identified one already."

By her expression, he could tell he wouldn't like what she had to say next.

"That doesn't sound like bad news to me, Sam. Who is it?"

Samantha took a deep breath. "The body was a male in his early thirties, and we found his wallet still in his pants."

"Just tell me."

"His name's Frank Scarnado."

He sighed. "That means what to me, Sam?"

"*Officer* Frank Scarnado."

A police officer may be involved in these killings. Great.

Nick shot Allen and Samantha a look. "Don't say anything to anyone about this. I don't want this leaking to the press before we know exactly what's going on, or I'll have someone's head. Is that understood?"

Both nodded.

Nick ordered, "Allen, you and Jason search those vehicles and have them all dusted for prints. I want to know everything about who worked here, what they were doing, and if their body isn't in this wreckage, I want to know where they are. Sam, work with forensics to help identify the bodies. We've got a lot to do."

Nick's team set up in Albany's headquarters so they could process the crime scene. They had almost nothing to go on with the previous murders, but now there was an overwhelming amount of evidence to sift through. The fingerprints were being processed and already there were two hits in IAFIS. The team met in one of the conference rooms.

Allen started off by reading his findings. "Our first hit was a woman by the name of Elizabeth Anne Mitchel, originally from Morristown, New Jersey." Allen handed out her mug shot for everyone to see. He continued, saying, "At the age of twelve she was in the foster care system and soon had a rap sheet ranging from petty theft to drugs and prostitution. When she was seventeen she graduated to murder—manslaughter, to be precise—and was sent to a high-security woman's facility. At the age of twenty-one in 2000 she was released and moved to Sussex. She fell off the radar two years later, according to her parole officer."

Samantha interjected, "Sounds like an upstanding citizen."

Nick could tell Jason had something to say so he nodded in his direction. Jason was the fourth member of their team, and Nick liked his laidback demeanor. However, having spent several years with the Bronx police, Jason was no pushover.

"I checked to see who owned the place," Jason said. "It's an extension of Saint Frances Hospital, but they closed it down a year ago. They claim to know nothing about what was happening in the place. I suggest we check the employee records for anyone named Elizabeth or Liz in the past year. I'm sure she didn't use her real name, but maybe a variation."

Nick nodded in agreement.

Allen tossed another photo onto the table. This one was of a pre-teen adolescent boy wearing a graduation uniform. "This is Tibon Agha, son of a United States ambassador to Jordan. Luckily for us, the entire family's prints are on file. Son of Jaleel and Durrdana, he was a child prodigy. IQ was off the charts. In 1987, at the age of twelve, Tibon graduated from a private high school. This is where it gets interesting. His family went on vacation after his graduation in Amman, Jordan, to visit relatives, only to be blown up in a freak car accident outside of the American Embassy. Guess who the only survivor was?"

Samantha answered, "Tibon."

Allen waved his hand in her direction. "Give that woman a prize. He was, however, paralyzed in his legs from a piece of metal that had nicked his spine. When he finally returned to the States, Tibon went to college at MIT and graduated at the top of his class. His major: biology and bioengineering. He was only seventeen when he got his doctorate. Unfortunately, that is all we have on him. Right after he graduated, he sold all of his family's estate and dropped out of sight. No one has seen him since. He should be about thirty-four now."

Allen finished and Nick closed the file in front of him. Turning toward Samantha, he said, "I want you to look up Tibon's old college friends and classmates. See what you can dig up on him. Someone has to know where he is. Follow up with the State Department and find out what hospital he was treated at. I want to know why his prints are at our crime scene."

"Jason, you need to follow up on the hospital and get me a list of all the employees who left in the last year. According to the registrations on the vehicles, several of the cars were registered to nurses. They're probably recruiting from within, like the last two murders."

Nick stood. "Allen, keep following up on the backgrounds of all the car owners. You know the drill." Nick hesitated, then walked over to the door and closed it. He turned to face all three members of his team and took a deliberate breath before speaking.

"What I'm about to ask of you is not to leave this room or to be discussed with anyone outside this room. If you're not comfortable with that, please leave now." Nick waited a couple of seconds. Just as he figured, his team was with him as they sat quietly waiting for what he was about to say. "Good. It has become painfully clear that whoever is responsible for these murders has inside information that can only be leaked from within the Bureau. This sicko has been one step in front of us from the beginning, and finding out an officer was involved tells me we can't trust anyone other than each other.

"Sam, I want you to make a list of all agents who had anything to do with this case. Start looking for any connections with past assignments they may have had with any of our known suspects. Do as much of a background check as you can, but keep it under the radar.

Jason, while you're at the hospital, check for anything or anyone from Poughkeepsie or the Hudson Valley area who would be linked to the Bureau. Family, friends...anyone who knew them. Does anyone have a problem with what I'm asking you to do?"

Nick looked each of them directly in the eyes. They were with him. "Good. I'm going to go meet with our professor from Columbia University, then the coroner. We have four IDs left unaccounted for and two unidentified cadavers. That means there are two possible witnesses out there. Let's go."

Nick walked into the evidence room where all of the computer parts that had been found at the crime scene were being kept. At the far end of the room sat a short dark-haired man with his back to Nick. The noise of typing on the computer told Nick his presence had been undetected. He cleared his throat in hopes of not startling the man, but still the typing continued.

Nick walked across the room to see what was so intriguing that it outweighed recognition of his existence. On the computer screen were several mathematical symbols and pictures of what he thought were DNA strands, but none of it made any sense to him.

The man continued to ignore Nick as he intermittently let out a "Hmm," and an "Oh, my."

Nick cleared his throat once again, only this time with a more aggressive sound. Finally the man stopped typing and jumped slightly as he turned to realize someone was standing right behind him.

"Thank you for coming, Dr. Yamugi. I'm Agent Nick Catlin."

The middle-aged Japanese man let out a nervous laugh as he replied, "So sorry. I...I...got caught up with what you have found...most fascinating, really. I was particularly interested in the—"

Nick cut Dr. Yamugi short. "Great, I see you've had some time to look at the computers we found."

"Why yes." The doctor seemed confused by the declaration of the obvious.

"Let's sit for a moment, shall we?" Nick pulled up a rolling seat.

"On behalf of the FBI, I'd like to thank you for coming on such short notice. When our technicians realized the type of technology we were dealing with in these computers, your name was on the top of our list."

Dr. Yamugi had a hard time keeping eye contact with Nick. He seemed uncomfortable with formalities and probably would have rather been looking at the computer than Nick.

"So, Doctor, what have you found out so far?"

Concern flickered in the doctor's eyes. "Well," he said, while at the same time looking at the ceiling, "to be completely frank with you, Agent Catlin, I'm dumbfounded."

"What do you mean? You couldn't find anything?"

"No, it's not that. Quite the opposite, actually."

Nick took a deep breath. "Please, whatever you did find, tell me."

"Well, it's clear that whatever this equipment was being used for has something to do with genetic manipulation or research."

"I know this already, Doctor," Nick said, holding his sarcasm to a minimum. "What I need to know is if you can give me more specifics."

"Yes, well, what I was going to add is that the modifications to the equipment are beyond anything I have ever seen before. I doubt anyone's ever seen the type of technology that you have recovered. Not anyone in the known world of science."

Now Nick was becoming interested. "How so?"

The doctor sat upright and stared at the ceiling as he formulated the thoughts in his head. "Where do I begin? The program on this computer has been modified to separate out sequences of a human's genetic code in ways that have never been thought of, let alone attempted. In fact—"

Nick hurried the doctor along. "I've heard many stories in the news and television of genetic manipulation before. Why is this different?"

The doctor became more animated, moving his hands in front of him. "You see, the genetic code is a set of rules by which information encoded in genetic material are translated into—"

"Stop." Nick didn't want to offend the doctor, but he needed answers now. "Give me the bottom line and in laymen's terms, please."

"Right. Sorry. The program on the computer that was recovered, if you have the knowledge, can be used to specify lines of DNA in a human and rewrite them. Imagine, if you will, changing your eye color or reversing your baldness. Let's go one step further. What if you wanted a better singing voice or to be taller? Even better, what if I wanted to be stronger, faster, more intelligent? The kind of genetic sequencing that this program does is so advanced that almost anything can be changed about a human being."

Nick didn't know what to say at first. "So what you're saying is that you could use this program to change, or say, *create,* a human being in whatever image you want? Like a 'God program'?"

The doctor tilted his head in a gesture of hesitation. "Yes and no. Like I said—*if* you have the knowledge. The program will create any genetic sequence you want and will target any part of the genetic code you want, but you must tell it where to look and what to change. The scientific community is not even close to understanding human DNA in the way this program is meant to work. The person using the program would have to have intimate, specific knowledge of which codes to change. In other words, the program is only as useful as the knowledge of the one using it. Whoever was using this program is beyond any genius you or I could imagine."

Nick replied, "I see. Let's say I am such a person and am able to create humans in any way I deem fit."

The doctor excitedly jumped in before Nick could finish his thought. "The problems that would arise from making any major changes to the genetic code would cause all sorts of physical and mental problems with the subjects in question. It would take literally thousands—possibly hundreds of thousands—of experiments before you got one viable subject who didn't have some sort of defect or mental disability. Not even with the intelligence level we are talking about can someone alter another human being's DNA and get it right the first time. There are just too many variables to consider and even then I doubt anyone could be successful."

The more Nick listened, the more disgusted he was becoming. "Is there anything more, Doctor?"

"I won't know until I've had more time to study the data on the computers."

Nick thanked the doctor and left. Finding the person responsible for these deaths had just become even more important to him. The case was no longer just about a murderer. The thought of creating children to experiment on them was on the same level as the Nazis, and Nick was even more determined to find whoever was responsible. He wished his father were still alive. He would know just what to say or do to cope with something so evil.

Four

Vengeance

Summer 1982
Amman, Jordan

The heat was almost unbearable to Tibon. Having grown up in New York State made it tough to deal with the summer temperatures in Amman, Jordan. Tibon had wanted to stay home, but his family went to visit their relatives every summer religiously. He had just graduated high school at the age of twelve and his parents wanted to throw a party for him with all their relatives in Amman. The sweat dripped down the sides of his face as he waited outside the embassy for his parents to get finished with their paperwork to enter the country. Despite the heat, he kept busy playing soccer in the courtyard with his two older brothers to pass the time.

Finally, after over an hour, his parents came out. His mother gestured for them to follow. Their diplomatic car was waiting just outside the embassy gate. He was in no hurry as he took up the rear. All the while he bounced the soccer ball on his feet. Tibon resented having to come to a country that he didn't feel was his home. What he wanted was to be back in the States with his friends. His brothers were already in the car as his mother yelled for him to hurry. It was just enough distraction for him to drop the ball.

"Hurry, now. Get your ball. We're already late," his mother chastised him.

Tibon could see his mother get into the car along with the rest of his family while he ran to the ball and picked it up off the sidewalk. Again he could hear his mother calling out for him as they held open one of the doors to the backseat.

When he looked back at the car something caught his attention. There was a light blinking under the back bumper of the car. At first he didn't realize what it was but then, without warning, the car exploded upward into the air several feet, knocking him backwards onto the road. The last sight he remembered seeing was flames shooting out of the car before everything went blank. There was something more he felt he should remember, but every time he tried to concentrate on what happened right after the explosion a loud buzzing noise filled his ears, making it impossible to concentrate. It didn't matter.

The official report from the United States was a fuel-line leak, but Tibon knew better. He spent months recovering from the surgery on his back after his family's deaths. He had lost the use of his legs and had been severely burnt on the left side of his torso, but he was alive. As long as he had that and his intelligence, there was nothing that was going to stop him from...

July 18, 2007

Tibon was brought out of his daydream as Liz Bolan walked into his office. Her long legs and pitch-black hair reminded him of his mother. He wasn't sure if that was why he felt so attached to her, or if it was her sadistic nature that drew him to her. Whatever the reason, she was loyal and easily manipulated. He had met her waiting tables at a diner several years earlier. The tattoos on her left arm told him she was an ex-convict, which was part of his attraction to her. Hardened and at the same time mentally fragile, Liz was a perfect target for his mental manipulations. He knew he could gain her trust and her loyalty to ensure his control over her. And that's exactly what he had done. He knew she would be loyal to him even up to her death.

After their close escape from being blown up the day before, he could see the swelling on the bridge of her nose had reduced considerably.

"Dr., I mean, Tibon, I'm sorry. It's become a habit." Liz smiled at him.

"Do we have the results back from the last batch of subjects?" He could see she was treading cautiously with him as she put the folder on his desk.

"I think you're going to like them, but I'm not the genius."

Tibon opened the folder, ignoring Liz's attempt at flattery. "This is good news. We can now move onto the next stage."

"What about the FBI?" she asked hesitantly. "We had to leave in a hurry."

He took a deep breath. "This is what I want you to do. I want you to take Damon to L.A. immediately. It's time for the next phase. Can you handle that?"

Liz seductively walked around the desk and sat right in front of him. She leaned forward and asked, "Have I ever failed you before?" She ran her fingers through his thick, prematurely graying hair and attempted to kiss him. He turned his head away.

Looking coldly into her dark blue eyes, he said, "Yes, yes you have, my love. I have five missing babies and two missing nurses, thanks to you and my incompetent staff. You had them and let them get away."

She slowly pulled back from Tibon.

"We don't need to worry about the babies, but the nurses, on the other hand, are a loose end that I hope for your sake doesn't become a problem."

"Won't your contact at the FBI be able to let us know if they find them?" Liz asked, diverting the subject from her failures.

"I'll handle it. You just worry about getting Damon set up. Don't screw up this time."

Liz nodded as she turned to leave. He could see the fear in her eyes. She wanted his approval again. He knew she would do as he asked.

"Go! I have a lot to do, and I don't need you in the way."

He smiled as he watched her leave his office. He needed to focus on the tasks at hand. These new results were the breakthrough he had spent the last twenty years doing research for. Now his real plans could begin.

Five

Barrus Ranch

July 18, 2007
Oklahoma

The Oklahoma sky shone brightly down on the Barrus Ranch as Leigh Barrus watched his workers from his office window. They were getting ready to take the herd down to one of the watering holes to give some relief to the cattle. Over the last two years it had become more difficult to manage the finances of the ranch. The economy was changing, and it seemed impossible to get caught up on the ever-piling bills in his office. Leigh had spent the better part of Saturday morning writing checks, now that money had been transferred from his family inheritance to his bank. There had been a lot of paperwork involved each time he dipped into it, but his men needed their pay and the bills wouldn't wait any longer. Leigh had crunched the figures and at the rate the ranch was going, he would lose everything in five to six years. The ranch had been in his family for three generations, but now it looked like he may have to let it go.

Leigh prepared himself as Blake headed toward the house. Tempers had been running high since none of Leigh's employees had been paid in over two weeks. It was time for him to make up for it. Blake had been his ranch manager for the last five years. He liked him a lot. In many ways he was the son Leigh never had. He was a good-looking fellow for the most part, and there were times he wished his niece had never left. The two of them would be a good fit. Blake was dependable, hard-working, and had an easygoing personality, just what his niece needed. Much like her first husband, God rest his soul.

"Howdy, Leigh. You got the boys' checks?" Leigh could see Blake was uncomfortable asking him that question, and it broke his heart that it was necessary.

"Here you go, Blake. I put a little extra in for each of you for being so understanding."

A visible relief came over Blake as he took the checks from Leigh. "Thanks. You know, Leigh, if there's something I can do you for, you'd ask me, right?"

Leigh smiled. "I appreciate the offer, but there ain't nothing wrong. Just having trouble with the bank, is all. Took a lot longer than I expected."

"You want to come over tonight and be with me and Rachael? My little ten-year-old makes a mighty fine meatloaf."

Leigh managed to smile at the invitation. "That's sounds great, Blake, but I'm still catching up on some bills and paperwork. Got some offers from a couple meat companies so there's that."

"If you can, it would be nice to have the company." Blake briefly took off his dark brown cowboy hat, soaked around the rim with sweat, so he could scratch his wavy black head of hair. "It's a hot one today. I'll make sure the boys are taken care of."

"I appreciate all you been doing and I'll try and make it by tonight. Go give the boys their checks before they lynch me from a tree."

They both laughed as Blake headed back to work. Leigh sat back in his chair. He was getting too old for this job. He was only fifty-three, but the last few years had been rough on him and he was feeling tired. It had been so much easier when his wife had been alive, and now that his niece had gone and moved out of state he felt alone and scared. If it hadn't been for Blake and his church family caring so much, he may have already hung up his hat and called it quits.

He tried to put that out of his head for the moment and get back to the bills, but there was a strange uneasiness inside his gut after thinking about his niece. He'd felt it all that morning, and now it was back again. He thought it was just worry over the bills needing to be paid, but the more he tried to ignore his feelings, the stronger they were becoming. After a few more minutes of not being able to shake the feeling, he stopped what he was doing and prayed.

Leigh could see his niece's face in his head as he prayed. He hadn't talked to her in a couple weeks. He had been trying to get through to her for several days, but she didn't return his messages. *One more try,* he thought to himself as he picked up the phone and dialed her number. Just like the other four times, the answering machine picked up. "Hi, it's Uncle Leigh. I hope all's well. Give a call when you get a chance. Love you."

Leigh was worried, but he had always been overprotective of her and needed to relax. He had plenty of work to do. If he was going to make it to Blake's for dinner, he knew he had better get busy.

Leigh looked out his office window again, only this time he saw a black SUV pulling up his driveway and park outside. He watched as two men in suits got out and headed toward his front door. He hurried to meet them. Strangers coming to his door didn't bode well with him. Horrible thoughts of what could have happened to his niece ran through his head as he opened the door.

"Hi. You are?" Leigh greeted them.

The older looking man asked, "Are you Leigh Barrus?"

Unexpectedly, Leigh found himself getting agitated at the fact the man didn't answer his question.

"Son, you knocked on my door. I can hear you folks ain't from around these parts, but in Oklahoma when someone knocks on another person's door and they're asking who you are, you better have the courtesy to answer."

The younger man pulled out a badge. "I'm very sorry, sir. I'm Agent Nick Catlin and this is Agent Allen Young. We're from the FBI. May we come in? It's in regards to your niece."

Leigh's heart sank, and he found himself speechless to ask the obvious question. With a wave of his arm he motioned for the two men to come in. Finally he managed to ask in a meek voice, "Is she all right?"

"That's what we're here about, Mr. Barrus. Have you seen her or talked to her recently?"

For an instant Leigh felt relieved the agents weren't there to tell him his niece was dead. Then his heart sank. "What has happened to her?" He instinctively apologized. "I'm sorry for being so short with you boys. I've been trying for days to get in touch but—where are my manners? Please sit."

They all sat in the living room as Agent Catlin started the conversation. "Mr. Barrus, we need—"

"What's happened to my little Janet?"

Agent Catlin continued, "Have you spoken to your niece anytime recently?"

"Like I said, not a peep in over a week. I've been trying her place in New York, but she hasn't returned my calls yet. What's this about? Has she gone missing?"

Agent Young answered, "There is an ongoing investigation involving several murders, and your niece's name has surfaced as a possible material witness, along with her friend Michele Townsend."

Leigh remembered Janet telling her about Michele and how they were becoming good friends. "Murder, you say? Oh my! Now you got me worried."

Murder and *material witness* were not words that had run through Leigh's thoughts up till now, and he was finding it hard to think clearly.

Agent Catlin asked, "So you haven't heard or seen Janet recently?"

"No sir, but if there is anything I can do to find them or help in any way—"

Agent Young pulled out one of his cards and handed it to him. "If she contacts you, please call us right away."

Leigh didn't want the men to leave yet. He had so many questions, but they seemed to elude him. Finally he asked, "What makes you think Janet is a witness?"

Agent Catlin replied, "Both her and Michele's fingerprints were found at the scene of a crime. So far we have accounted for everyone involved except for them. Leigh, the last time you spoke with Janet, did she say what she was doing or tell you anything about her job?"

Leigh didn't miss the intentional changing of the subject. He thought about that for a moment. "Not really. About six or seven months ago she said something about working on a project at the hospital, but she didn't tell me much more than that. Actually, she never spoke much about work to me."

Agent Young asked, "Any place you know of that she would stay or hide if she felt she was in trouble? Like with family or friends?"

Leigh shook his head. "No sir, I'm all she's got. Her father died when she was only two years old, and both her mother and aunt died in a car crash when she was fifteen. I'm all she has left, after her husband died." Leigh trailed off into thought at how much death his niece has had to endure throughout her life. And now she was in some sort of trouble, which he felt helpless to do anything about. "That girl's been through the ringer all her life." Leigh's eyes watered. "If anything's happened to her, I don't know what—"

"We'll do our best to find her. Sorry to have taken up your time. You don't mind if we call you just in case there are more questions?"

Leigh was so deep in thought, it took a moment to register that Nick had asked him a question. "Oh, I'm sorry. Of course."

The two agents stood up, and Leigh shook their hands before they made their way out the front door. Again Leigh sat back down and prayed for his niece and her safety. The bills would have to wait.

Six

The Cabin

The next day Leigh woke up at 4:15 in the morning. He had been up late the night before, unable to sleep. He tried to do his normal routine just like always, but it was difficult to concentrate. After showering and getting dressed, he headed to the kitchen to make his coffee. Several times he caught himself staring at the telephone, hoping it would ring, and Janet's voice would call out to him. He sat down at his kitchen table and automatically grabbed his Bible, like he did every morning. The desire to read eluded him. *Janet, where are you?*

The last time he had seen his niece face to face was over two years ago at her husband's funeral. She was the daughter he never had, the child he never had. His brother, Gene, had died on the missionary field when she wasn't even two years old. He asked her mother, Anna, to come live with him and his wife, Jenny, at the ranch. A smile curled at the sides of his mouth at the memory of the little red-haired tyke. She looked so much like her mother, bright hazel eyes and a smile that melted your heart. It didn't take long for him and Janet to become inseparable. Everywhere he went she tried to follow. He truly loved her as his own.

Life was good for a long time—until the accident. His heart skipped a beat at the memory. It was just before Janet's sixteenth birthday when it happened. His wife, Jenny, and Janet's mother, Anna, were hit by a tractor-trailer during a rainstorm. It was an accident, and no one was to blame, but that wasn't much of a comfort. The only family that either of them had left was each other.

It took a few years, but eventually Janet came out of her emotional shell. He remembered the day she brought home Marcus for the first time to meet him. She had just graduated college with her nursing degree and was working at the local hospital just outside of Tulsa. He was a fine man and a good fit for Janet. It was all going so well for her life. They got married and wanted to start a family, but then...on a flight heading to Buffalo, N.Y., Marcus's plane crashed, killing over forty passengers and crew. They said it was an electrical failure, but no excuse could console Janet.

The funeral was one of the hardest things he had ever gone through, even more difficult than burying his own wife and sister-in-law. Janet's eyes told him everything he needed to know about how she was feeling. Despair and anger had taken the place of the joyous woman he had come to know.

The week following the funeral was when the argument happened. Her bitterness toward God had become evident, and no matter what he said to her he couldn't help take any of it away. The thought of that fight being the last time he would see his niece was unthinkable....

At a quarter to five Blake pulled up the driveway and helped him concentrate on the day ahead. They had to repair one of the wells that broke down. The plan was to have prayer and then work on fixing it afterwards. Thankfully they had plenty of water for the cattle, but the well couldn't wait any longer.

Blake walked in just as Leigh was pouring them coffee. He took off his hat and shook the water from it. "Morning, Leigh. It's going to be a wet one out there." He hung up his coat and hat. "Were you up at the cabin last night? We missed you at dinner."

"It's a long story. Yesterday I found out—" Leigh stopped when he fully realized what Blake had just asked him. "Why would I have gone up to the cabin? I haven't been there in a couple years."

"I could see fresh car tracks in the mud going up into the woods. Right where the old dirt road is."

Leigh put down his cup of coffee. Several times he had caught Bradley Cooper from town hunting up on his property, and the thought of him using the cabin rubbed Leigh the wrong way. In fact, everything about Bradley rubbed him the wrong way.

At the door Leigh jerked on his boots and grabbed a shotgun from a nearby cabinet. Blake did the same and followed him out the door.

"I take it the well can wait?" Blake asked.

Leigh didn't answer.

Blake hopped into the truck beside Leigh, and they headed up into the hills following the tracks. Since it took about forty minutes to get to the cabin, he tried to calm himself. About a mile away from the lake, Leigh could see smoke rising in the distance through an opening in the forest tree line. When they finally pulled up to the cabin there was an old blue Buick station wagon parked outside. Leigh parked next to it and got out of the truck with his shotgun in hand. He loaded his shotgun with Blake behind him.

"Now, Leigh, we're just going to scare them, right?"

He shot Blake a sideways glance of indignation at the question.

Leigh expected to hear men's voices as he listened from the front porch doorway, but instead he heard babies crying. What were Bradley and his boys doing with babies? He stepped through the front door. There were no lights on as a faint glow came from the fireplace. Sitting on the floor in front of the fireplace was a blond-haired woman with her back to him. The babies were spread out in front of her, lying on bedsheets.

Leigh stepped cautiously toward the woman.

Blake cleared his throat. "Um, Leigh?"

A gun cocked beside his ear. He froze.

A familiar voice ordered, "Don't move, or I'll put a bullet in your head."

"Janet?" Leigh turned around slowly, "Oh dear Lord, thank you! You're okay."

Janet immediately lowered the police revolver as he hugged her tight. When she wept on his shoulder, Leigh knew his niece was in trouble.

"It's all right, sweetheart," he said calmly. "Whatever happened, I'm here for you."

The rain was letting up outside as Leigh sat at the dining room table with his niece and Blake. She looked so tired. Her long red hair was matted to her head, and the bruise marks on her forehead made his heart long to take her in his arms and make the pain go away. To see her so beaten and weary was difficult to deal with.

"Start from the beginning, Janet. You've been so secretive about what's been happening."

She nodded. "Okay, I'll try and stay on point, since there's so much to tell. We were working at Saint Luke's Hospital in Poughkeepsie when a friend from work approached us about a new project that needed a couple night nurses." She stopped and took a deep breath. "Her name was Liz Bolan, and up to that point, I liked her. She said that the project was a drug study for a new medicine that would help women who are unable to have children carry a pregnancy to full term. Michele and I thought it'd be great to be a part of it. We should have known better. For starters, the building that this so called 'drug study' was being held in was out in the middle of nowhere. Also, none of the ten women who participated in the project spoke any English. We had to have an interpreter on staff at all times. Who brings in people from out of the country to do a drug study? Makes no sense. None of the women had any visitors, and since all of them were in their second trimester when we started the project, you would think someone would have wanted to check up on them. Not a single call came in the entire six months we were there."

Janet took another deep breath. "For some reason they had split up the ten participants. Michele and I were only responsible for five of them. The other wing of the facility housed the other five participants. There was no reason to have us separate, but I didn't say or question anything because they were paying really good money. Stupid!"

Leigh was about to console her, but she kept speaking. "We did all sorts of blood tests and administered drugs that we thought were helping the women, but I don't think that's what they were for. I'm not even sure the drugs had anything to do with what was going on."

Michele stood in the kitchen just outside the dining room, trying to rock the baby in her arms to sleep. "Tell them about Terresa or Tavita, whatever her name was. Tell them what happened."

"Right," Janet agreed. "Even though we didn't speak our patients' languages, I got to know this one participant really well. She was a sweet young girl, maybe twenty years old, if that. Probably from the Middle East somewhere, but I couldn't tell exactly. We were told her name was Terresa, but obviously that was a lie also. I got to know her pretty well, and since we had the night shift, there was plenty of time to kill. During the late evening hours Terresa and I would play checkers or watch TV together.

"Well, a couple weeks before Terresa's due date, I came to her room with her evening meds. When I got there, she was doubled over the back of the couch, trying to hold herself up. I ran over and examined her. I thought something was wrong with the baby, but before I could call for the interpreter and Michele, she grabbed my hand and led me to the bathroom. At the time I didn't know what to make of it.

"When we were in the bathroom, she closed the door and put on the shower. I tried to ask her several times what was wrong, but she kept shushing me. Once the shower was on, she gave me a hug and pulled my head close to hers. In broken English she said, 'My name is Tavita. I want to thank you for being a friend. Please take care of my baby when I am gone.' Needless to say I was shocked, not just by the fact she could speak pretty good English, but that she thought we were going to take away her baby. Once she said that to me she turned off the shower and walked back to her bedroom. She never spoke another word to me after that.

"Anyway, on Michele's and my shift a couple days before Terresa's due date, she went into labor. Needless to say, we were quite excited. Oh, I forgot to tell you. Let me back up a little so you understand better. Liz Bolan, the lady who had offered us the job, was our direct supervisor. I thought she was a nice person until we started working for her. I've never met a more cold-hearted person in my life. It was like she turned into a completely different person once we were working on this project. The real craziness started when Dr. Scharf started hanging around with her all hours of the night...in his office."

Leigh had been able to follow up to this point, but now he was confused. "Who's Dr. Scharf?"

"Sorry. Dr. Scharf is the man responsible for the project. For the first three months he was nowhere to be found. We were told about him but had never met him till the beginning of the third trimester. He ran more tests on the participants and stayed during our shift. To be honest, I wasn't sure who was more cold-hearted—Liz or Dr. Scharf. They certainly belonged together."

In the living room Michele scoffed.

"Anyway, when Terresa went into labor, Wheels and Bolan were right—"

Leigh put up his hand for her to stop. "Okay, who's Wheels?"

"Sorry again. That was our nickname for Dr. Scharf." She looked down, ashamed. "I forgot to mention he was in a wheelchair."

Leigh shook his head as he tried to keep it all straight. "Go on."

"Like I said, they were both there when we delivered Terresa's baby. A healthy baby boy after only four hours of labor. I've never seen a woman give birth so quickly in my life."

"I don't mean to be rude, sweetheart, but how did you end up here with five babies? I'm guessing they ain't yours."

Janet smiled at him. "I'm getting there. I tried to hand the baby to Terresa to hold, but Liz stopped me. She took the baby out of my hands and handed the boy to a technician. She told the technician to take him away, which caused Terresa to freak out. I couldn't blame her. I was pretty upset myself. So much so that I got in Liz's face and told her to back off and let the girl hold her child. That's when Dr. Scharf spoke softly into Terresa's ear. I didn't hear everything, but what I could make out was something to the effect of, 'Remember what we talked about' and 'You understood the deal.' After that, we were told to take the rest of the night off.

"When we got to work the next day, all five of our patients had been induced into labor, and all five infants were under guard in the nursery. We weren't allowed to see the mothers or the infants. Instead, we were told that there was to be an emergency staff meeting in a half hour, and we were not allowed to leave the building. I was so scared, Uncle Leigh. Something very wrong was happening, and neither of us knew what to do. So we went to the back of the building by the gas tanks and utility rooms where we usually went for our break. Only problem was that there were a couple of men dressed in black standing just outside the doorway holding guns strapped around their shoulders.

Thankfully they didn't hear us, but we could hear them. One of them relayed their orders to kill the entire staff and the five unwanted children. At first I thought I was hearing things, but one of them mentioned they had to hurry because Dr. Scharf's informant in the FBI said they needed to."

Blake asked, "They said there was an informant in the FBI?"

Wide-eyed, Janet nodded. "I know. Fear got the better of us, and we ran back to our wing. They were going to kill us all, and I couldn't let them kill those children."

Uncle Leigh sat upright in his chair. "How in the world did you get out of there?"

"I don't know, to be honest, Uncle Leigh. When we got back inside, the guards had gone into the conference room. We put the babies in a transfer cart built for all five of them and hid initially in the ladies' room."

At those words, Michele started laughing in the other room.

"Oh, yeah," Janet said, "we ran into Liz Bolan in there. I kind of decked her and broke her nose." A sheepish grin of satisfaction curled the sides of her mouth.

"Anyway, we waited for the two men from the back entrance to pass the ladies' room before we made our move. As soon as the coast was clear, we ran to the back entrance by the utility room. We could hear gunfire and people screaming in the distance, which made us move even quicker. We almost made it, but not before they found us. What happened next is still a blur. I remember pushing Michele and the babies out the door as bullets started whizzing by my head. I fell forward through the doorway just as a large explosion went off. I don't know if a bullet hit a gas line or what. The next thing I know I'm on the pavement next to a Jeep™, the five babies are laying everywhere, and Michele is unconscious. I checked the Jeep™ and found the keys had been left in it. I dragged Michele into the backseat and placed the babies on the floor next to her. Then there were more explosions. I didn't wait around to find out if anyone even saw us or not. We would have gone to the police, but the Jeep™ we took had a badge in the ashtray. We didn't know who we could trust."

There was a long pause; the rain hitting the roof filled the void.

Leigh finally said, "You two are staying here with those children. There's no record of this cabin in town, so nobody's going to come looking for you here."

Janet sighed in relief.

Michele reluctantly asked, "We're going to need some help with diapers and whatnot. We have a few bucks left, but—"

Leigh lifted a hand. "I'll take care of everything. You two just take care of those little ones and don't worry about the rest. Okay?"

With that Leigh took Blake back to the ranch. He didn't want to leave, but they had already been away for too long. He had a lot to do and very little time to do it. When he got back to the ranch a couple of his ranch hands were sitting around in the barns waiting for them to show up. He didn't want to, but he left Blake with the workers to fix up the well and run the ranch while he went and got supplies for the cabin. There was a lot involved if someone was going to live at the cabin. It was Sunday, so Leigh knew he wasn't going to be able to get everything he needed right away.

Over the next week Leigh left Blake in charge of the ranch while he fixed up the cabin. He had bought several rechargeable marine batteries so the girls would have electricity and also replaced the pump he used for the plumbing. The old system ran down to the lake, but everything was rotting away. Leigh had to pull more money out of his family inheritance to fix up the cabin. When he was done, everything worked great. New mattresses and cribs for the babies, along with a new refrigerator and propane stove, made the cabin a home.

Both Janet and Michele seemed to be settling in and adjusting to their new place. Leigh was grateful he could be helping. He wasn't sure how this was all going to work out with the priorities at the ranch, but Leigh had a sense of peace about it all. His little Janet was home and that was all that mattered.

Seven

Growing Up

Janet sat on the dock taking a break from watching the children. Lake Elim always looked so pretty. The summer breeze, a family of ducks swimming along the shoreline, and the sun reflecting off the water brought back childhood memories. She remembered Uncle Leigh and Aunt Jenny bringing her and her mother up to this cabin for weekend getaways. She'd learned how to fish on this very same dock with Uncle Leigh. She smiled as she recalled those peaceful, innocent times.

Everything around her invoked emotions long forgotten: visions of Aunt Jenny playing her guitar while everyone sang hymns and church choruses by the fireplace. She had given her life to Christ during one of those weekends. She tried to remember back. It took a moment, but finally it came to her. She was seven when she was baptized, only feet away from where she was now sitting. Both her mother and Uncle Leigh had done the honors while Aunt Jenny took pictures. It was one of the most wonderful days in her life. Her childhood had been filled with such love and joy, something she wished had never ended.

The sadness returned as she returned to reality. She could hear several of the babies crying inside and knew that Michele had her hands full. As she ran inside to help, Janet couldn't help but feel uneasy by the way the children were beginning to behave. It had only been three weeks, and already they were eating more than was normal for their age. Something seemed odd about the children. Her nursing experience told her she needed to start documenting the children's behaviors and development. Michele agreed with her, so they both kept an eye on the children for anything abnormal.

36

* **
** *

That night Janet sat alone in her room staring into the cracked mirror that had once been her aunt's. How had she gotten to this place in her life? She had been worried about returning home, yet now she was home. Everything she had been running from lingered like shadows everywhere she looked. Her childhood, her family, her marriage— memories she didn't want to revisit—had been forced back into her life. *Why, God?*

She loved her uncle very much, but it was difficult facing him the last few months. The things she'd said to him after her husband Marcus died had erected an emotional wall between them. He welcomed her with open arms, but she wasn't ready to let down her guard.

Pushing aside her feelings, Janet grabbed the notebook and pen from her bedside table and wrote.

Friday, August 10, 2007
The five children are only twenty-four days old, and already they are starting to need solid foods. Their hunger is almost overwhelming at times. Uncle Leigh has been so helpful, bringing us everything we need each week, but I'm concerned for him. He's looking tired.

Uncle Leigh suggested we name the children today. He said that they are our children now, and it only seemed right we call them by name. Michele and I didn't want to name them given that we didn't know what was going to happen, but he's right. We both sat down and named each of them. Michele let me go first, so I named the boy we knew was Teresa's child Marcus, because his dark blue eyes reminded me of my late husband. Michele chose to name one of the girls Angela, after her Aunt Angie who raised her most of her life. Michele said it was because she smiled like her aunt does.

I named the other girl, who seems to be the neediest out of all the babies, Anna—after my mother because of her auburn hair. Michele named the blond boy Zack after her grandfather she knew as a child. And I named the last boy Sampson. He is the biggest of all the children, and one of the strongest. His little hand grips my fingers so tightly sometimes that it's actually uncomfortable.

Monday, September 17, 2007
The children are just nine weeks old, but Michele pointed out that all of them can flip over by themselves. This is something that a four-month-old would do, but it just confirms my original observation. They are all growing at an abnormal rate—even their weight is more like a child twice their age. The only exception is Sampson. He was already larger than the other children, but it is becoming very clear that he is going to be a very large boy. When I pick him up, he feels like he has lead for bones, he's so heavy.

Saturday, October 20, 2007
All of them are crawling, and it's hard to keep up with them. It's a challenge taking care of all five at once, and Michele isn't dealing with it as well as I am. Anna has been acting strange with Michele lately. She only wants me to pick her up, for some reason. Anna's been the most sensitive of all the children so far; maybe she's reading Michele's tension.

Uncle Leigh came up to the cabin to bring more supplies and to play with the kids. I forgot how much he loves children. It was good that he came because Sampson broke some of the bars on his crib. Uncle Leigh ended up spending most of the day fixing them.

He also made an observation that I was surprised I didn't notice. Uncle Leigh pointed out that none of the children have had any sickness or medical issues. I know they are only about three months old, but it seemed odd.

Friday, November 2, 2007
It's begun. Today Sampson said his first word. He called Michele "Selwee." We have been telling the children that we were Janet and Shelly, and apparently he picked up on it. I cannot believe that a four-month-old could start talking. I can't really look at any of them as four months old, I guess, since Sampson already looks like

a one-year-old and the rest look twice their age. I suppose I shouldn't be that surprised, given everything that is happening.

Uncle Leigh gave us an early Christmas present this week. He asked Blake to help him install a satellite dish. I don't know where he finds the time or the money, but when I ask him about it he avoids answering me. Uncle Leigh's looking older to me than I think he should. I'm concerned.

Wednesday, November 7, 2007

Okay, the rest of the gang is talking now. Michele is becoming distant as of late. I think it's because she's unable to deal with the weird changes in the children. She hasn't said anything to me about it, but I can see it in her.

On a brighter note, it's been soooo nice to have a TV and computer. Not having access to the outside world and reading old books for the last four months has been hard on both of us.

I looked up INYO industries today and found almost nothing on the Internet about them except a small news article saying they are a foreign drug manufacturer. No official website or other information. I feel really stupid working for a company I knew nothing about. The money was good, but still.

Monday December 24, 2007
Christmas Eve

All of the children are growing so fast it never stops to amaze me. It's been a little over five months, and from what Michele and I can see, they're growing at about twice the rate of normal children. It's hard to say they are only five months old because they are the size of ten- or eleven-month-olds. Sampson looks even older.

Today Angie surprised us; she stood up and walked effortlessly. Both our jaws dropped as she slowly ran around the living room, laughing and giggling while the other children watched her. What was even more amazing was the fact she never fell. I don't know what they did to these children, but they are not normal.

Marcus is the child I'm most concerned about. We've been seeing signs of what can only be called *seizures*. At first we thought he was just throwing a temper tantrum, but the more episodes he has, the more convinced I am that something is wrong. Marcus will be playing with all of the other children on the floor, get angry for no reason, then fall down, shaking uncontrollably. After several minutes of shaking, he sits up and seems fine, but it's been scary to watch, and we can't take him to the hospital for testing. Motherhood is not happening the way I thought it would.

Thursday, January 10, 2008
I was brushing Anna's hair today and explaining that my mama brushed my hair when I was really young. I just wanted to pass the time, but these children are so smart. Anna turned around and called me "Mama" for the first time. I didn't know what to say to her because it didn't seem right with both Michele and I taking care of the children.

Before I could do anything about it, Anna was following me all around the house, calling me "Mama," which got the other children to start calling me "Mama." I could see the hurt in Michele's eyes. I tried to explain to her what happened. She just told the children that they should call me "Mama" and her "Aunt Shelly." She tried to blow it off, but I knew it really bothered her. It's been even more difficult now that the children are walking and talking at only six months. I can't emphasize enough how strange it is to look at these children and imagine they are that young when they are as big as a twelve-month-old or older.

We had a big scare yesterday when Uncle Leigh was at the cabin recharging the marine batteries. I wasn't there to see it, but he said Zack came up to him to be held, and before Uncle Leigh could react, the boy grabbed the live wires attached to one of the batteries—without being hurt. I don't even know what to say about that, other than I'm not surprised.

Wednesday, March 5, 2008
Marcus is having more fits of uncontrolled rage and seizures. Both Zack and he have been closer to each other than to any of the other children. Poor Zack gets the brunt of Marcus's episodes. The

other day was the worst one yet. The two of them were fighting over a toy, and it got out of hand. Michele had to break them up, but Marcus wouldn't stop. Michele had to pick him up and bring him into her bedroom for almost an hour. When I went in to see how he was, Marcus was standing in the middle of the room shaking uncontrollably and gritting his teeth. He looked mad and upset, but I know it's not his fault. Whatever this is, I hope he grows out of it and soon.

I have not mentioned just how fast Zack is. Now that he is up and running around it's very clear that he has exceptional speed. I saw him carrying his truck to take outside when he dropped it. Most kids wouldn't have the coordination to catch or stop the truck from falling, but Zack's reflexes were faster than I've seen in most adults. He hardly even looked at the truck when he grabbed it out of the air as it was falling to the floor.

As I'm sitting here writing, I remember the scare that Michele and I had last week. We were in the living room, and Michele looked upstairs to the balcony area. There was Angie, walking tightrope fashion along the banister. When I turned around and saw her, I screamed for her to get down. She jumped off the railing down into the living room and landed behind the couch I was sitting on. Her little head popped up, smiling at me. I almost fainted from the rush of blood draining from my head. Michele didn't say a word, but I could tell she was freaked out by it.

Sunday, April 20, 2008

It has been apparent for a while that these children are exceptionally smart, but I didn't really know how smart until today. This afternoon I was playing Mahjong on the computer, and Angie wanted to come and sit with me instead of playing with her dolls. As she sat on my lap, several times she tried to grab the mouse from me until I let her play with it. What I expected her to do and what she did were completely opposite: I thought she would just move the cursor around for a while, but instead she solved a puzzle I hadn't been able to break in over an hour. On top of it, she did it in less than three minutes. Needless to say, I was shocked and speechless as the picture behind the puzzle came alive. Angie started giggling.

The children are about the size of eighteen-month-olds, even though it's only been a little over nine months. I am starting to get used to it. One of the major downsides to this is the feeling of time passing really quickly and the illusion that you are older than you really are.

One of the things I wanted to note was about Anna. There is something very strange about her that I can't put my finger on yet. She has been following me everywhere I go, whether it is cleaning, cooking, or taking out the garbage. Anna doesn't play much with the other children but instead watches them from a distance. She's not unfriendly, but more of a loner. The really strange part is her ability to read my thoughts. I know she isn't, but several times I may have a thought about grabbing the sugar for my coffee, and Anna will grab it before I do and hand it to me. Or I will be sitting watching TV and think I need to brush my teeth before bed, and she will bring me my toothbrush. It's creepy, and I know that Michele tries to stay away from Anna as much as possible because of it.

Uncle Leigh brought up Aunt Jenny's guitar today after church and played hymns and choruses for the children. They really liked it. I laughed as Angie and Sampson both danced while he played "Blessed Be the Rock" for them. It brought back some old memories, seeing him play that guitar. I know Uncle Leigh wants to talk to me about the day I left, but I'm just not ready yet. I'm still angry with God, and I don't know if I'm strong enough yet to deal with it.

Eight

New Lead

June 2008
Nearly a year since the Poughkeepsie murders

Nick sat alone in his office and once again found himself reading over the case file on the Poughkeepsie murders. His team had been able to gather a lot of evidence, but it only brought up more questions than answers. A lot of pressure was coming from his superiors to get this case solved. Having two dead police officers at the scene didn't help with the publicity of the case. From state officials to the White House, his team was under scrutiny.

Given Tibon's background, he was their main suspect as to who was behind the murders. Although they didn't have any proof, the facts all pointed logically to him. Problem was, no one who knew him had seen Tibon in years. Samantha was digging up any possible contacts in Amman, Jordan, since all of their local contacts had been dead ends. Jason and Nick were following up on a possible lead about Damon's whereabouts. Just one lead—that was all Nick wanted. This case was wearing him down. His emotions were becoming frazzled, but he'd never admit that to anyone. He sat back and purposefully exhaled.

Sam interrupted his thoughts as she tapped gently on his door. "Got a sec?" She smirked at him.

Whenever she smirked like that, Nick knew it was because of good news. He waved for her to come in. "Talk to me."

She hurried into his office and closed the door behind her. This must be really good news.

"I finally tracked down two of Tibon's old college buddies. I wouldn't categorize them as 'buddies;' let's say 'known associates.' Well, they hated him, really." She laughed at her own attempt at humor.

"You're killing me, Sam."

"Okay, okay!" She took a deep breath. Sitting down across from Nick, she continued. "Neither was very close to Tibon, but both said he had no love for America and even said they heard him mention he blamed our government for his family's death."

There was an awkward silence for a few seconds.

"That it?" Nick couldn't hide his disappointment.

She feigned being hurt. "Sheesh, we're cranky. No, that's not it. In fact, that was just to bust your chops. No, here is the real gem."

Her smile got bigger by the second as she pulled out a note and placed it in front of him. "This is the address of a three o'clock appointment we have in Boston tomorrow. I took the liberty of looking up the address and booking us a flight."

His confused expression must have told her he didn't understand. "Bear with me on this. I finally tracked down the hospital that did the surgery on Tibon when he was injured in the car explosion. It wasn't easy. All the diplomatic channels I had to go through with the Amman government—not to mention how long ago his surgery was—but I managed to track down some of the staff from the operation."

"I don't get how this helps us."

"There's more. By a stroke of pure luck, one of the nurses who assisted lives here in the States now. I've contacted her, and she is willing to meet with us."

"I still don't see how this is supposed to help us." They already knew Tibon was in a wheelchair.

Samantha sat back and gave him a look of a cat that just ate a bird. "When I mentioned we were investigating an incident that Tibon may be involved in, she didn't believe me. She questioned whether we had the same Tibon but wouldn't elaborate why. This obviously piqued my interest, and she agreed to meet with us at a diner in Boston."

Nick wasn't sure where this was going to lead, but they didn't have much to go on so far. If the Tibon they were looking for was a different person, then they had better investigate what this woman had to say. He closed the file in front of him and stood up. "Well then, let's get packed."

The woman sitting across from Nick stirred her tea thoughtfully as the waitress brought Samantha and him their coffees. She looked sad and a little nervous, so he decided to tread lightly with his questions.

"So, Mrs. Thomas," Nick started off.

"Please, call me Val. Thomas was my married name."

Her thick Middle Eastern accent was hard at first to get used to, but Nick continued. "Okay, Val, I understand you were one of the assisting nurses present during Tibon Agha's surgery. At the time he would have been twelve years old. Is that correct?"

Val didn't meet his eyes when she answered. "That is correct."

Sam asked, "On the phone, you wanted to know if we had the right Tibon. Can you tell us why you asked me about that?"

The woman seemed to respond to Sam better than to Nick.

Val looked up at Sam. "It was a long time ago, but his surgery I remember very well." She pushed her graying black hair from her face and took a sip of her tea. Nick noticed her hands were shaking. "They brought the boy into surgery with two pieces of shrapnel imbedded in his lower abdomen. One of them had hit Tibon's spine."

She paused, then stared into her teacup and seemed to drift off.

Nick prompted her. "We understand this is what paralyzed him from the waist down."

For the first time Val gazed at him directly. "No, no. That is why he died."

Sam shot him a quick look of confusion before asking Val, "What do you mean 'died'? Our records show that Tibon was paralyzed and returned back here to the United States to go to college."

Val's eyes narrowed, revealing wrinkles around her eyes that showed her age. After a nervous glance around the almost-empty diner, she said, "I do not know of such a thing that you speak of." Her eyes filled with tears as she surveyed the street through the window.

"Are you sure?" Nick asked. "This happened a very long time ago."

She continued to look out the window. "I am very sure, Agent Catlin."

Sam reached out and put her hand gently on the woman's arm. "Why are you so sure, Val?"

The woman pulled her arm away. "Because I was told never to speak of the boy's death. The men who told me this did so at gunpoint to both my husband and myself. But if people are being killed, then the truth must be known."

Nick asked, "Who threatened you?"

Val grabbed her purse and slid out of the booth. "I'm sorry. I must go now."

"Please wait," Nick said as he got up to follow the woman heading out of the diner.

Val ignored him and left. Sam and he stood at the diner doorway, watching her hurry across the street, when she suddenly dropped. They both ran to see what was wrong as traffic stopped in both directions. Blood poured from her chest, and Sam immediately applied pressure to stop the bleeding. Nick scanned the surrounding buildings.

There, standing across the street on the rooftop, was Damon, smiling down at Nick as he held his rifle.

Immediately Nick ran across the street and into the apartment building where Damon was. Nick sprinted up the seven stories of stairs and crashed through the rooftop door with his gun pointed forward. Nothing. There was no sign of Damon, not even footprints in the gravel.

The only sound was that of the crowd gathering below and blowing car horns. Why would Damon kill this woman? Who told her not to speak? The list of questions was getting longer and longer as Nick made his way back down to help Samantha. When he finally got back down to the street, Val was dead.

Nine

Janet's Memoirs

We celebrated the children's first birthday today. Wow. I can't believe how time flies. They all look like they are at least two years old—Sampson looks more like three. I keep asking myself the same question day in and day out. *What did they do to these children to make them like this?* Michele and I talk a lot about it with Uncle Leigh when he comes to visit.

To be honest, none of us really knows. You see these movies and TV shows about people playing God by experimenting with human tissues and genetic alterations, but having lived with these five children over the last year I'm beginning to wonder how much of this stuff is fiction, and how much is real. All of the stories tell about superhuman abilities that are used for good or evil, but they never show the other consequences of the gifts.

I am sure we haven't seen the extent of the children's abilities, but so far Anna cries at the slightest raise of your voice and has nightmares all the time. Marcus sleeps maybe five hours a night, if that. Michele and I have to take turns getting up early with him, just so he isn't running around unsupervised. Sampson is one of the strongest children I have ever seen and is constantly breaking toys on accident. I've lost count how many times Uncle Leigh has fixed his bed. It got so bad that we finally just put the mattress on the floor and threw out the frame. Angie gets stuck in between the staircase railings and chairs in the dining room when she tries to slip through them. I don't think I ever mentioned she is double-jointed. Unbelievable.

Zack is constantly running into walls or furniture because he is too fast for his own good. Every day I hear him crying because he ran into something. Marcus is a whole other ball game. The seizures have not stopped, and the fits of rage that precede them are getting worse as he gets older. One minute he will be happy and playful, and the next he is trying to break a toy or starts pounding on the sofa, screaming. He hasn't really hurt anybody or himself yet, but they are all getting so big, and I worry about what damage he will do if he doesn't get control.

Thursday, November 27, 2008
Thanksgiving Day

I haven't written in a couple months, so I thought I had better give an update. Nothing much has changed with the children. They are still growing at an accelerated rate, and all of them are suffering for it. There isn't a day that goes by that each of them doesn't complain about being in pain, Sampson especially. I think they are getting used to the pain to some extent, but it's got to be hard. I can't imagine.

Uncle Leigh came to the cabin with Blake to celebrate Thanksgiving. I was wondering where Blake's daughter, Rachael, was. When I asked, it was clear I hit a sore spot with Blake. Apparently Rachael's mother had her this Thanksgiving, and it was written all over Blake's face that he didn't approve.

A strange thing happened after that. Michele flirted with Blake a little during the evening. I don't know if Michele was trying to get his mind off of his ex-wife, or it was just her normal behavior coming out, but I found myself getting upset. Blake was very polite to her and didn't reciprocate any feelings, which made me happy. I don't know why I felt that way.

Friday, January 2, 2009

I know I have harped on this several times, but I really want to emphasize what is happening with these children. They were all born on July 17th 2007, except for Marcus, who was born the day before. In a couple weeks these children will be only a year and a half, but you would never know it by looking at them. All of them look more like three-year-olds and Sampson even older, of course, but even more difficult to explain is the intellectual development of each child.

Even though they look three, they sound more like six-year-olds with IQs that I can't begin to measure. The only thing holding them back is Michele's and my lack of knowledge to teach them. For Christmas Uncle Leigh bought a bunch of learning CDs for the computer to teach the children math, English, social studies, and some science programs. Already they have mastered each of them. I think we're going to start looking up some material on the Internet for them. It should be interesting to see just how smart these children are. I find myself having conversations with Anna sometimes, and I almost forget she's just a small child.

Speaking of Anna, there is a wisdom that comes from her at times way beyond someone with a high IQ. For instance, the other day we were both sitting in the dining room finishing our lunch while the rest of the children played in the living room, and Marcus kept throwing his football up in the air. Several times I called out and told him to stop, but he ignored me. Finally I said that he had till the count of three to stop. As I started counting Anna asked me why I was giving him till the count of three.

I didn't really have an answer for her and said the first thing that came to my mind: that I wanted to give him a chance to obey me. Anna replied that I had already given him more than enough chances to obey and that giving him a count only gives him control, not me. I sat for a moment looking at her—she was right. I immediately took the ball away from him and sent him to his room. Marcus has been quicker to listen to me since I did that. How can someone so young have that kind of insight? Excuse me, one-and-a-half-year-old.

Monday, May 18, 2009
Uncle Leigh showed up this afternoon unexpectedly and didn't look very happy. He took Michele and me into the dining room

and showed us a credit card bill in the name of Jennifer Barrus, my deceased aunt, but that wasn't the real shocking part. The card had a twenty-thousand-dollar limit, and it was maxed out. We told him that we had no idea about the card and that we had nothing to do with it. As we were speaking, little Angie came into the room crying. When Michele asked her what was wrong, she confessed that she signed up for the card and was using it for online classes.

We all stared at her in shock. Uncle Leigh told her to show him what she was signed up for. Angie showed us the courses she had taken. There was one class in mathematics and a couple others in science. What was even crazier was she passed them all with perfect scores. We explained to her the seriousness of what she had done and that she would be punished by not being allowed to use the computer for the time being.

Uncle Leigh was speechless at first as we sat in the living room discussing what we needed to do. Finally he shook his head and suggested we monitor the computer time more closely with all the children. He would try and find some college-level courses for the children.

Apparently they aren't getting all the teaching they need.

Ten

L.A.

Nick walked off the plane into the warm spring-like air of California. He was unprepared for the heat. Januarys in Pittsburgh were brutally cold most of the time, and having gone from freezing temperatures to Los Angeles made him feel overdressed and uncomfortable.

Allen was standing in the distance. He had gone ahead to investigate the lead they had on Damon Hannah. They watched for more than an hour while the other passengers picked up luggage. With each passing minute Nick was getting more agitated. He just wanted to get situated in his hotel room and change his clothes. The humidity added to his already poor attitude until finally he went over to the service desk.

"My luggage is missing." Nick flashed his badge at the squirrelly man behind the desk.

The man didn't flinch or change his blank expression when he asked, "What flight were you on, sir?"

Nick pulled out his ticket stub and placed it on the counter without saying anything. The man stared at his computer screen for several seconds until finally he looked up at Nick.

Wide-eyed, the man said, "Oh, dear. I'm sorry, sir, but apparently there has been a slight miscalculation with your luggage."

"Miscalculation? What do you mean, *miscalculation?*"

"Well, sir, apparently your luggage ended up in Seattle."

Nick shook his head. "Please give me your supervisor."

The man scurried away and soon came back with his supervisor.

Nick stood around another fifteen minutes arguing with her, but the best they could do was to get his luggage to L.A. by morning. He found it funny that of all the FBI shows he had seen over the years the agents flew on private jets and here he was, flying coach. It didn't seem right to him, somehow...and now his luggage was missing.

They soon got to the parking lot and Allen drove them out of the airport.

"We need to stop at a clothing store. I can't stay in this suit all day."

"I really don't know L.A. Let me call Sam. Her family lives around here. She'll know a good place." He connected his headset and called her on his cell phone. "Hey, Sam, it's Allen. We need a favor. Nick's luggage won't be in till tomorrow, and he wants to buy a change of clothes. We're just south of Inglewood on the freeway. Any ideas?" He waited for a reply. "Thanks. I see it up ahead. See you in a bit."

Nick thanked Allen as they pulled off the freeway. They drove for only a few blocks before pulling up to a men's clothing store off South Prairie Avenue. Nick told Allen to wait for him in the car, because he didn't plan on taking very long. He made his way into the store and quickly spotted the men's suits in the back. Nick chuckled as he checked some of the prices. He had forgotten he was in L.A. Everything was outrageously priced, as far as he was concerned. He had never paid more than a couple hundred for a suit before.

A young woman with long blond hair and bright blue eyes walked over to him and smiled. "Can I help you find anything?"

Flustered by her beauty, he awkwardly replied, "Sorry, yes. I mean no, I'm good. I'm good. Thanks."

The girl smiled again and gave a slight giggle as she walked away. Just then a man came out of a dressing room from the back. Nick couldn't see him because of the rack of suits he was looking at.

As Nick tried to decide which suit he was going to buy to max out his credit card with, the same young woman approached the man who just came out of the dressing room.

She asked, "Did you like what you tried on, Mr. Montresor?"

The man replied, "Looks nice. I'll take them all."

Nick didn't really pay much attention to their conversation, but for some reason the name *Montresor* sounded familiar, though he couldn't place it. The man paid at the counter for his clothes as Nick mulled over the name again and again. He couldn't shake the feeling that he knew that name. After the man left the store it stuck him. The name Montresor was the main character in the book *The Cask of Amontillado* by Edgar Allen Poe. He had read it in college. He darted for the front door of the store. The young woman tried to get his attention, but Nick ignored her. He needed to see the man who had just left.

Nick watched as a car exited the parking lot with Damon Hannah in the driver's seat. Thankfully Damon didn't see him as he made his way back to Allen and jumped into the car yelling, "Follow now!"

"Follow what?"

Nick impatiently pointed to the back end of the black Volvo™ pulling out of the parking lot. "That car! Come on, before we lose him!"

Allen already had their sedan moving and followed the Volvo™. Nick didn't say anything at first so Allen finally asked, "And who are we tailing?"

Nick smiled as he kept his eyes on the road. "Damon Hannah."

Allen's surprise was what Nick expected because that had been his initial reaction. "You're kiddin', right?"

"Nope. He was buying clothes. Believe that?"

Allen shook his head at Nick's question. They followed Damon to a warehouse district and watched him park his car in an empty parking lot. They watched from the end of the block as he got out of his car and headed into the warehouse. Nick knew protocol was to call for backup, but he also didn't want to take a chance that Damon would get away again. Reluctantly he pulled out his cell phone and called Samantha to get down to their location on West 111th Street with backup.

They pulled into a parking lot across the street and Nick rolled down the window. He pulled a pair of binoculars from the glove compartment, hoping to see something. Unfortunately there was nothing. There were no windows he could get a clear view through. They were all dark. Everything inside him wanted to rush into the warehouse and grab Damon.

Allen asked, "Do you want to go for it? I'll back you up."

"No. We can't," Nick said, frustrated. "We need to wait."

A few more seconds passed. Bursts of gunfire came from within the warehouse, followed by a woman's scream. That was all Nick could take. Both men were out of the car with guns drawn as they crossed the street toward the warehouse. Nick motioned for Allen to take the front as he circled around the back. Nick approached the back doorway and peered into one of the windows. He couldn't see anything at first. Then he caught the back of Damon walking behind a shelf and out of his sight. As quietly as he could, Nick opened the door and moved inside.

The warehouse smelled of oil and sawdust. In the middle of the room there were several cutting tables covered in wood and dirt. By the looks of them, they hadn't been used in quite some time. Nick tried to be light-footed, but the floor was rotting wood that squeaked with every step. He made his way along a shelf that stood about thirteen feet high. Several cardboard boxes were stacked along it covered in dust and cobwebs. With the dim light coming through the windows it was hard for Nick to see very clearly. He maneuvered his way to where he had last seen Damon.

He could hear heavy breathing coming from several feet away. He looked around the corner of the shelves to see a dark-haired woman lying facedown on the wood floor. There was no one else around, but Damon had to be nearby. Slowly Nick made his way toward the woman. There were no wounds or blood that he could see, but she was breathing in quick succession, as if having trouble catching her breath.

Nick kept his eyes open for any movement around the room as he knelt down next to the woman and whispered, "Miss, are you all right? Are you hurt?"

The woman didn't move or say anything. Nick was hesitant to give much attention to her until he knew where Damon was. Once they had him in custody, then Nick could examine the woman more closely.

He stood up and continued to survey his surroundings. The place was probably once a lumber manufacturer, given the amount of wood chips and sawdust lying around. Debris was lying everywhere, ranging from broken motor parts to light bulbs. Nick peered down to see if he could track Damon's footprints in the dirt. His eyes were drawn to the piece of mirror leaning up against one of the saw tables. He could see the woman's body in the reflection. She rolled onto her side, allowing him to see her face. It took him a moment to recognize the woman's face. *Elizabeth Mitchel.* She pulled out a gun from underneath her body.

Instinctively Nick turned and kicked the gun from her hands, sending it across the room as a shot went off. He immediately pointed his gun at her but was shocked to see her smiling at him. Nick thought it odd that she would be smiling, but then dread swept over him. Nick didn't see anyone at first, but something inside him told him to look up.

It was too late. Across the room Damon sat on a ledge at the top of another shelf. His gun fired before Nick could react. He was forced backwards from the bullet as it went through his right shoulder. Nick fell over Liz and to the floor. His body was running on pure survival as he rolled behind one of the sawing tables for cover. That's when Nick realized he had dropped his gun. He had to move now. Damon shot two more times. The bullets bounced off the tabletop Nick was hiding behind. Gathering all of his strength, Nick leaped to his feet and ran for the back door. Several shots fired. One of them went into the wood floor in front of Nick.

A loud cracking echoed off the walls as he fell through the floor to the basement. He awoke to find himself lying on a pile of broken wood. He tried to sit up, but his shoulder cried out with pain. He could barely see anything through the small amount of light coming from the hole above his head. The dust was still settling in the air. He must have blacked out for a few seconds.

Once again he tried to sit up, only to feel the broken ribs that now accompanied his shoulder wound. He needed to get away from the hole overhead before Damon or Liz saw him and finished the job they started.

Two more gunshots rang from the other side of the warehouse. Allen's voice cried out in pain as Nick listened helplessly. It would still be a few minutes before the rest of the team showed up with the police. Damon and Liz weren't going to let him live. One of them would come down to find him.

He felt around the floor for some sort of weapon until he finally found something that would do. A link chain lay at Nick's feet. He wrapped it around his left hand. He was right-handed, but the gunshot to his shoulder was making it almost impossible to lift anything. Nick struggled to find a place to hide. Footsteps crossed the basement floor.

It was hard to tell which of the two had come for him, but Nick was pretty sure it was only one set of footsteps. He tried to keep quiet and breathe slowly, but the pain and the blood loss made it difficult to concentrate. The footsteps got closer as Nick fought off light-headedness.

Waiting. Waiting. Closer. Closer. Nick's eyes had adjusted to the dark, helping him see a hand holding a pistol just before he attacked. With what little strength he had left, Nick lashed out with the chain and smashed it hard alongside the pistol. Damon let out a shriek of surprise and pain as the pistol shot into the floor and fell from his hand. He brought the chain around and whipped it alongside Damon's head. He fell backwards and tripped over the fallen wood. Damon fought to regain his balance while Nick came forward again with the chain. Beating hard down onto his shooter's back, he sent Damon to the floor, crying in pain.

Nick could see his attacker better now that he was lying where he had been only moments before, underneath the hole. Again and again Nick came down hard, as the rage and fear became one massive adrenaline rush. Damon lay unconscious, but fury had taken Nick over as he raised the chain with both hands over his head. He was just about to come down with all of his strength, his pain forgotten momentarily, when his eyes caught Liz standing at the edge of the hole pointing her gun at him. There was no time to react.

The first shot went into Nick's right abdomen, and time seemed to stand still for him. The second shot hit his left rib cage. This was the end. He watched in slow motion as the last gunshot exploded from Liz's gun. It hit him in the right side of his forehead, sending him backwards onto the floor. Darkness was the only thing that followed. After what seemed like an eternity Nick could hear the faint voice of a woman. She sounded familiar, but it was hard to think.

A voice said, "He's down here."

Nick woke up to beeping and hissing. He struggled to focus his eyes. Several minutes passed before he was able to see clearly. Exhaustion kept trying to overtake him, but the fear of not remembering how he got here won out. He was in a hospital—that much was sure by the machine attached to the tube running down his throat. The on and off pressure in his lungs told him they were helping him breathe. Instinctively Nick tried to move his hands and feet. It was difficult, but he had mobility. Along his chest he could see a cast and nothing more.

As he lay awake Nick tried to remember anything that would help him understand what had happened to him, but nothing came. *I need to go back to the last thing I can remember.*

It was difficult at first. Did he have amnesia? He remembered his name who he was and what he did for a living. *Come on Nick, think*, he pushed himself.

What was the last thing he could remember? The plane ride to L.A. His lost luggage. Allen. Damon. The memories only came in flashes. He had gone into the warehouse and found a woman on the floor. He fell through the floor and heard Allen cry out. There was more. It was like a faint dream right after waking up. Particulars didn't come, only feelings.

A picture of Elizabeth Mitchel's face flashed before his eyes. The monitor beeped faster. Elizabeth had pointed a gun at him. Tears flowed from his eyes as the pain and fear all rushed back.

A nurse finally came into the room to check on him. He was grateful to see another face.

"The doctor will be in shortly," she said.

The nurse came back within minutes with the doctor. Nick could see that there were two police officers standing outside his room.

The doctor pulled out the chart that hung at the end of the bed and opened it up before speaking to Nick. "My name is Dr. Thomson, and you are a very lucky man. Can you remember who you are? Just squeeze my finger once for yes and twice for no."

Nick squeezed the doctor's finger once.

"Great, Agent Catlin. For all intents and purposes, you should be dead, but apparently one near-death experience saved you from another. According to your chart, you had a brain aneurism as a teen and they put a plate in your head."

The doctor gave a slight smile at the irony of the situation. "This is one for the books. You've got an angel looking out for you. As for the rest of your injuries: You were shot in the left side of your chest, which shattered three of your ribs and punctured your lung. There was extensive damage done, but no arteries were hit. You will probably be on the respirator for a while longer until you heal sufficiently. The shot to your abdomen went through your right kidney. We had to remove it. It's going to take a long time for you to heal completely, but the good news is that you will."

The door opened again and Allen rolled into the room in a wheelchair. His left leg had a cast on it and around his neck was a brace. Nick wished he could tell his friend how glad he was to see him alive.

"I'll give you a few minutes, and then I want to do some tests, Agent Catlin." With that the doctor left.

Allen pulled up next to Nick's bed and smiled. "You have no idea how grateful I'm you're still alive." Nick could see the tears welling up in Allen's eyes. "I know you're probably tired, and apparently this is a one-way conversation, so I'll be quick. I barely escaped myself. After I heard the shots and you yelling I came running. I didn't see you, but I did see that psycho, Elizabeth. I followed her to the front of the warehouse. I guess she saw me. I barely made it out alive. I ended up pinned behind some barrels. When all was said and done, I took a bullet in my leg. It broke the bone, but other than that only got a few minor scrapes and bruises."

Nick so badly wanted to say something, but even if he didn't have a tube down his throat he didn't think he would have the strength.

Allen reached up and put his hand on Nick's arm to comfort him. "There's more, but it can wait until you're better."

Nick grabbed Allen's wrist as he tried to pull away. Nick really wanted to know what he had to say.

Allen said, "All right. I didn't want to tell you this, but Sam was found shot in her home. Her husband came home to find her dead. Thankfully the children were at a friend's house when it happened. I did some checking, and it looks like she had an offshore account set up. I hate to say it, Nick, but it looks like Sam was the leak. We must have been getting too close, and now they're getting rid of loose ends."

Samantha? How could she do something like this? It was out of character, yet the pieces fit. She was the one who suggested the clothing store, and it wouldn't be too hard for a federal agent to reroute someone's luggage. But even after thinking it through logically, he still couldn't picture it. There should have been signs telling them something was wrong.

"I need to get back to my room. FYI, there's press everywhere in the hospital. Someone leaked we had a lead on the case, and we're plastered all over the ten o'clock news."

Allen left the room. Nick realized why he had two police officers at his door. They wanted to keep the press out. He wanted nothing more than to stop whoever was behind these killings and close this case. It didn't matter anymore. The case would be handed over to another team now. Nick had never understood true fear until now, and a large part of him was happy to be relieved of the burden. He knew the only thing for him to do now was heal. Everything else would have to wait.

Eleven

Prophetess

Janet's Journal
Friday, November 20, 2009

It's been several months since I wrote in my journal. Again the children have continued to grow far too quickly, and Uncle Leigh, Michele, and I have all speculated as to what may have been done to them. I know we may never know exactly what was done, but I believe that it has something to do with genetic research. It may even be some sort of government experiment.

What really scares me the most about these children is the fact I have fallen in love with them. They are the family I always wanted to have with my husband, Marcus. The reason I'm scared is because we cannot hide in these woods forever. What kind of life are these children going to have? We're afraid to go to the authorities. Someone involved with the killers may find out about us and, given the children's special gifts, they may end up being some sort of lab experiments for the government. No, I want them to be able to have a life. Maybe once they are old enough we can find a place outside of these woods and live normal lives. Until then we need to hide.

Leigh drove his truck next to his mailbox. He had been in town that evening at a church dinner to raise money for missionaries. It was always nice to give when he could, but money was becoming a topic that brought knots to his stomach. As he grabbed his mail, the cold winter air reminded him that it was only a few weeks till Christmas. Not only was the money tight and he worried about buying presents, but the FBI was watching his every move.

After Angie had used the credit card, Leigh was brought in for questioning. They thought he was funding Janet and Michele but couldn't trace the online transactions. Thankfully Angie had somehow covered her tracks. Leigh smirked as he thought about how smart the children were—even the FBI was baffled. Ever since that time agents had been camped just outside the ranch. Having been raised on the ranch, Leigh knew nearly everyone in town, and that made spotting the FBI too easy at times. They did create a big problem, however. It was difficult to buy groceries or go shopping without being followed. Thankfully, Blake helped out a lot. They weren't focusing on him that much, and it was easier to have him pick up the supplies for Janet and the children.

Up the road a quarter mile, Leigh could see their car with the lights out. He shook his head at the situation as he gazed at the mail. The dread and nerves that had been haunting Leigh came back as he saw his tax statement for the ranch. It was a couple months overdue, and there was no more delaying. Leigh knew he would have to use the last of his family's savings in order to keep the ranch going for a few more months. The money was almost gone, and it was time to let Janet and Michele know the situation.

Leigh pulled up to his house and around the back, away from prying eyes. He was grateful that the hills to get to the cabin couldn't be seen from the roadside. It was one less thing he had to worry about. The realization of what his niece and Michele would have to do scared him. They would be forced to go to the FBI and pray for the best. More than ever, he needed to keep his eyes on God and not the problems.

He showed up around seven that Saturday night and found everyone sitting around the fireplace. The children were playing quietly together for once, and both Janet and Michele waved at him from the couch. They had been watching *Veggie Tales™*. Leigh had no idea how many times they had watched those videos, but it always seemed to be the same ones every time he came to the cabin.

He wiped his shoes and closed the door behind him, which alerted the children he was there. All of them got up off the floor, yelling "Uncle Leigh!" and rushed to hug him. He greeted them all and gave each of them a kiss on the forehead. Janet offered him some coffee, which he gladly accepted. The children went back to half-watching the show and half playing with toys in the living room.

As Leigh and Janet sat in the dining room drinking coffee, Michele stayed with the children. At first he was just going to blurt it all out about the money. But since Michele would be as much affected by this as any of them, he figured he should wait until the children went to bed.

So the two of them sat and shared how each of their weeks had been, nothing deep. Janet had a list of things that needed to be done around the cabin, and Leigh felt his heart sink. The roof had started to leak, but that would have to wait until spring to fix properly. Leigh wasn't even sure they had that long. Also, the marine batteries needed to be charged again and possibly replaced. Leigh had noticed that they weren't holding a charge for as long as they should be lately. As for the children, they needed more clothes, especially Sampson.

Leigh didn't know how he was going to keep up with how fast the children were growing. Every few months he had been asking Blake to pick up clothes for them. He didn't want to take advantage of the help. Blake had understood at first, but lately Leigh had noticed an almost resentful attitude whenever he asked for a favor. He would cross that bridge later.

The more Janet talked, the tighter the knot in his stomach became, as the feeling of being overwhelmed combined with exhaustion crept in. Finally it ended when she got up and excused herself to head for the bathroom. Leigh tried to get his wits about him. He was so distracted that he almost didn't notice little Anna was standing at his side. Her pretty hazel eyes somehow comforted him as she raised her arms, wanting him to pick her up.

As tired and upset as Leigh was, he still couldn't help but smile at the child. He set her on his lap and gave her a kiss on the forehead. It never ceased to amaze him how fast they were all growing. To an outsider Anna would look to be a normal healthy five-year-old, yet she wasn't quite two and a half. More difficult was keeping a perspective on the children's intellectual levels. Each was brilliant, to say the least, and had his or her own strengths.

Angie was the computer whiz, which had already proven to be dangerous. Sampson was the philosopher of the group. He had taken up reading anything and everything that Leigh had brought to the cabin, including the Bible. What was even more amazing was the fact he memorized everything he read. Often Leigh would ask him where a certain Bible verse was, and the boy didn't hesitate to answer.

Marcus was the tough one of the group, and it showed. His constant fighting and hyper personality made him hard to deal with, but he could pick up any sport or physical challenge. His body was the only thing holding him back from being the greatest athlete Leigh had ever seen. He knew that once Marcus was old enough, there would be no stopping the boy at whatever he wanted to do.

As for Zack, he was a cross between Angie and Marcus. His ability to do calculations in his head was remarkable, and his speed and reflexes were far beyond anything that even an adult could do. He also liked to tinker with things. Leigh had brought a remote control car for the children to play with, and the following week Zack had completely disassembled it. That wasn't quite as impressive as when he put it back together in perfect working order.

Each of the children was unique and gifted, but Anna was the one Leigh found the most interesting and strange. It had been obvious to all of the adults that her perception of others' feelings was beyond any normal human being. It was eerie. He didn't think someone could be genetically altered to read another person's thoughts. What did he know? He was only a country boy.

Leigh forced a smile. "How's my little girl?"

Anna kept looking down at the floor. It was clear to see she was pondering something.

"What's wrong, sweetheart?"

Finally she replied, "Don't tell Mama yet, Uncle Leigh."

Her answer shocked him. All he could do was stare at her for a few seconds. "Why do you say that?"

Still she didn't look up at him. She was uncomfortable. That much was clear as she continued to stare at the floor.

"Go on. It's all right," he coaxed her.

Finally she said, "He told me to tell you."

This was not what Leigh had expected. Actually, he didn't know what to expect, but the idea that the girl was hearing voices hadn't crossed his mind. Pressing the issue, he asked, "Who's 'he'?"

Tears welled up in her eyes. "Jesus."

Again Leigh didn't know what to say.

How could that be? He tried to wrap his mind around what the little girl was saying. "Are you telling me that God told you to say that to me?"

Anna just nodded. Tears ran down her cheeks. The sight of her crying broke Leigh's heart. He pulled her closer. "You don't need to be afraid, Anna. I just want to understand what's happening. So you hear God speak to you, and He told you to not talk to Mama about what?"

She finally gazed into his face as if he had asked her a silly question and said, "The money. God's going to take care of it for us."

Once she said that, he didn't know what to say or think. Was it possible she was truly hearing from God, or was this part of what was done to these children? Leigh was deep in thought with these questions when Anna said, "It's God. He told me to say that to you too."

His face went pale. He looked into Anna's eyes. Anna took the opportunity to speak thoughts that Leigh realized she had never felt she could share before. She said, "I didn't want to tell Mama 'cause she's been mad at God, and I didn't want her mad at me, too. Aunt Shelly doesn't like me much. I think she's scared of me."

Leigh finished her thought for her. "And I'm the only one who'll believe you." He hugged her. He had heard of people in other churches who had ministries of a prophetic nature. He had never actually met one before. This was all new to Leigh, and he wasn't sure how to handle it. To be safe, he would heed the little girl's advice and keep quiet about the money for the time being.

For a few seconds Anna lay against her uncle's chest. Finally she said, "Aunt Shelly wants to leave."

Leigh had barely recovered from the first shock when Anna laid this revelation on him. "We scare her, and she wants to leave. We need to let her go."

Just at that moment they both could hear Janet coming back down the hallway toward them.

Leigh put Anna down. "Go play in the living room with your brothers and sister. I want to talk to Mama."

As his niece walked into dining room past Anna, Leigh said, "We need to talk."

Twelve

Storm

May 2010

Spring was in full bloom and the children continued to grow. Janet was still dealing with what Uncle Leigh had told her about Anna's gift of prophesy and about Michele wanting to leave. At first she didn't want to believe any of it, but over the past five months she changed her mind. She noticed little things that Anna would say or do that certainly made it seem like she was hearing from God or reading people's minds. Also, she watched Michele more closely.

Her friend's reactions to the children and their gifts made it evident to Janet that what Uncle Leigh said was true. She wanted to leave. Janet hadn't wanted to acknowledge the truth that had been right before her eyes. Michele's feelings became clearer when Janet helped Uncle Leigh baptize the children in the lake. Michele refused to participate, and Janet could see the children were disappointed—especially Marcus. He had grown the closest to Michele. This was another reason Janet put off talking to her. She knew it was selfish, but she had gotten used to having Michele there for support. Although the main reason was mostly selfish, there was also the children's feelings to consider. They loved Michele, despite her lack of interest in them.

After several weeks had passed, it became easier for Janet to put off talking to Michele about the subject, and with Blake and Uncle Leigh starting work on the roof it made it even easier to ignore. Janet found ways of keeping the children out of Michele's way, in hopes of lightening the tension, which always grew when Blake was around. Janet even tried to hide her feelings for Blake, because it only added to Michele's bad attitude. She could only imagine the thoughts going through her friend's mind. She knew Michele liked Blake too and probably resented her for stealing the only viable relationship they might be able to have.

As Uncle Leigh and Blake worked on the roof, Janet decided it would probably be best if she took the children for a walk. The children were all excited when she told them they were going to go pick berries to make a pie later. Anything was better than dealing with Michele.

After lunch Janet gathered all the children and headed east toward a field that she remembered from when she had been a child. At the far end had been a large row of blackberry bushes, and she hoped they were still there.

It took them about fifteen minutes to get to the field, and when they did, it was much larger than Janet remembered. All the grass was overgrown and the path she remembered was gone—but she wasn't going to let that stop her. The children followed right behind her as she made a path with a stick she picked up along the way. As the sun beat down on them, she realized that the children probably shouldn't be out in the heat for too long. She quickened her pace when the blackberry bushes came into view. The children saw them and grew excited.

Soon they made it across the long field and Janet handed them each a plastic bag to put the berries in. They would probably eat most of what they picked, but that was the fun of picking the berries. Each of them eagerly ran over to the bushes.

A short while later Janet was glad she'd come prepared. She pulled out a couple of washcloths and poured some water on them. The children had already made a mess of themselves, and Janet laughed at the sight of blackberry juice all over their faces and hands. Each of them beamed with pleasure as she managed to wash their faces. Every now and then one of them would toss a couple berries into their bag, but not often.

"Make sure you get some in your bags," she reminded them, smiling.

As they were in the middle of feasting, Janet heard something in the distance. She couldn't make out what it was at first. She stopped picking berries for a minute to listen for the sound again. It came. *Thunder.* Janet looked up to see a cloud forming in the sky. A brisk breeze was building, causing her hair to blow into her eyes. She hadn't thought there would be any rain today, but clearly they needed to get back to the cabin.

"Okay, everyone, finish wiping your hands and mouths. Make sure you have your bags with you. We need to go back now."

There was a collective sigh and some whining—all except Zack. He looked pale.

"Are you feeling okay, Zack?" She placed a hand to his forehead. He was running a fever. "Can you walk back, sweetheart?"

Zack didn't say anything but nodded.

She felt bad now having taken them out on a walk in this heat. She ordered, "All right, everyone, follow me. Hurry now."

Janet led them back along the path she had made earlier, only this time she hurried her pace. As they made their way across the field, several more clouds filled the air. The wind was picking up speed also. She only took a few glances back at the children to make sure they were keeping up with her.

At the other end of the field, she looked back. Zack was standing in the middle of the field, bent over, with his hands on his thighs. He looked very sick, and Janet berated herself for not keeping a better eye on him. She told the children to wait while she went to go get Zack. The rain had just begun to pour down as a thunderclap exploded overhead. The force of the thunder vibrated through Janet's body, forcing her to cover her ears.

When she looked up again, Zack was standing, staring into the sky. Tears poured down his face; Janet could see the boy was terrified. The clouds overhead became almost black as another thunderclap rocked the field and caused Janet to once again cover her ears and stop. She was only about twenty feet away from Zack when it happened.

The first bolt of lightning blinded Janet and sent her backwards onto the ground. As her sight finally came back, another bolt of lightning struck. This time she shielded her eyes with her arm. She could see briefly what was happening as she lay in the grass. The lightning struck Zack several times. Janet could only watch in horror the vision of her little boy glowing in the middle of the field in between bolts. Then another bolt of lightning hit him, then another. Janet couldn't believe her eyes. She screamed out Zack's name, only to be drowned out by the deafening thunder overhead. Fear of losing Zack overtook her. Janet got to her feet and ran toward him in disregard of her own safety. Another bolt struck her boy. Again she fell to the ground, hitting her head.

Zack's screaming brought her back. His voice was heart-wrenching and almost unworldly as Janet lifted her head to see. Zack was glowing so brightly it was almost impossible to look directly at him. Then with a jerk of his hands over his head Zack let out an even louder scream, releasing a burst of energy from his hands into the clouds overhead. It seemed to last forever, but when it ended she watched Zack finally fall to the ground, followed by a loud thunderclap that dispersed the clouds. A single ray of light broke through from overhead and shone down on Zack's body.

Janet was frozen momentarily at the sight, even though every part of her being wanted to run to her boy. With great effort she got to her feet, fighting off the fear that was trying to paralyze her, and ran to Zack's side. She knelt down beside him and hurried to put her ear to his mouth to see if he was breathing. Janet cried in relief when she heard his tiny breaths. It was difficult to see around her as she picked up Zack. The smoke from the ground that had been singed made it difficult to find her direction. His body felt like it was on fire. Her adrenaline helped her ignore the pain from the heat. Finally Janet was able to see the other children standing where she had left them and ran as fast as she could.

The rain dissipated the closer she got to the edge of the trees, and she found herself having a hard time breathing because of the heat radiating from Zack. The rain was evaporating off of the boy, making Janet feel like she was running in a sauna.

"Everyone come! Now!" she yelled out to the children.

Janet didn't wait to see if they were doing as she asked but instead kept running straight toward the cabin. Unsure of how much further she could run with Zack before collapsing, she pushed forward. She collapsed from exhaustion and relief when she saw Blake running toward her.

Janet looked up at Blake as he yelled, "What happened?"

All she could do was shake her head. The shock of what just happened made her incapable of saying anything at that moment.

Blake grabbed Zack out of her arms. "Janet, you need to get the other children back to the cabin. Do you understand me?"

Janet didn't reply.

"JANET!"

This shook her out of her daze. "I have the children. Go," she said weakly. She watched as Blake ran off with Zack.

Dazed and confused, Janet somehow managed to gather all the children and walk them back to the cabin. When she got back, Zack was laying on the sofa with his shirt off and an ice pack on his head. Michele was kneeling down beside him, taking his pulse, as both Blake and Uncle Leigh stood by.

As Janet walked through the front door, Uncle Leigh said, "Blake, do me a favor and take the children outside so they don't see Zack like this."

Janet stood fixated on Zack.

"Well, what happened out there? We heard the thunder and then we saw the lightning striking. Did he get hit?" Uncle Leigh asked her.

She ignored his question as memories of losing her husband ran through her head.

Uncle Leigh grabbed her by the shoulders and forced her to look at him. "Did he get hit?"

Janet finally was able to focus. "Yes. Yes!"

"There's not a scratch on him. Are you sure he was struck?" Michele asked.

"I watched it with my own eyes," Janet said as she cried. "Over and over. I thought it wasn't going to stop. I couldn't help him."

"Well, there's no sign of injuries, but he is burning up. His temperature is well over 106. If we don't get it down, he'll die. He's in some sort of comatose state right now, and his pulse is way down, which makes no sense with the fever he has. I don't know what we can do for him."

There was another pause as all three studied Zack, lying on the sofa. Janet was just about to say something when Uncle Leigh stepped over to Zack and knelt down on one knee next to him. She watched as her uncle placed his hand on Zack's chest and lowered his head. She wasn't sure what he was doing at first, but then she heard him.

"Father, in the name of Jesus, spare this boy's life and heal him. Take away this fever and give him health again. Your Word says by Your stripes we are healed, please..." He couldn't finish speaking.

There was a long, awkward silence as Uncle Leigh kept his hand on Zack. Janet could hear him praying quietly. She could see that Michele was having the same reaction she was. She didn't know what to say or think. Janet hadn't seen him pray like that in years. She wasn't sure why it was shocking to her. Michele stared at her, as if asking for guidance as to what they should be doing. Janet thought about saying something to her uncle, but she didn't want to hurt his feelings.

Michele left the room and went into the kitchen, leaving Janet alone with her thoughts. She finally put her hand on his shoulder. When he didn't look up, Janet figured she had better say something. She jumped and screamed when Zack arched his back. The boy took a deep breath as his eyes opened wide.

Zack quickly sat upright and hugged Uncle Leigh. Janet joined in the hug as all cried from relief. After a minute Zack calmed down, and Uncle Leigh stood up to let Janet examine him more closely. His temperature was back to normal; the boy was going to be fine.

Janet grabbed Zack back into her arms once again. She looked up at her uncle, unsure what to say to him. There was an understanding between them.

Leigh was the first to break the silence. "Don't ever tell me God doesn't care."

Janet knew what he was referring to. The night of their argument after her husband died.

She had yelled at Uncle Leigh, "God doesn't care." His only offense was trying to comfort her through her pain. She wanted desperately to say, "I'm sorry," but her emotional walls wouldn't allow her. Instead she squeezed Zack a little tighter.

Later that night Janet sat in the living room with Uncle Leigh and Michele. They were discussing what had happened that day in more detail.

"This is ridiculous," Michele blurted out. "How are we supposed to raise kids like this?"

Janet shared Michele's frustration. "Uncle Leigh, what are we supposed to do? A kid gets hit by lightning repeatedly and lives. Another has the strength of five men. I mean, look at Anna. No one should be able to read another human being the way she can. What I'm afraid of is that we haven't seen everything."

Uncle Leigh didn't say anything right away, but Janet knew that look. His brow was slanted slightly, and the lines at the side of his eyes became more defined. He was working on sharing something profound.

Michele didn't wait for Uncle Leigh. "She's right. Something's going on with Marcus, too. The pain he's going through. It's almost like something is changing inside him. How he can take the pain is beyond me."

Janet sat further back in her chair and let out a sigh of frustration. "It's like something out of a comic book or movie."

All were silent until Uncle Leigh finally spoke up. "I'm sorry I don't have all the answers for you two. What's going on with these youngsters is a lot to take in. They ain't normal, but I know one thing to be true. They were brought into this world for a reason. I see God's hand on each of them, so hold strong, girls. I think we are just caretakers of something far more important than any of us can imagine."

Quiet reigned once again. There was another moment of silence.

"Why don't we call it a night? It's been a long day." Janet suggested.

"Good idea," her uncle agreed.

Once Uncle Leigh left, Janet went straight to her bedroom. It was hard to sleep. She wrestled with her conflicting feelings of anger and resentment from the past. She knew God was speaking to her, no matter how hard she fought him. For the first time since her husband died, Janet felt something alive inside her spirit, and she didn't want to fight it anymore.

Thirteen

Plans

The view of the city at night was breathtaking with all the lights and traffic moving like rivers of stars below. Tibon gazed from his twenty-third-story office window, deep in thought. The windows went from floor to ceiling in a half circle around his desk. It made for easy viewing of the Hudson River and the Empire State Building.

He looked into the window at himself. CEO of a corporation was a perfect cover. He admired his dark gray three-piece suit and bright red necktie. He could see the gradual graying of his once-black hair as he entered his forties. The look was exactly what he was going for, given he now owned all of INYO industries. This building was one of its subsidiaries, and he made sure there was no connection that could be trailed from his mother company.

He continued to amaze himself at how he was able to accumulate the funding for his project in such short a time. In the last two years alone he had advanced his research ahead of schedule. And now he was on the verge of his first real breakthrough. It was time to test his findings, but he found himself hesitant to proceed. He weighed the pros and cons of what he was about to do, which caused the memories to rush through his mind yet again. The explosion, the lies, the cover-ups…they all needed to be punished for what they had done. The feelings of anger and hatred welled up inside of him as he replayed the day his family was murdered. There was something else in the back of his thoughts. Always out of memory's reach, like a dream you knew only a moment ago but have now forgotten….

The intercom from his desk buzzed and brought him back to the present. Tibon turned in his wheelchair to answer.

"What is it?" he snapped.

"Sir, I think you will want to come down to Examination Room Three. It's happened again," a man's voice rang out.

Tibon's eyes narrowed in disgust. "I'll be right down."

He jerked his wheelchair around his desk and followed a ramp that encircled the entire office. Actually, his office was more equivalent to a large presidential suite. There was a sunken living room with ramps for his wheelchair. Dark brown leather furniture accompanied by a fully stocked bar set the tone for success. He moved along a ramp that ran along the edges of the office. To the left-hand side of the room was a private elevator that fit in nicely with the mahogany paneling.

Tibon opened up the elevator and headed down to the basement level. Once there he rolled down the hallway, ignoring the handful of personnel walking by. He could see they were afraid to look him in the eyes, but each nodded as he passed. They were afraid of him—just the way he wanted it. Every employee knew their place. They were more like slaves, really. It wasn't fear of their own lives that kept them motivated, no. It was fear for their families. Thanks to his financial backers, he not only received funding for his project but also workers. Their families were held as collateral. The moment they displeased him a family member paid the price back home. The price was death.

He wheeled into Examination Room Three as the medic who had called him stood next to a covered body lying on one of the tables. His eyes showed panic as Tibon pulled up next to the body on the opposite side of the table. With a flick of a switch on his wheelchair, his seat rose to a more appropriate height to view the body.

In anticipation of his question, the medic pulled the cover back, revealing a beautiful young girl about six years old. There were no visible marks or bruises on her, but he knew she was dead, just like the others.

"Have you found anything this time?" he asked sharply.

"No sir, not yet, but I was about to start the autopsy on her and thought you would want to see her before I started. All of her blood work was normal, and I already pumped her stomach. I found nothing to suggest poison, but this is only preliminary."

He was surrounded by a group of idiots. He should shoot the man, but this idiot was one of his best and he needed him. Tibon shot a look of anger at the man to make sure he understood his life was in the balance.

"I do have some good news," the medic hurried to add. "The genetic markers you asked us to isolate have been completed and are ready for testing, sir."

This last bit of news caused Tibon to let go of the fact they had just lost the fourth test subject, leaving only one left from the original ten from Poughkeepsie. Liz still hadn't found the other five children and the two nurses yet. He doubted they would at this point. He shook off the frustration that accompanied thinking about Liz's failures and focused on moving forward with his plans. Thanks to the test results born out of that project, he was now hopeful to complete what he had begun.

Fourteen

Surprise

June 2011

Summer was in full bloom on the Barrus Ranch. It was another hot day well over ninety degrees. Leigh sat in his office staring at the bills and payroll with a knot in his stomach. He had been selling off several acres of forest to pay the bills, but that had come to an end once the conservationists found out and declared part of his property wetlands. Every option except selling the ranch had been taken away. But he couldn't sell because of Janet and the children. Once again he sat with his eyes closed and prayed to God for help, but before he could truly start, the front door opened.

Blake walked toward him. "Did I catch you at a bad time, Leigh?"

He waved Blake in with a smile. "Nah, come on in. I could use a break. What can I do you for? Or are you just here taking a breather in the air conditioning?"

Blake smiled at Leigh as he placed a pile of mail on the desk. "I got the mail for you."

Leigh looked at the ever-increasing pile of bills on his desk and forced a smile. "Thanks, son. I appreciate it."

Blake turned to leave, then stopped. Facing Leigh again, he asked, "You sure there's nothing I can do? You've been real distant the last few months. I know it's none of my business, but is something wrong?"

Blake had become like a son to Leigh over the years, and his fatherly instincts wanted to protect everyone from the problems he was dealing with. A part of him knew it wasn't necessarily the right thing to do, but he didn't want anyone else to have to worry about the finances. He kept strong in his faith that God was going to see them through, no matter what happened.

Leigh replied, "I much appreciate it, son, but I'm fine. Just got a lot on my mind right now is all."

With a hesitant nod Blake turned and left. Leigh fumbled through the new mail, sorting out all of the bills from the junk, but one envelope caught his eye. It was from his investment bank that held what little was left of his family's inheritance. Dread came over him as he opened it. Thoughts of seeing the account closed or the bank taking what little was left ran through his mind.

Holding his breath, he read the notice and…was shocked. It was a simple statement of his account and all of the recent transactions. Leigh sat staring at the piece of paper for several seconds before blinking. He kept re-reading it because what he saw didn't make sense. It must be a mistake.

The balance of the account last month had been just under a couple thousand dollars, which wouldn't even cover the taxes for this quarter. Now it was showing exactly $358,233.51!

Leigh snapped out of his shocked state and called his investment bank to confirm. After holding for nearly twenty minutes, he got a live person. They went over the account and all of the transactions with him. Apparently Leigh had made several online transactions over the bank's Internet website that involved his stocks—107, to be exact. Leigh thanked the person and hung up. He smiled to himself as he headed out the door to his truck.

Sniffling and quick short breaths filled the room as Michele sat on her bed holding Marcus. She had closed the curtains so the sunlight wouldn't add to the pain he was already feeling. She rocked him slowly while he clenched his eyes shut and covered his ears in an attempt to fight off the pain. He had been experiencing migraines accompanied by severe earaches for a couple of months now, and she was the one he ran to when they started. She could feel the weight of the boy's body leaning hard against her. He had grown into a very muscular eight-year-old with an uncontrolled temper. She knew that whatever had been done four years ago when the children were born was causing the outbursts, but they hadn't found anything to help the boy.

She wasn't sure why Marcus was the only one of the children who had grown attached to her. He ran to her for comfort when the bouts of pain would begin. Thankfully they only lasted for a few minutes, but it seemed like an eternity sometimes. What really surprised Michele was the fact Marcus never cried. He simply would hold his ears and rock back and forth. He never verbalized his anguish, and Michele was sure he was in horrible pain. It broke her heart that there was nothing they could do to help him through these episodes. As far as anyone could tell, there was nothing wrong with him medically. Then again, they couldn't take him to a hospital to run tests.

The only upside to the problem was that once the pain went away Marcus didn't seem to be affected. He simply went back to playing or doing chores. He was probably the toughest boy she had ever seen and one of the strongest, except for Sampson.

At last the pain subsided, and Michele watched from her window as Marcus went outside. He started hitting the punching bag that Leigh brought him to work out with. It helped Marcus focus his anger and frustration. Instead of fighting with the other children, he took out his inner demons on the bag. Because of his growing attachment to her, she decided to try and make the best of her situation. The longer she stayed, more torn she became.

She loved Janet like a sister. No matter how hard she tried to get used to the children and living isolated, she still wanted desperately to leave. Now Marcus growing so close to her made it even more difficult.

"Uncle Leigh's coming!" The children yelled, interrupting her thoughts. He wasn't supposed to be visiting till the evening. What was the occasion?

Janet stood on the porch with Anna at her side, watching the other children run to greet Uncle Leigh. It was a normal sight to her, but to an outsider it may have looked strange. If she didn't know better, it looked like three eight-year-olds and a short man hugging and kissing Uncle Leigh. Sampson had grown to just over five feet tall. Over the last year the boy had grown much faster than the other children, and both he and Marcus had begun to grow facial hair. It was just another side effect from the project. Sampson wasn't so fond of shaving or having his hair cut every week, so he decided to let his hair grow out and pulled it back into a ponytail to go along with his ever-growing full beard.

His increasing size, both in height and width, gave him a look of a full-grown man, and to see him hugging and kissing Uncle Leigh was strange. Everything about these children was strange, but she loved them.

Leigh made his way toward the porch, and Janet could see he was trying to hide a smile. Most of his glances were focused on Anna, as he came closer to the porch. Before Janet could say hello to Uncle Leigh, Anna said in a low voice, "He knows, Mama."

"Howdy there, little lady," Leigh greeted Anna with his arms opened wide.

When Anna didn't come to him, Janet said, "We got to talk."

It was Leigh who now looked ashamed. "Yeah, sure."

Janet told the children, "Stay outside for a few minutes and play. The grownups need to have a little discussion."

Michele had come out of her room and followed Janet and Leigh into the dining room.

"What's up, Leigh?" Michele greeted.

Leigh moved toward a chair. "How could you?" Janet hissed. She could see her tone caught both Uncle Leigh and Michele by surprise. By the look in his eyes he knew why she was angry.

"Please don't be upset, Janet. I was handling the situation as best as I could. I didn't see any reason to go and add to your worries."

Janet kicked the table. "When were you going to say something? When it was too late?"

Michele stepped between them. "I don't mean to seem like an idiot, but what's wrong with you two? What's this about?"

Janet shot a glare at Uncle Leigh as if to say, "You tell her." She crossed her arms and waited.

"Michele, the ranch hasn't been doing so good the last few years, and I've been using up my life savings to keep us afloat. The taxes been late getting paid, and I've had a sell off several acres of forest to keep us going."

Janet waited for Michele's reaction.

"Oh." Michele frowned. "Are you saying we're going to have to move?"

Leigh pulled out a piece of paper from his shirt and slid it across the dining room table. Michele picked it up and read as Leigh said to her, "No, young lady. No one's going to be going anywhere anytime soon. That's the new balance in my account. Should be enough to last us awhile."

Michele appeared even more confused than she had been previously, and Leigh tried to clarify for her. "My best guess, Michele, is that Janet here has been getting some help from our five geniuses."

"Yes," Janet admitted. "I made Anna tell me what was wrong with you, Uncle Leigh. I knew something had been bothering you for a long time. At first I was shocked and scared, but Anna offered a solution. She said with Angie's help she could get your stocks back up. So I helped them by telling them your personal information. I was surprised how much I remembered from the time I used to do the books for you."

Janet smiled. "They were amazing. For two months Anna studied the stocks and different markets. I made notes for her as both of them went from one website to another, pulling up news articles and stock reports. I don't know how they did it, but Angie was able to create an online account in your name, and they sat at the computer trading and buying stocks. Each day the account went up higher and higher until I finally had to say enough."

"Janet, I'm sorry I didn't tell you. I love you, and like I said, I didn't want for you to worry."

"I know," Janet said as the frustration finally subsided. "But if we're a family, then you can't be keeping things like this from me."

"What?" Michele snapped at her. "Family! What do you know about family? You stand here and say to him that he shouldn't keep things from you, yet that's exactly what you did to me! When were you going to say something to me? Huh? Or am I not a part of this family? This is unbelievable. You—"

Michele stopped herself. It was clear she couldn't continue the conversation, and she turned away to go back to her room. Janet called for her to come back, but Leigh put up a hand to warn her to let Michele go. There was an awkward silence as both sat and replayed what had just happened.

"You've put it off for too long. She's right, you know? Just like you were right that I should have said something to you sooner. You know she's not happy here, and you know that you got to let her go. That's why you didn't tell her what was happening. You need to let go of your fears and talk to her."

Janet didn't say anything. She nodded weakly at Uncle Leigh. He was right, and she knew it. It was time.

That evening Leigh helped put all the children to bed while Janet cleaned up the dinner dishes. He could tell the children sensed something was wrong, so he took them to bed individually himself and prayed with them. When he came downstairs, Janet brought a sandwich on a plate to Michele's room. He watched out of the corner of his eye as Janet knocked on the door and waited for a reply.

After a few seconds he could hear Janet ask, "Can I come in? I need to talk with you."

Then Janet disappeared into the bedroom. At the same time, Leigh could hear one of the doors opening from upstairs. He glanced up to see Marcus leaning over the railing. He looked worried, and Leigh felt sorry for the boy. He waved him to come down to the living room and within seconds Marcus was in his uncle's lap.

"Can't sleep, hey?"

Marcus replied with a slight shake of his head.

"You know what helps me relax sometimes is a glass of milk. Would you like to have some with me?"

Marcus nodded at Leigh. He smiled at the boy and set him in a chair while he went to get them milk. Leigh wasn't sure when it happened, but as he poured milk into their glasses he glanced back at Marcus and could see the pain on the boy's face as he held his ears. Another episode.

Marcus sat upright in the chair as the twinges ached in his ears. Instinctively he placed his hands over them, but this time the pain became more of a throbbing sensation rather than sharp, knifing pains. It was strange at first. Even though he covered his ears, he could still hear. It sounded like someone had turned up the volume in his head as the sounds around him became an onslaught of noise. The milk pouring into the glass sounded like a waterfall and the ticking of the clock on the mantle echoed as if he had it pressed against his ear. Both his and Uncle Leigh's heartbeats pounded in his mind. Every sound flooded him as if they had been amplified through a loudspeaker. It hurt at first, but as the thudding approach of Uncle Leigh's footsteps grew closer, Marcus slowly removed his hands from his head.

Uncle Leigh asked, "ARE YOU OKAY, MARCUS?"

His uncle's voice boomed in his head and made him wince. The flood of noises continued: wind in the trees outside and the splash of a fish jumping in the lake. It sounded like he was standing only a few feet away. More sounds bombarded him as he fought off the pain. He could hear Zack coughing upstairs in their room and Anna talking with Angie as they whispered about Aunt Shelly and Mama.

"Marcus?" Uncle Leigh's voice sounded softer. "Are you all right, son?"

The intensity of the sounds was fading, yet Marcus could still hear each of them. He nodded to Uncle Leigh. "Yes, sir."

Marcus stared at the wall as he allowed all of the sounds resonate in his head. With each second passing by he found himself able to discern and isolate them. Something changed. All the other sounds faded as a new noise made its way to the foreground. It was Mama and Aunt Shelly in the other room. The voices were faint at first, but the more he focused his concentration on their words the clearer they became. It took a minute, but he was finally able to hear clearly.

Janet cut off Michele when she tried to make light of what happened earlier. "Michele, please hear me out. This has been a long time coming, and I owe you an apology."

She leaned up against the windowsill while Michele sat on her bed. "I'm sorry that I didn't tell you about the money issue. I guess I am more like my uncle than I'd like to admit. Our friendship means so much to me. I consider you family, and so do the children. That's why this is so hard for me to say. It's clear you're not happy here, and I've been selfish not wanting you to leave. I feared raising the kids on my own, but that shouldn't come at the expense of your happiness. What I'm trying to say to you is that if you want to leave, I won't be hurt and I'll understand completely."

Janet crossed over to the bed and sat next to Michele. "There'll be no hard feelings, I promise you. Just know you owe me nothing. Actually, I owe you more than you will ever know."

There was a long pause. Janet wasn't sure how her friend was going to react.

"Thank you," Michele said softly. "I do love you, Janet. You're my sister. And I love the children. But sometimes it's just been…" She choked on her words.

Janet patted her on the back gently and put her arm around her shoulders. "I know, I know. But it's going to be all right. We're going to be fine, and so are you."

They hugged each other and Michele said, "Maybe we should go talk to Uncle Leigh and get his input on how we should handle this."

"That's a good idea." A huge weight lifted from Janet's shoulders. One glance at Michelle, and Janet could tell her friend felt the same way. Janet followed Michele to the door, but when it opened, they found Marcus standing in the hallway. He stood wide-eyed as he looked up at Michele. At first Janet thought he was having another one of his headache episodes, but as she gazed into his eyes she could tell it was something much more serious. His eyes conveyed the fear he was feeling, along with betrayal. Before she could say anything, Marcus turned away from them and ran out the front door into the night.

Uncle Leigh ran to the door calling for Marcus to come back, but after a few seconds Janet realized he wasn't coming back. Leigh faced her and Michele and asked, "What happened?"

Janet replied, "I was about to ask you the same question."

"He was sitting drinking a glass of milk with me one moment, and the next he's rushing to your bedroom. I asked him what was wrong, but your door opened and he bolted."

Michele said, "He heard us talking."

Uncle Leigh shook his head and replied, "There's no way he heard you. He was sitting with me the whole time."

"I don't know how he heard, Uncle Leigh, but his eyes said that he did."

Fifteen

Rush

The clear night sky was fading from his vision as a cool summer breeze blew across his face. Marcus could feel the life draining from his body as the blood continued to pour from his leg that was now broken and encased in a metal trap. He cried as he recalled the events of the night and the feelings of fear and abandonment.

He had run out of the cabin as fast as he could with only the sound of Uncle Leigh crying out after him. At first he didn't know where he was running to, but at least it was away from the betrayal he was feeling. He had only his pajamas on and was barefoot, but he didn't care. Fear drove him to keep running. His eyes had not adjusted to the darkness. Several times he cut his arms and legs on tree branches. It didn't slow him down. The adrenaline running through his body masked the pain.

The rush of adrenaline made his stomach warm. It felt like a fever beginning to rise up within him. His strength and agility grew with each passing minute. Soon it became a flood of fire within him as he picked up more speed. Marcus wasn't sure when it happened, but his eyes had adjusted to the night and everything became clear to him. With his new vision he was able to run even faster. His entire focus was now on the overwhelming flood of power running through his body. Every muscle flowed with adrenaline. His sight, smell, touch, hearing had all been heightened beyond anything he had experienced before. The power seemed to come in waves. With each one he became stronger.

He shot out of the tree line and into an open field. His opportunity to release all of his speed and strength had come. Marcus willed his body to run faster. He could see in the middle of the field a family of deer eating. He tried to follow them. He caught up to one of the bucks. He was beautiful. He had never seen a deer that close up.

Up ahead his eyes focused on the thirty-foot trench in the middle of the field and away from the creature. This part of the woods was new to him. He had no idea how deep the trench went. Something inside him said to go faster. Nothing was going to slow him down. Without any hesitation Marcus reached the edge of the ravine and leaped several feet into the air. He rotated his hands to keep his balance as he soared over the gaping hole below him. When he landed he instinctively tucked and rolled several times. Immediately he sprang back to his feet and continued running. It only took a few seconds before he was back in the forest.

He felt tiny raindrops hit his face. The effect was the equivalent to throwing a bucket of cold water over his head. His attention was now focused on the thunder in the distance. In between the trees he could see clouds rolling in. His strength left his body. He became painfully aware of his wounds all at once—his arms, his legs, and especially his feet. Violently he fell to the ground. His entire body screamed from the exhaustion and injuries.

The rain poured down harder while the leaves from the trees helped shield him, but only slightly. He examined his feet and cringed. There were twigs and small stones imbedded in his feet. Marcus realized that he didn't know where he was or how far away from home he had gone. He was alone, lost, and wounded. Marcus wanted to cry but his instincts to survive overcome his self-pity.

The sudden chill he felt from the rain pouring down upon his body helped him realize he had lost his pajama top somewhere along the way. His pants were almost shredded completely off of his legs. He examined his body more closely. Bleeding came from several gashes along his arms and legs. Several of them were already beginning to heal.

The rain intensified and lightning lit up the sky, which helped Marcus see that his vision had faded some, now that the rush of adrenaline had left his body. What he needed to focus on was his feet. He could feel and see that he had several broken toes. There was nothing he could do about them, but he needed to remove the pebbles and sticks embedded in his feet. One by one he pulled them out. The pain was hard to bear at first, but he knew if he couldn't walk, he wasn't ever going to make it back to his family.

He had learned enough from Mama and Aunt Shelly that with all the punctures in his feet he would surely bleed to death if he didn't do something. Once he had pulled out as much debris as possible from his feet he tore off what little of his pajama bottoms that were left and wrapped his feet to stop the flow of blood.

Now came the hard part, standing. Marcus looked around the forest floor for any kind of branch or stick that he could use to help him walk. He timed his search as the lightning flashed and finally found a limb in the distance that had fallen off one of the trees. He pulled himself on his hands through the puddles of mud that had now been formed all along the ground around him. He made his way to where the tree limb lay and broke off a big enough stick for him to use. It took some work because the wood was wet, but survival outweighed any deterrent at this point.

Using the broken tree limb he pulled himself up onto his feet and immediately fell back to the ground in pain. There were still pieces of wood in his feet, causing knifing pains up into his legs. Several times he tried to get to his feet but fell back down. Determined, he got to his feet with the help of the stick. The pain didn't go away, but he accepted it, just like he had done with the ear and headaches. There was no other option at this point.

Slowly and methodically he made his way back toward the open field. He wasn't sure how long he had been walking when he saw the ravine in the distance. The clouds were beginning to fade and the rain had begun to subside. The closer he got to the middle of the field he could see that the ravine ran the length of the field. There was no way he would be able to climb down and then back up. He could barely walk.

With stick clutched in both hands he trekked around the ravine. The pain in his feet had died down slightly, making it a little easier to navigate. He quickened his pace along the forest edge. As he approached the other side of the ravine, he stopped. He had no idea which direction he came from. Panic. *Which way do I go?* The rain had washed away any tracks of his run earlier. *I want to go home* was his only thought. Aunt Shelly leaving didn't feel as overwhelming.

Uncle Leigh would know what to do. Mama always went to him when she needed help. Prayer. That's what his uncle would do. He bowed his head and prayed a silent prayer to God. Hopes of hearing Mama or Uncle Leigh crying out for him kept him listening, but all he could hear was the diminishing rain and the wind rustling through the forest.

Marcus had almost made it back to where he thought he had come from. Stopping, he hoped to find some clue as to the way home. He would have to guess. The rain stopped and the skies had begun to clear up, revealing all of God's creation above. Dozens of stars filled the sky. Marcus focused on their beauty while walking. His footing had become steadier as more time went by, and the pain had lessened. He found his pace had picked up, but he still wasn't sure if he was going in the right direction.

Just as this thought went through his head he heard a loud clanking of metal below him, followed by pain. Marcus had no idea how long he had been unconscious, but he wished he hadn't awakened. The intensity of the pain running up his leg was excruciating. He cried out in pain as he fought to see what was causing it. Wrapped around his leg was some sort of trap. It had nearly severed his right leg. He could see his foot in an unnatural direction, pointing almost opposite of his kneecap.

The blood was pouring out of him onto the muddy ground, and he could feel the life within him fading with each heartbeat. He laid back down, looking up into the night sky and prayed with what little strength he had left in him. The last thing Marcus saw was a faint light in the distance, and he lost consciousness once again.

Leigh had waited for almost a half hour before going to the ranch and getting the horses. Leigh brought Janet with him and saddled up a horse for her. He directed her to head in the general direction that Marcus ran off. All of the children had gotten up when they heard Uncle Leigh calling out, so he suggested Michele stay at the cabin with them. If she was the reason Marcus ran off in the first place, then he thought it wise that she not come right now.

Leigh had no idea just how far Marcus had gone, and it had already been a couple hours. With flashlight in hand the two of them spread out within shouting distance. Leigh and Janet searched for any sign of the boy until well past midnight.

Leigh could smell a storm moving in. He continued to offer up a silent prayer for Marcus, because that was the only way they were going to find him. The thought of the boy alone and scared in the middle of the forest at night was bad enough, but it was dangerous too. There were animals of all sorts that could mistake him for a meal. Leigh pressed on quicker, and he yelled out to Janet to do the same.

They had searched for several miles, and the rain had begun to pour down, making it even harder to see anything. Not that stopping was an option, and he was sure Janet felt the same. Hope slipped away as he fought off the overwhelming feeling of futility. Janet cried out, and Leigh pulled his horse over to her to see what the fuss was about. As he approached he could see Janet had gotten off her horse and was holding what looked like a piece of Marcus's blue pajamas. Hope resurged. Marcus had come this way.

They were already at least five miles from the cabin and Leigh shook his head as he silently asked himself, *How far did that boy run?*

He jumped back onto his horse and the two of them spanned out again. It wasn't long before Leigh came to a large open field. He could see Janet in the distance to his right was still with him.

The rain finally let up and he yelled out to Janet, "Head across the field."

As they made their way through the field Leigh kept calling out, "Marcus!" His voice was beginning to go. Janet was having the same problem. They needed to find the boy and soon. Leigh flashed his light several feet in front of him and yelled out to Janet, "Watch out for the trench ahead!"

He pulled up to the edge of it and flashed his light, searching for a sign that maybe the boy had fallen in. Given how dark it was, it would have been easy to fall in without noticing in time. After several minutes of moving up and down the ravine there was no sign of Marcus. Again hope was dwindling as the minutes passed by. Leigh pulled up next to Janet. The sky had cleared up, and the moon was shining brightly, which made it easier to see one another.

"There's no way he made it past this. We should go back and fan out again in a different direction."

Janet nodded her agreement, and they headed back into the woods again. Leigh moved even quicker this time as the pressure mounted to find Marcus. He flashed his light from left to right, scanning the forest floor ahead.

Leigh almost missed it at first, but as he brought the flashlight back around something reflected in the distance. He was only twenty feet away when his heart stopped at the site of Marcus on the forest floor. The boy was lying motionless. As Leigh ran to him he could see the metal trap latched around his leg.

Michele sat half asleep on the couch with Anna's head lying on her lap. All of the children had tried to stay up waiting for Mama and Uncle Leigh to come back with Marcus, but sometime after one in the morning they faded to sleep. Michele had gotten pillows and blankets for them as they lay side by side on the living room floor.

The time seemed to drag on as one a.m. turned into two a.m.. The last time Michele checked the clock it was well past three-thirty in the morning. The rainfall on the roof made staying awake an experiment in torture as every instinct in her body wanted to sleep. But her fear and love for Marcus outweighed her desire to sleep while she continued listening for horses outside.

Finally she heard a faint whinnying in the distance. It broke through the silence of the night now that the rain had stopped. She gently slid out from underneath Anna's head and stared through the screen door. The sounds were getting closer, even though she still couldn't see anything. Finally two horses came into sight with Janet and Uncle Leigh on them. She gasped as her vision became clearer and she could see Marcus lying lifelessly over Uncle Leigh's horse.

She ran out to meet them crying, "No, no, no!"

Uncle Leigh ordered, "Out of the way, Michele!" as she tried to get to Marcus.

She could see the trap in Uncle Leigh's hand was wrapped around the boy's leg as he slid Marcus gently off of the horse. Janet had already gotten off of her horse and was helping Leigh move Marcus into the cabin. Michele followed as they made their way inside. She felt that this was all her fault, and she was helpless to do anything about it. Leigh and Janet placed Marcus on the dining room table while she tried to keep all the children back. They had awakened and were standing waiting in the living room when their brother was brought in. She could see they were just as worried as she was, but again she was at a loss as to what to do.

She could see they had put a tourniquet on his leg to stop the bleeding, but his skin was so pale that he already looked dead. Uncle Leigh grabbed at the trap to try and open it up and remove Marcus's leg, but it was rusted shut.

"I need my tools, but I left them back at the ranch," Leigh exclaimed.

Michele watched Janet check Marcus's pulse and, judging by her reaction it wasn't good. Uncle Leigh turned toward Janet and Michele with a look she didn't often see—panic. There was a moment of indecision.

Anna broke the silence. "Sampson, take the trap off of Marcus but be careful with his leg."

Sampson did as she asked. With one pull of his hands the trap snapped open, revealing the broken bone and muscles.

Anna put her hands on both Janet and Michelle. "We need you to go and get clean cloths and hot water along with the first-aid kit and sewing needles." Michele didn't know why, but she did exactly as Anna asked without question. She hurried to the kitchen. She took some towels out of the cabinet along with the water and placed it next to Marcus on the table.

Michele could hear Anna handing out more orders.

"Uncle Leigh, you'll need to get a couple of small pieces of flat wood to use as a splint."

Uncle Leigh headed outside.

Anna continued to direct everyone. "Zack and Angie, you need to set the bone. It looks like a clean break, so we may be able to save his leg."

Michele carried the pitcher of hot water and some clothes and set them on the table next to Marcus.

"Take the cloths and clean the leg and be quick about it. We may not have much time."

Again Michele felt compelled to do what Anna said. It was a strange sensation. She felt like she was watching someone else doing the cleaning of the wound—as if she were standing back watching herself. Angie and Zack held the leg as Michele cleaned the best she could around the gaping wound.

Anna inspected her work. "That's good. It looks like the muscles weren't severed. Zack, hold the leg in the upright position and Angie, you align the bones. You have to feel inside to do it properly, but make sure it's lined up." She turned to Sampson. "We're going to need twine to hold his leg in place. I believe there is some in the shed. Go get it, and bring it back with a knife to cut with."

Sampson ran out the back door. Janet had returned with the sewing needles and thread while Michele continued cleaning around the wound. Anna grabbed one of the blankets from the living room and placed it over Marcus as Uncle Leigh came back with four good pieces of wood to use.

Once everyone was back, Anna got on top of the table and sewed up the wound while Zack and Angie held the leg in place. It was amazing to watch as she sutured Marcus's leg like a professional.

When Anna finished she looked at Uncle Leigh. "Please take off the tourniquet now."

They could see the blood slowly filling the leg as he removed the tourniquet.

Anna asked Janet, "Check his pulse again."

Janet did as she was asked. "It's faint but steady."

Anna looked around at everyone. "We should pray."

Sixteen

Good-bye

October 2011

The morning sun shone over the treetops and caused a glittering effect along the gentle waves on the lake. Leigh had been sitting on the dock for a couple hours praying for Marcus and waiting to see if he was going to live. The exhaustion was becoming a permanent state of being. He took in a deep breath and turned his face upward toward the sky.

Janet called down, "Uncle Leigh, come inside."

He looked at his watch. It was 6:53 a.m. With what little strength he had in him, he walked back up to the cabin. Inside, the children were still sleeping on the floor in the living room. Marcus was lying on his back, his legs propped up by pillows on the couch. Some color had come back to the boy's face, which was a good sign. Janet met him with a large cup of coffee in her hands and invited him to the dining room.

As they both sat down she said, "I needed some company." She forced a smile, even though he could see she was fighting to stay awake. "This is my fifth cup already. It ain't workin'."

Leigh managed a chuckle as he drank his coffee. "I've been running everything over and over in my head. Strange night."

Janet nodded. "So much happened at once, and I'm still trying to sort it all out. The strangest part was Anna."

"Yeah, same for me. When she started telling us what to do, it was like I was sleepwalking or in some sort of daze that I couldn't snap out of."

"Me too. I mean, I knew what was happening, but it was like watching myself from the outside."

"Another gift?" he asked.

"I don't know. But we were all affected by it. The strangest part was the fact she knew exactly what to do. She probably saved Marcus's life this morning."

"I've been praying so."

Janet looked away for a moment. Leigh could see God was still a sore subject for her, but then she said, "I've found myself praying a lot lately. I owe you an apology for the things I said when I left."

Leigh said, "Janet, you don't owe me anything."

"Yes, I do." She finally looked him in the eyes. "I do owe you, more than you'll ever know. When Mama and Aunt Jenny died in the car accident, it was you being there for me that kept me strong, and then when my Marcus died, you were just trying to do the same. I pushed you away and said some horrible things. If it weren't for you being here for us right now, I don't know if I could cope." She choked up.

"I love you too, sweetheart," he said softly, "and I forgave all of that a long time ago. Why don't you go and get some rest, and I'll watch over the kids if they get up?"

Leigh thought she was going to take him up on his offer when a voice called out, "Mama."

Both Leigh and Janet immediately went out into the living room to find Marcus awake. He was still groggy.

Janet leaned over and kissed the boy on the cheek. "I'm here, sweetheart." She knelt down next to him. "Don't speak; just rest. You've had a rough night, and we can talk about it later, okay?"

The boy immediately closed his eyes and fell back to sleep. Janet's emotions flooded to the surface. Uncle Leigh took her in his arms and held her as she released all the tears she'd bottled up all night.

When they were done, Janet wiped her face. "I love you. I can't sleep right now, so if you need to, go back to the ranch."

She was right. He had left everything, once again, for Blake to take care of without notifying him. Going to the dining room, he grabbed the broken trap and headed back to the ranch. He had been trying not to dwell on his growing anger, but he couldn't stop it any longer. Leigh tossed the trap in the back of his pickup with more force than he intended to. *This hunting is going to stop.*

The truck flew by Sheriff Webber's vehicle, doing well over fifty-five miles an hour in a thirty-five zone. He set down his sandwich. A second truck flew past close behind the first truck. *Great.* He didn't even get a bite.

The sheriff flipped on his lights and gave chase. He moved in. Both vehicles looked familiar. The closest was Blake Heroux's truck. Blake was behind the wheel. He knew Blake well. Their daughters went to school together. It was out of character for Blake to be speeding through town like this. Despite his lights and siren, neither truck slowed down. As he reached for the radio to call for backup, the lead truck slowed down and then pulled into a driveway just on the outskirts of town. The house belonged to Bradley Cooper, and Sheriff Webber had a revelation as to who was driving the lead truck.

Leigh Barrus and Bradley Cooper had had a bad relationship for years, stemming all the way back to high school. Bradley was a bad seed, and for some reason he took out his anger on Leigh any chance he could. He could see Leigh getting out of his truck. Leigh grabbed what looked like a trap from the back of his pickup. It made sense now. Blake got out of his truck and attempted to stop Leigh. Bradley often went onto Leigh's property hunting illegally, and it looked like one of the traps he used had been found.

Sheriff Webber quickened his pace to get to the front door. Leigh banged on the door as Blake stood uncomfortably at his side.

Blake had seen that look in Leigh's eyes before. Leigh was mad, and Blake knew he had better stay close to him just in case. Bradley Cooper opened the door, a beer in his hand. He was wearing a stained T-shirt and overalls. It was clear he had not expected company or, more likely, didn't care.

"What do you want, rich boy?"

Leigh threw the broken trap at Bradley's feet and nearly hit him with it. "Is this yours? *Is it?*"

Blake put a hand on Leigh's shoulder. He pushed it away.

"You accusing me of something, Mr. Barrus?"

"Next time I see you in my woods I'll mistake you for a deer. Understand me, Cooper?"

Sheriff Webber stepped between the two men. "You listen here, Leigh, if you have a problem, you come to me. What's gotten into you anyway?"

Bradley stepped forward. "Yeah, get off my property, rich boy, before I have you arrested for tresspassin'."

The sheriff spun. "Shut up, Bradley! If I find out you've been on his property hunting illegally again the only thing you're going to see is the inside of my jail. Got it?"

Bradley backed off some as the sheriff turned to Leigh. "Go home. Now! Or you're going to give me no choice, Leigh. Blake, take him home."

Blake grabbed Leigh by the arm and walked him to his truck with the sheriff right behind them. Leigh kicked his truck tire. Sheriff Weber asked, "Leigh, what's gotten into you? This ain't nothing new with Bradley, but I've never seen you like this before."

Blake spoke up. "It's been a rough few weeks. Last night we birthed new calves. Not enough sleep is all."

That seemed to appease the sheriff's curiosity. "Go home, you two. I'm letting you get away with the speeding this time, but don't make it a habit."

Leigh sighed. "Thanks, Tommy. I'm sorry for the headache. Say hi to Melanie for me."

The sheriff shot a smile at Leigh. "You can do that tomorrow at church. We'll keep this little incident between us. Ain't nobody perfect. Now go home."

With that, the sheriff watched from his vehicle as Blake talked with Leigh for a moment alone.

Leigh said, "You didn't have to lie for me like that."

Blake shot him a frustrated look. "Who was lying? I was up all night with those two calves. Where were you? You knew they were due and didn't even check in. I'm getting a little tired of running the ranch all by myself. You don't pay me enough, Leigh. If you weren't like family to me, I would've walked a long time ago." Blake hesitated.

"What happened, anyways? One moment we're looking at the trap, the next you're jumping in the truck and taking off like a mad man."

"I'm just tired. I saw Bradley's initials on the inside of the trap and the fact that Marcus almost died last night, well, I don't know. I snapped. And I'm so sorry I've been looking so much to you for helping around the ranch lately. I've been taking advantage. I'm sorry."

Blake smacked Leigh's shoulder. "Let's go back to the house and get some rest. Both of us need a break."

He could see Leigh was trying to force a smile as he got back into his truck. Blake hadn't realized Marcus had gotten stuck in one of Bradley's traps. He worried about the boy and wanted to go up to the cabin to support Janet, but duties at the ranch kept him from going to her side. He didn't think that he could feel for another woman after his wife left him and his daughter, Rachael, nine years ago. Given the circumstances, it was doubtful anything could come of it, but there was always hope.

The next day Janet watched as Anna removed the splint from Marcus's leg. She asked Anna several times, "Are you sure we should be doing this?"

"Yes, Mama," came Anna's reply each time.

As a nurse, Janet's instinct was fighting against removing the splint, but after what had happened the night before she gave Anna the benefit of the doubt. She helped Marcus sit up because he was still exhausted from losing so much blood.

Janet asked, "How does it feel?"

Marcus was hesitant to move his leg at first but finally he grabbed a hold of her arm and pulled himself up. He took several steps on his leg. He was already healed. Michele walked into the living room at that very moment. By her wide-eyed expression, she was just as surprised and Janet. Marcus and Michele locked gazes. The hurt in his eyes told Janet everything. He sat back down on the couch, turning away from

Michele. Janet could see how hurt she was. Now came the truly difficult part. She gathered all of the children together, along with Michele, and explained what was going to happen.

The news that Aunt Shelly was leaving was hard for them all to handle, especially for Marcus. Over the next month, though, Janet noticed they were all coping. The children even chipped in to help get their Aunt Shelly ready. Zack, Sampson, and Marcus helped Uncle Leigh work on getting the blue Buick station wagon that had been sitting for several years fixed and running. The girls had something else they were doing to prepare for their Aunt Shelly's departure, but they wouldn't let anyone know what it was. All Janet knew was that Angie and Anna asked Uncle Leigh to get them some odd supplies.

After several weeks the day had finally come. The plan was that Michele would move to the West Coast under a new name. It would be difficult, but Janet was coming to terms herself. Once the station wagon had been packed, everyone stood on the porch to say good-bye. Janet found it hard to know what to say or do as she awkwardly tried to find the right words.

Thankfully, Uncle Leigh interrupted the good-byes and handed Michele an envelope. "This will help get you started."

Michele opened up the envelope to find a stack of one-hundred-dollar bills inside. "There's twenty thousand to help get you going, and another fifty in your suitcase. Saying no isn't an option, young lady."

Michele hugged Uncle Leigh tightly. "Thank you," Michele managed.

"Oh, and there's one more gift." Leigh stepped aside as Angie came forward. "They've been makin' you something, but they won't tell us what."

Michele smiled at Angie who was now holding out a small letterbox wrapped in Christmas paper and ribbon.

Angie said, "Aunt Shelly, this is to help you start a new life in California. We wanted to make sure you'd be okay."

Michele took the present and opened it up. Janet was just as curious to see what the children had made. She moved to Michele's side to see what it was. Inside the box was a California driver's license, birth certificate and social security card, all perfectly forged with the name *Shelly Renard* on them.

As all three adults stared at what the children had done, Angie said, "You will always be a part of our family. Oh, and you will need to have the address changed on the license once you find a place to live." She looked down a little ashamed. "I hacked into the DMV so you're on record. You shouldn't have any problems."

Janet was stunned. Finally Michele bent down and hugged Angie, then all of the children, as she thanked them. It was time. She walked Michele to the station wagon as everyone waved good-bye.

Janet gave her one last hug. "You will always be welcome. E-mail us once you are settled in, okay?"

Holding back the tears, Michele said, "Will do."

"Now get going. There're maps on the seat for you."

With that Michele got into the vehicle. She waved as she pulled away. Uncle Leigh walked over to Janet and put an arm around her shoulders. "Did the right thing. I'm proud of you."

Janet leaned her head onto his shoulder. It was done. She felt like a new chapter was beginning in her and the children's life somehow. She felt scared and liberated all at the same time.

Seventeen

Loose Ends

October 2011

Nick had gotten used to the smell of stale beer and cigarette smoke that accompanied his favorite bar. All alone he sat in the booth with his shot glass and a three-quarters-filled bottle of whiskey. He stared blankly at the table in front of him, thoughtfully running his right hand along his forehead where the ten-inch scar ran along his hairline. Repeatedly he replayed the last four years in his head. He couldn't get a grasp of what he was feeling. Was he feeling fear, anxiety, disbelief, or was it just futility? It didn't matter now. It had been bad enough finding out that Samantha was the killer's informant, but what he just experienced made everything that happened even harder to swallow.

Self-pity. That was what he was feeling. His failure as a husband and father had been just the tip of the iceberg. Now that failure had poured over into the only thing he had ever been good at—his job. When Samantha had been able to get only minor background information on Tibon, he should have known, shouldn't he? Every lead or sting operation had all ended up as wild chases and a waste of the Bureau's resources. His bags at the airport being sent to the wrong city and the chance encounter with Damon in L.A.… it all could have easily been Samantha's doing. How could he have been so stupid?

His incompetence almost cost him his and Allen's life. The Bureau had been coming down hard on him from the start to get this case solved, and the pressure clouded his judgment. In hindsight he was surprised they let him go this long without any results, especially when they found out there had been cops involved.

Anyway, none of it mattered. He took another shot. The sight of his own hand made him stop and stare. Forty-eight hours ago they had Damon in their grasp, but any hopes of redeeming his career or his life vanished in a matter of seconds. He remembered getting the anonymous call.

Forty-eight hours earlier

Buzz. Buzz. Nick's cell phone vibrated. He didn't recognize the number but he answered anyway.

"Hello."

"Agent Catlin, listen very closely to what I'm about to tell you. Write this down," a soft feminine voice said.

Nick caught himself grabbing for a pen on his desk. "Who is this and how did—"

"Norfolk, Virginia: Super 8 Motel, 1010 West Ocean View Avenue. Do you have that? 1010 West Ocean View Avenue."

He hurried to scribble the address down. "What's this about? Who am I speaking—"

"Poughkeepsie, Chicago and all the others—you want answers, and here is where you'll find some of them. Go quickly before they find out I helped you."

The connection went dead.

He remembered the excitement at finally getting a break on the case. He knew he was breaking every protocol there was in the Bureau by going alone. The thought of another goose chase and coming up empty was not something he was willing to share with another living being. He wasn't sure he could handle another failure....

Two hours later he was standing in the lobby of the motel talking to a middle-aged woman who reeked of stale cigarettes.

He flashed his badge to the woman. "I need to ask you a couple questions. I'm Agent Catlin. How many people have signed in over the last twenty-four hours?"

The lady starred at him for a moment.

"Today would be nice."

She cleared her throat. "There've only been two," she said in a raspy smoker's voice.

"Can I have their names, please?"

She let out a slight exasperated sigh and said, "Ain't this against the law or something?"

One of Nick's pet peeves was someone who was clueless like this woman was. "No, it 'ain't' against the law, but will this make you feel more comfortable?" Nick handed her a fifty-dollar bill.

The woman snatched the fifty and slid it into her bra. She tapped on the keyboard and said, "A couple came in late last night under the name *Jones*. Yeah, right. The other was a guy by the name of James Fortunato. Little stuck on himself, if you ask me."

"What did Fortunato look like?"

"About your size, but an Italian guy with a lot of jewelry. Acted like he was better than everyone around him. You know the type. Why he was staying here, I have no idea."

The man wanted to stay low or maybe he didn't have as much money as he tried to lead on. Whatever the answer was, Nick's heart raced. "What room is he in?"

"He's not in a room. Left sometime this morning."

"He checked out?" Nick felt a sudden bottoming-out of his excitement.

She waved her hand. "No, I mean he's not in his room *now*. He'll be back. The room number is 113. It's just outside, around the left of the building."

He took a deep breath. "Thank you so much for your cooperation."

She smiled at him. "No problem. Anything to help."

As he turned around, in the fading evening light, the sight of Damon walking past the front doors heading toward his room caused him to stop in his tracks. Before he knew what he was doing Nick was out the doors and tackled Damon to the ground. The fear in Damon's eyes as he tried to reach for his pistol inside his jacket told him Damon was completely surprised to see him.

Nick wasn't about to give him a chance to escape this time. Several blows to the head calmed Damon down. A surprising feeling of enjoyment at Damon's pain caused Nick to assess just how angry he really was.

"You're under arrest for the murder of Taghreed Hikmat Thomas." Nick had waited a long time say those words. "And for the attempted murder of yours truly." He pushed Damon's head hard into the pavement and a sick thud accompanied a cry of pain. Nick leaned close to his ear and whispered, "Give me a reason to kill you. Please resist." Rage started to escalate. "Resist. *Resist!*"

Damon just smiled as blood dripped from his lower lip and nose.

The rapid breathing and anger subsided as Nick handcuffed Damon and yanked him to his feet. How was he going to explain this back in Philadelphia? It didn't matter. He had his man and possibly some answers.

The vision is going to haunt me for a long time, Nick thought as he shook his head and downed another shot….

He had arranged an armored bus to transport Damon from Norfolk to Philadelphia. Flying wasn't an option. There were too many possible scenarios to consider. No, he was going to follow the bus back to Philadelphia and keep a close eye on his key witness.

It was well into the evening and traffic was almost nonexistent at 9 p.m. The bus and Nick were somewhere in the middle of the mountains. In a couple hours they'd be back home.

"I know, Allen. You don't have to lecture me. I'm sure I'll get a good reaming for this." Nick was beginning to wonder why he had telephoned his former partner in the first place.

Allen's voice sounded like a scolding parent. "You're unbeli….when…there…"

"Look, I'll tell you the whole thing in the morning. We should be in a little after 11. I've got to go. We're up in these hills, and I'm losing reception."

That's when it happened. There were no other cars around as the bus in front of him came to a stop for a traffic light. The small town had already closed up for the night, and there wasn't a soul out on the sidewalks. A strange vibration caused his car to rock slightly as he came to a stop behind the bus. Then another came but more violent.

Without warning Nick watched the bus in front of him hurl into the air sideways. In shock he watched as the bus rolled over and over until it finally crashed into a nearby gas station. His sight was drawn back to the figure standing in front of his car. It was nighttime, so the creature's face and details were hard to read. What he saw was nothing short of impossible. It stood the same height as the traffic light and was wider than his car. The size of the creature's arms and legs was immense. Nick almost passed out from the rush of blood from his head at the sight of it.

Thud, thud, thud. The creature walked over to the bus. The vehicle was beginning to catch fire as gas sprayed in the air. In horror Nick watched as the creature thrust its fist into the side of the tipped-over bus and yanked Damon out like a wet rag. Three or four times it bashed Damon's lifeless body to the pavement, then dropped him.

Nick wasn't sure why he did it, but he got out of the car finally and pulled his gun. With its back still turned away from him, Nick unloaded his clip at the creature. It spun around and let out a horrifying wail. Nick immediately got back into his car.

Thud, thud, thud. It was heading right for him. Nick immediately floored the gas pedal and sped down the road. Nick kept checking his rearview mirror. The creature stayed right behind him. How fast was this thing? Once he hit fifty miles per hour the creature disappeared from sight, but the panic didn't go that easily.

Over the next couple hours Nick kept driving. He turned off his cell phone because he didn't want to try and explain what had just happened. Mile after mile he drove until he ended up at the bar across the street from his apartment.

No one was going to believe him. He still couldn't believe it himself. The thought of having to explain all this tomorrow was exactly what he was hoping to drown in liquor, but it wasn't working. Frustrated, Nick got up from the booth and tossed some money down on the bar. It was time to sleep off the living nightmare he had just experienced, and he hoped that tomorrow it would all go away. A slight chuckle came out of him at the absurdity of his thoughts.

The room was dimly lit as Liz walked in. She could see Tibon lying quietly in his recovery room bed. His eyes were closed when he said, "Report."

Liz was mildly impressed at his detection of her. She had tried to be as silent as possible. It was a game she played regularly around him. The thought that one day she would kill him crossed her mind several times, but her heart wouldn't allow her so far. She loved this psychopath, even though she knew he had no true feelings toward her. He had been the only person in her life who had showed any interest or need for her. Plus, there was a connection that she had with Tibon. They both enjoyed hurting others. He had helped her to release an underlying anger that she had fought to extinguish for years. She needed to grab hold of the pain, the anger, the abandonment, and give it an outlet, just as Tibon had taught her.

She replied, "He's been taken care of, my love."

"Damon was an idiot. I should have gotten rid of him earlier. I think I'm getting soft in my old age." It was clear that he didn't expect any sort of reply, so Liz stood silently.

"Help me sit up."

She hurried to his side and grabbed his legs with one hand and his arm with the other. Tibon sat upright on his bed with a slight smirk on his face. "After I'm done with my treatments, you'll be next."

She didn't really understand all that Tibon had been doing with his experiments, but she wasn't too fond of the idea of being a lab rat for him. The things he promised her were very enticing, though. Nonetheless, she feared what he was planning on doing to her, and she tried to hide it.

"The funding has already been promised. It's just a matter of a few visual aids to secure it. I need you to be a part of this." He grabbed her arm and pulled her down so he could be face to face with her. "Thank you for taking care of Damon for me. I know I can always count on you to do what is needed." He pulled her to himself. They kissed.

When their lips parted, he said, "Go get the doctor. I want to get started early today." Liz smiled at Tibon and then left to do as he asked. She watched from the hallway as he grabbed a folder off his nightstand and opened it. She knew it was the results from the latest tests, which brought a smile to his face.

Liz turned away and made her way down two flights of stairs, then opened up a pair of swinging doors that led to the testing area. The long hallway gradually filled with the crying of infants as she drew near its end. She opened the doors. The full volume of the cries enveloped her as she walked into the large auditorium filled with babies. They were being monitored in examination bays. There were more than three hundred infants, all crying out as dozens of lab technicians and doctors prodded and examined them.

Liz surveyed the room for Tibon's personal doctor to tell him that the testing was to begin. She knew she should feel some sort of outrage or sympathy at what he was doing to the children, but she felt nothing. That was the way she liked it—empty and dead inside. This way no one could ever hurt her again.

Eighteen

Changes

May 2013

Spring was in full bloom and it wouldn't be long before the children's sixth birthday. It had been hard on Janet these last couple years with Michele gone, but eventually she started to adjust. Thankfully, so did the children. It helped that Michele sent e-mails updating the kids and her letting them know how things were going. The latest e-mail said Michele had gotten involved with a local church and seemed very happy. She was glad for her friend but wished Michele were here to help her.

Even though the children were only going to be six, Janet had begun to deal with them entering the age of puberty, and it was manifesting itself in more ways than one. The girls already needed training bras. From that point on, the all-around attitude seemed to decline. She needed to deal with the children as if they were a bunch of preteens, which was what they were physically. It also marked the beginning of new abilities and problems the children had to face.

Anna was having dreams or visions during the night that would cause her to wake up screaming. She would tell Janet in great detail events that, she said, would happen sometime in the future. Her retelling of the dreams was so vivid and disturbing that Janet began to write them down. The visions were of battles in large cities and of multitudes of people dying. Others were of deformed children and monsters, but the common theme throughout the dreams was the family. They were all there, and Anna felt these events were going to take place soon.

When Janet told Uncle Leigh, he listened patiently. His only comments were, "These kids were born for a reason. I wouldn't be surprised if she's right." This wasn't comforting, but what could she do?

One of the other major problems was that over the last two years Sampson had grown to almost seven feet tall. It wasn't just his height that had changed—his entire body was getting wider and larger in sheer mass. His muscles had grown to abnormal proportions and he weighed more than what the floors could withstand in the cabin. Uncle Leigh and Blake had to reinforce the floors and move Sampson downstairs into Michele's old room. They put a door going outside from the bedroom just so he could get in and out without breaking anything in the house.

What was hardest for Janet to watch was the pain he was going through. His body was growing at such an accelerated rate, even compared to the other children, that it caused sharp pains in all of his joints. Janet tried giving him aspirin or ibuprofen, but it just wasn't helping. Sampson had to take at least triple the amount that a normal sized person to have any effect.

He had his good days and bad. When the pain was bad he found it difficult to walk. Even when it wasn't as severe he often stumbled. Sampson hardly ever complained. It broke Janet's heart to see him like this. She prayed it'd pass, hoping his body would get used to it, but she could see how difficult it was for him.

Sampson sat quietly on a nearby tree stump, pretending to read his Bible as he watched his brother Marcus do his daily workout. He was feeling pretty good today, thankfully, and the idea of doing nothing was eating at him. Sampson found himself counting his brother's pushups that were now over two hundred and still going strong. How come none of his brothers or sisters had the problems he had? He couldn't help but notice Marcus was growing into a well-defined young man. It was hard to miss when he worked out with no shirt on. His brother was amazing when it came to physical activities. Not a single drop of sweat had fallen from Marcus over the last five minutes.

A thought came to him as he watched his brother. *What if I worked out? Maybe the pain wouldn't be as bad if I strengthen my body.* He didn't like bothering his brothers and sisters, but maybe Marcus could help him.

After deliberating whether he should or not for several minutes, Sampson finally got up the nerve to go over to Marcus. He started to get up. *No.* He hesitated. *What if he rejects me again? Makes fun of me like he often does? I'm too big to play with.* His insecurities and fear ran rampant.

Over the last few months Marcus had begun to show more signs of frustration and was having fits of rage. His brother was not the nicest to deal with if he was in a bad mood. Again he sat back down. Uncle Leigh's voice echoed in his head. *"Don't let fear dictate your actions."*

Sampson stood up once again, determined. "Marcus, do you think it be okay if I worked out too?"

His brother didn't miss a push-up. He threw a sideward glance of surprise. "Sure. No prob."

At first Sampson wasn't sure what he should do, but then he decided he had best copy some of the things that he had seen Marcus do a thousand times before. He started with stretches and then a few sit-ups. The pain wasn't that bad, and it actually lessened the more his body's muscles warmed up. Sampson found that he liked the rush of adrenaline he was getting from the exercises. The pain was gone. He started to get excited at his discovery and changed to push-ups. This was going better than he thought. There was also the feeling that he was a part of something with Marcus. The punching bag was next.

He knew Marcus was touchy about the bag so he asked, "Marcus, can I work on the bag a little?"

Again Marcus shot him a questioning glance. "Go for it."

Having permission now, he walked over to the bag. At first he didn't know what to do, but then he replayed all the times he had seen his brother hitting it. He should probably do the same. Setting his feet into place, he jabbed at the bag with his fists. Sampson didn't hit it very hard to start off. He just wanted to get a feel for it. This seemed to catch Marcus's attention and he came over to watch. Sampson felt strange at first, but after a little while Marcus nodded in approval.

"That's it. You got the idea."

A feeling of acceptance overwhelmed Sampson as his brother gave his approval. He had never done anything like this before.

"No, no. You're doin' it all wrong," Marcus criticized. "You want to stay more on your toes and shift your weight into the punch. Come on, do it right. Someone your size can do better than that. Turn with the punch. Aim beyond the bag and drive your fist. That's pathetic. Harder. *Harder*. Come on, what's wrong with you?"

The harsher the remarks became, the more Sampson lost focus and finally stopped all together. He stood silently, filled with failure and rejection. It wasn't an uncommon feeling for Sampson. After having tasted a small glimpse of belonging and acceptance, it amplified his pain. He just wanted Marcus to stop, but for some reason the insults kept coming. It was so unlike Marcus, who usually knew when enough was enough.

"Are you a moron? Someone like you can't hit a small bag. Why did you come over here anyway? You're just getting in my way. Go away. Come back when you want to be serious."

Sampson snapped. All the years of frustration came out of him at once. "You want me to hit the bag?" He gave the bag a hard hit, and it nearly wrapped around the tree limb it was hanging from.

Marcus's eyes went big as he watched his bag fall back down hard, still connected to its chains. "Hey, be careful, you big ox!"

"I thought you wanted me to hit it! I'M HITTING IT!" With that Sampson let all his anger out and punched the bag with all his force. There was a loud cracking of wood as the tree branch broke off and went sailing through the air, still attached to the punching bag. As Marcus watched his bag flying away, Sampson shoved him and sent his brother falling to the ground. "You're so mean!"

He stopped at the sight of Marcus lying on the ground. His brother was holding his left arm. "I'm sorry, Marcus. I didn't mean to hurt you."

In an instant the shock left Marcus's eyes and was replaced with a look of pure madness. Marcus was upon him. With a fury that he had never seen before in his brother, Sampson tried to fight off punches and kicks as they landed on his legs and ribs. He stood more than a couple feet taller than Marcus, but that didn't deter the attack. Sampson tried to push Marcus off of him, but he couldn't. His brother was moving so fast from side to side. The only thing he could do was try and back away. At first the blows didn't really make an impact, but Marcus kept landing harder and harder punches and kicks. It was as if his brother's strength was increasing.

Mama yelled out for them to stop. Sampson couldn't obey. Marcus landed hits to his head and neck. He tried to protect his head with his massive arms, but then that left his midsection open. His brother took advantage of every opening. Sampson was having trouble breathing. He tripped over the woodpile around the corner of the cabin. Marcus was on him, out of control.

"I'm sorry! I'm sorry!"

Marcus didn't diminish his attack.

Then, suddenly, the hitting finally stopped. Sampson took his hands away from his face to see Zack standing over him with a log.

He looked over to see that Marcus had rolled several feet from him. His brother jumped to his feet, crazed. Blood was all over his torso, hands and face. The entire family stood around him, staring at Marcus in disbelief.

Marcus's insane expression turned to fear when he saw the blood on his hands. "I'm sorry, I didn't mean to."

Without warning, Marcus turned away and ran through the woods. Mama tried calling out for him, but it was no use. Marcus was gone.

The tears poured down Marcus's face almost as fast as he ran through the woods. The horror and shame at attacking his brother like he did fueled his desire to get away from the cabin. He picked up more and more speed as his tears evaporated off his cheeks from the wind hitting his face. Running on pure instinct, Marcus dodged tree branches and ditches as he navigated his way, though he didn't know where he was going. Effortlessly he jumped over logs and obstacles as he felt the rush of adrenaline flowing through his veins.

Marcus didn't know how long he had been running, but up ahead he could see Uncle Leigh's house. He had only been there once or twice and it had always been at nighttime. He slowed up as he came to the forest's edge and surveyed his surroundings. Uncle Leigh had said never to come to the house unless he was with them, but Marcus was desperate. He wanted to dash toward the house, but Uncle Leigh wouldn't probably be there. He would be out working at this time in the afternoon.

Uncertain as to what he should do, Marcus started to cry again. Just then, out of the corner of his eye, he could see Blake coming out the back of the barn. It was several yards away, and he didn't see anyone else with Blake, so he ran to him as fast as he could. Blake had only walked a handful of steps before he turned to see Marcus running toward him.

Blake looked worried, but Marcus didn't care. His anxiety was driving him, and all he could say to Blake was, "Uncle Leigh. I need Uncle Leigh!"

"Calm down now. You all right, son?"

Marcus was catching his breath as he said even more anxiously, "I need Uncle Leigh!"

"Okay, okay, I'll go get him. He's just over the west ridge, but you stay here, you understand?"

He did as he was told and waited for Blake to come back with Uncle Leigh. Finally, his uncle's truck came over the hill with Blake in the passenger seat.

Uncle Leigh got out and ran to Marcus. "Are you hurt, boy?"

"I'm sorry, I'm sorry. I didn't mean to hurt him. I lost control, and I hurt him bad, Uncle Leigh. I didn't mean…"

"Calm down, boy. We can handle this, you hear me?" He pulled Marcus gently by the shoulders and looked him in the eyes.

Marcus nodded.

"Good. Now get in the truck. I'm taking you back home."

Marcus did as Uncle Leigh asked him to.

Blake said, "I'll take over for the rest of the day. You go."

"Thank you, son."

Marcus couldn't help the waves of shame and self-loathing he was feeling as his tears kept pouring forth. When Uncle Leigh got in the truck with him, he calmed down. He had always felt safe with his uncle and longed to make him proud. After today, though, he wondered if his uncle would hate him.

It seemed like a long time had passed before Uncle Leigh asked him, "You going to tell me what happened now?"

He still wasn't completely ready to admit to what he had done. "Sampson broke my bag and pushed me."

"And why did Sampson break your bag and push you?"

"I was calling him names and being mean to him. I don't know why I did, but I couldn't help it."

His uncle's voice was still calm, to his surprise. "Still having trouble with losing your temper, huh?"

Marcus nodded, "It's gotten worse lately. I hate me! What's wrong with me?"

Uncle Leigh didn't say anything to him for several minutes. They drove in silence and Marcus was beginning to think his uncle hated him. "I don't know what's worse: my temper, not sleeping at night, or the accidents." He realized he had verbalized his thoughts.

His uncle asked him, "What do you mean, *accidents?*"

Marcus blushed, "Well—"

Uncle Leigh reassured him, saying, "Marcus, whatever you tell me will be between us. I went through a lot of what you're dealing with, so I won't be shocked."

"Well, I only sleep about three hours a night, but when I do I have...well...I don't really know what they are, but I call them *accidents.*" He still didn't want to look at his uncle in fear of rejection.

"I see. How often does this happen?"

Marcus thought for a second, "Maybe four to six times."

Uncle Leigh didn't seem shocked. "That's to be expected for someone at your age, I guess. I know you kids are going to be six in a couple months, but you got to understand that your body is going into a stage of life that most twelve- to thirteen-year-olds go through. Some even earlier. Four to six a week isn't that unheard of."

For a second Marcus was feeling better, but when his uncle didn't understand, the hopelessness rose up again. He replied sharply, "Not a week, Uncle Leigh. A night. I can't stop it. I fall asleep, and there's nothing I can do."

Leigh stopped the truck and put it into park as he turned to face

Marcus. "A night?"

Marcus could see on his uncle's face that he had shocked him. He nodded. "A night! I don't know what's worse—the accidents or the anger fits that hit me. I can't control any of it, and now I hurt Sampson. Everyone's going to be mad at me. I hate myself, Uncle Leigh. I want to stop being like this!"

Uncle Leigh placed his arm around his shoulders and pulled him close. "We're going to see this through. I'm not sure what we can do about 'the accidents' right now, 'cause I think that's just something you're going to have to live with. But we can do something about that temper of yours." Uncle Leigh asked, "How long did it take you to run to the ranch, son?"

It seemed like an odd question, but Marcus thought hard. He really didn't have any idea.

"Son, it takes me about forty minutes to drive up to the cabin from the ranch in the truck. You must have taken, what, maybe a couple hours, right?"

Marcus knew that couldn't be right and started shaking his head. "I don't think so, Uncle Leigh."

"It had to. I drive about forty miles an hour up these dirt roads."

Marcus continued to shake his head, "Sampson and I just fought a little while ago. I don't even think an hour."

Marcus waited for a reply, but none came. Instead Uncle Leigh put the truck back into gear and continued back to the cabin.

There was another long silence before his uncle asked, "Do you think the run is too far for you to do each day?"

"Nah. That was nothing."

"Okay, then. Every morning I get up at 4:15 a.m. and spend a half hour in prayer and reading the Bible. I want you to be careful so that no one sees you, but I think it'd be good for you to come each morning. What do you say?"

"Sure!" More time with Uncle Leigh was like a gift.

"Then it's settled. We will burn some of that testosterone and energy running through you and help you get focused."

Marcus's excitement dimmed. Now for the hard part—asking Sampson for forgiveness.

* **
** *

Leigh was happy to see that Sampson wasn't as hurt as the blood on Marcus made it seem. Marcus had done a thorough job of beating on his brother, who was a couple feet taller than him and much larger. Leigh felt guilty for being impressed at Marcus's strength. The boy needed to get it under control before he truly hurt someone. Both he and Janet stood by while the two brothers made up. They didn't hear all of the conversation, but there was a lot of crying and even a couple hugs. Leigh did hear one remark from Marcus that told him the boy was truly sorry.

Marcus said to Sampson as they hugged, "I love you, and I will always be there for you."

It was a mature statement for the boy to make, and Leigh was impressed. When the two brothers were done, they both started to head for the front door.

Janet sternly asked, "And where do you think you are going?"

Both boys turned around with shamed expressions.

"I want both of you in your rooms. This isn't over. I'll decide what kind of punishment you'll be getting in a bit. Until then I want you in your rooms, and I don't want to hear a peep out of you. Understood?"

Both boys simultaneously said, "Yes, Mama," and headed to their respective bedrooms.

Once the boys were gone, Leigh said, "I can see that Sampson is already healing from his beating."

"Yeah, I noticed that too. Probably all the kids have enhanced immune systems. In fact, I don't think I can ever remember them being truly sick at all."

Janet took a seat in the recliner and Leigh sat on the couch arm across from her. "Just out of curiosity, when I showed up with Marcus, how long had he been gone?"

She looked at the clock and said, "Oh, just over an hour. Maybe an hour and twenty minutes tops. Why?"

Leigh shook his head. "That can't be."

"Sure it is," Janet said. Then she seemed to understand his question.

116

"Oh, wow."

"You sure about that time?"

Janet's eyes were wide; she looked at the clock again. "Yeah."

"That boy ran faster than I can drive here, if that's true."

Janet called out, "Marcus, get down here."

The boy hurried down the stairs from his bedroom and stood right next to her.

She asked, "How fast can you run?"

Marcus shrugged. "Pretty fast, I guess. I don't have any way to tell, but Zack's quicker than me anyways."

Leigh knew he shouldn't be shocked, but he couldn't help himself. "How do you know that, son?"

"Well, we go over to the field to the east and play deer tag. We wait behind the trees at the edge and wait until a herd or family of deer start grazing. Then whoever can tag the most deer before they run into the woods wins." Marcus said this as if it was something normal that most children would do in their surroundings. "Zack holds the record right now at six, but I don't think the babies should count. They're too easy to tag. Besides, sometimes the other deer get mad and start chasing us back."

Leigh let out a laugh of unbelief at what he was hearing. Janet sat staring at Marcus with her mouth hanging open. Marcus looked at both of them, waiting to see if there were any more questions.

"Okay, Marcus. Thank you. No go back to your room and wait for me," Janet finally said.

Leigh looked at her and smiled. "Never dull 'round here."

Janet kissed Leigh before he headed back to the ranch. He wondered what other surprises these kids would come up with.

Wednesday, May 29, 2013

It has been a long time since my last journal entry. I guess I have gotten so used to the strange things happening with the children that I haven't even thought twice about writing it down. Just for the record, the children have continued to grow at the same accelerated rate. They are going to be six years old soon, but puberty is already starting for many of them. Their abilities have increased, and every day I wonder what will be next. On a side note, I was glad to see Blake again this past weekend. I never thought I would feel attracted to another man after losing Marcus, but I have to admit I like him a lot. We took a walk together, thanks to Uncle Leigh, who watched the children for us. He talked about his daughter, Rachael, and his ex-wife, who had left them both. Seems I'm not the only one around with emotional scars to deal with. He is a quiet man for the most part, and he has been very helpful to Uncle Leigh and us as a family.

I see Marcus watching everything that Blake does. I get the impression that he looks up to Blake. I can't blame him. From what I am seeing, Blake's wife was foolish to leave.

Nineteen

Storm

Whack, thud, crack went the sounds of stick fighting in the part of the forest the children had named Clay Valley. It was a small ravine, just south of the cabin, where the ground had a layer of clay on the topsoil. When it rained, like it had that morning, the ground became very slick and muddy, creating puddles of grayish brown liquid. It was just the way Marcus liked it.

It was late August, just a month past his sixth birthday, and Marcus was sure he wasn't the only one going stir crazy looking for something to do. It was his idea to have a stick duel and Zack was glad to oblige him. Marcus loved having everyone together watching him and Zack spar off. Both his sisters and Sampson watched from the ridge above. Angie sat on Sampson's shoulders and yelled out strategies to Marcus and Zack as they parried and thrust their sticks at each other. Marcus continued his attack and every now and then he would catch Zack on the arm and vice versa. It was a close match. The rules were simple—no hitting in the head or groin, and the best two out of three falls wins.

He and Zack were completely covered in mud from knocking each other down. It made it difficult to keep a good grasp on their sticks, but that didn't slow Marcus down. He kept track of the falls in his head, one fall apiece so far. Marcus was trying to be cautious because the next fall would crown the champ.

He had a difficult time seeing everything clearly because his brother was extremely fast with his attacks. Sometimes the only way Marcus knew they connected was the sound of the sticks hitting. Marcus circled around the left side of Zack, looking for an opening.

Angie yelled out, "Oh, come on already, guys. Someone take a chance."

He agreed with Angie's assessment. Zack was faster than him and if he didn't go on the offensive it was only a matter of time before his brother knocked him down again. Marcus moved in closer and attacked with a series of quick, short jabs, causing Zack to back away. He thought he had his brother on the defensive until he walked right into a ray of sun coming through the trees. For a split second he couldn't see clearly. His brother ducked down low and swung his stick at his feet. His legs were pulled out from underneath him. He landed in a large puddle that splashed everyone with mud. Marcus pounded his arms down in frustration causing another large splash.

Several "heys" and "watch-its" rang out as Marcus got to his feet. Zack bowed mockingly to everyone as if they had been giving him a standing ovation.

Angie wiped some mud away from her face and said, "Oh, please. Spare us. Marcus would have beat you if he had paid attention to his surroundings."

"Oh yeah, little sis? I don't see you down here," Zack countered.

"Excuse me, Sampson," Angie leaped off of his shoulders down into the fighting area. She landed in one of the puddles, only this time the mud hit Zack in the face. He spit it out and wiped his eyes as Marcus presented her with his stick as if it were Excalibur. Angie gave him a royal nod and a smile as she accepted.

Marcus walked past her and whispered, "Remember what I taught you."

Angie nodded. Marcus watched as his brother and sister got into their fighting stances and circled each other.

Marcus called up to Anna, "Do you want to do the honors?"

"Let the match begin!" Anna called out in an official voice.

At first Marcus noticed Zack was taking it slow for Angie. It was clear he didn't want to really hurt her. She was still their little sister, even with all the playful banter. The others cheered Angie on. She was certainly the underdog of this match. She stood several inches shorter than Zack and was a lot smaller, but both were cocky. Both had blond hair and dark blue eyes, which often made Marcus wonder if Zack and Angie were actually blood related. Angie's eyes were much larger than Zack's, though, and her cheekbones were higher. Her complexion was more of a chestnut color in contrast to the pale complexion of Zack.

Marcus cheered Angie on, and the match began. The two sticks collided a few times, echoing through the forest. Zack took a step back from the force of the impact on the sticks. Marcus laughed at his wide-eyed stare. His brother hadn't expected that.

Zack sped up his attacks, only to be met with Angie's counterattacks. Again Zack's was surprised at his sister's agility. Marcus knew Zack was faster. Angie had no real chance of winning, but it was good to see some humility in his brother.

With each swing Zack quickened his attack. A jab to her midsection nearly connected. With cat-like speed she dodged the attack. Again Zack swung his stick at her feet and just barely missed. With a leap Angie jumped over the attack, all the while continuing to back away. It wasn't long before Angie was up against the rotted tree stump that adorned the western part of the ravine.

Angie smiled playfully at Zack as she smacked her stick into a puddle next to her. The mud splattered all over Zack's face and yellow t-shirt. With a graceful leap she jumped onto the stump. Before Zack could wipe the filth from his eyes, Angie had flipped over his head. Zack was met with a jab to his ribs, putting him on the defense. He doubled over, protecting his sore rib. Angie tried to strike again at his legs. Zack barely deflected the attack and was now being backed against the tree stump himself. A sense of pride filled Marcus briefly. His little sister was no slouch when it came to fighting.

She attacked with a sense of urgency just the way he had taught her. After several close hits Zack's eyebrows furrowed. Marcus knew his brother was done playing around. Zack attacked. Angie was forced to retreat. He knew she would have to outsmart Zack if she were going to win.

The sunshine faded overhead, causing Marcus to look up and see clouds rolling in. It was soon followed by the sound of thunder in the distance. He put his focus back on the match and saw that Zack was landing slight hits on Angie's arms and legs. Angie looked at her surroundings like he had taught her. She needed an advantage. Zack was cutting off maneuvering space. Soon she would find herself up against the ravine wall. Angie thrust her stick toward Zack's stomach as her only option. He could hear the stick hit its mark. He watched in shock as Zack fell to one knee in pain.

Something was wrong. Marcus had hit his brother a lot harder than that in the stomach and never got this kind of reaction. For a moment he thought Zack was just pretending, but the look on his brother's face told him that the pained look was real. The thunder rumbled again in the distance, right as Angie took advantage of her brother's opening. She swept the stick behind the leg he was leaning on and sent Zack falling onto his side.

Angie yelled out, "Winner! Winner!"

Sampson joined in with her.

Zack wasn't moving.

Marcus ran to his side. Zack lay in a fetal position holding his arms over his stomach. Angie leaned over to check on Zack and reached out to touch his shoulder.

"No, don't!" was all that Marcus could say.

A sudden burst of light exploded from Zack, sending Angie backwards through the air. She landed several feet away.

Sampson and Anna ran to their sister's side to help while Marcus examined Zack.

Through clenched teeth Zack said, "Don't touch me!"

Out of the corner of Marcus's eye he saw Angie shaking her head. Anna grabbed Angie's right hand and held it up to examine. From what Marcus could see she had been burnt severely.

Sampson's deep voice rang out saying, "It looks like she has electrical burns. Like the ones that Uncle Leigh had gotten when putting in the new marine batteries last fall, only worse."

Marcus said, "Sampson and Anna, take Angie back to the cabin and have Mama look at her hand. Don't tell her about Zack just yet."

Anna opened her mouth to say something. "Just do it!" The tone of his voice was harsher than he intended, but he needed them to leave. Marcus tried to be slightly less abrasive when he said, "I'll take care of Zack. He's going to be fine. Now go. Go, already!"

The other kids stared briefly at him then did as he asked. Once they were far enough away, he asked, "Another one?"

Zack could only nod as he fought with the pain.

"It looks like it's worse than the last time. You got to let it out, Zack. I know it hurts but it's not going to go away until you do."

It was obvious that Zack couldn't handle the pain much longer but Marcus knew it was going to hurt more in a moment.

He tried to encourage Zack saying, "Come on! You can do this! Take the pain! Stand up and take the pain! The quicker you do this, the faster it's over with."

At first Zack didn't respond so Marcus said again, "Zack, you're tougher than this. I'm here for you. Get it over with."

With much reluctance Zack stood up. Marcus could see a soft red glow coming from his brother's midsection.

Marcus stepped a few feet away. "That's it! Now focus on the tree stump! Let it all out! Don't hold back!"

Marcus watched as Zack took one final deep breath and exhaled. He could feel the electricity filling the air. Two bursts of energy shot from Zack's hands into the tree stump. Bark and wood exploded in every direction. Zack screamed a horrific cry of pain. Immediately his brother dropped down to his knees. Marcus walked over slowly and tapped Zack. There was no more electrical buildup.

"Can you walk?"

Zack could barely speak through his crying, and Marcus realized how difficult it must be for his brother. He sat down next to Zack and put his hand on his brother's arm. Right now what he needed was to rest, but Marcus could hear the thunder in the distance. Since he was getting no answer or reaction, he needed to take matters into his own hands. He stood to his feet and lifted Zack over his shoulder. Marcus was slightly taller than his brother and definitely larger in build, so it was easy for him to carry his brother. Several yards to the west the sound of rainfall could be heard as Marcus hurried back to the cabin. The last thing they needed was to be out in the middle of another lightning storm.

By the time Marcus made it back to the cabin Zack was walking on his own. Although neither he nor Zack said anything, they would have to explain to Mama what had happened. Marcus had known about the episodes for a while, but Zack had asked him not to say anything. His brother was scared of what he may become.

When they got back, Mama was waiting on the front porch sitting on the steps. Marcus could tell by the look on her face that one of the others blabbed the whole story to her. He tried to take the brunt of her wrath as he stepped in front of Zack.

"Mama, it's my fault."

She put up her hand to silence him. He knew better than to disobey her when she was like this.

"Zack," Mama said with a low ominous voice. "Come here."

His brother slowly walked up to Mama. "Yes, Mama."

"How long has this been happening to you? And don't play stupid with me."

Zack didn't answer her right away, and it was obvious to Marcus that he was embarrassed. That was the reason why he hadn't said something to Mama or anyone else in the first place. Marcus had been the only one Zack trusted with his problem.

"It's been a couple months," Marcus spoke out.

"Thank you, Marcus, but I didn't ask you. Now, Zack, is this true?"

A thunderclap in the distance rang out, and Marcus was getting nervous standing outside with his brother when a storm was approaching. Finally Zack nodded.

This apparently appeased her. "Zack, go inside and get those filthy clothes off. I want to hear the shower running in five minutes. You hear me?"

"Yes, Mama," he mumbled.

Marcus went to follow his brother but Mama stopped him. "Where do you think you're going?"

He thought it was too good to be true.

"Now, son." Whenever Mama called him "son," he knew she was very, very serious. "I've noticed that all your brothers and sisters look up to you. Whether you asked for that or not, it's a fact. I know you want to look out for them, but not telling me what happened was stupid. Whatever is happening with Zack is very dangerous. It's not only dangerous to him, but to the whole family."

"He was so ashamed of what was happening, and we didn't want you to worry. I hear you talking to Uncle Leigh about us. I don't mean to eavesdrop, but sometimes I can't help but hear everything in the house. We have so many problems, and you worry for us all the time. So does Uncle Leigh. I just thought that whatever was happening to Zack would fade away and you wouldn't have to worry about another new problem. I'm sorry, Mama."

She didn't respond at first; then she hugged him tightly.

"I'm sorry," she said. Marcus could tell by the tone of her voice that she was upset. "Oh . . ." She pushed him away from her and looked down at her shirt. "Look at this mess, young man. Now get yourself up to your room and get ready to jump in the shower the second your brother is done."

Marcus smiled at her and ran inside to his room. He was glad that he was honest with Mama about how he was feeling. Uncle Leigh would be proud of him.

376, 377, 378...Marcus counted quietly to himself while doing sit-ups on the living room floor. The room was pitch black except for a small red ember in the fireplace from a couple hours earlier. The exercises were a part of his discipleship with Uncle Leigh. Since he had started running to the ranch every morning for prayer, they had worked out a physical regimen to help him burn up the energy that his body was creating. Since Marcus was only sleeping about three hours a night, he had a lot of time on his hands. Exercise was his main outlet.

It had been a sore subject with the other kids—Marcus having one-on-one prayer time with Uncle Leigh—but none of them could run as far as he could, not even Zack. Although his brother was faster than he was, Zack could not keep up with Marcus's endurance. He could run for several miles before feeling any effects physically. Marcus could tell his brothers and sisters resented being left out, so as a peace offering he shared whatever Scriptures he read with Uncle Leigh that morning with everyone. They seemed to like this idea, so Marcus began an early-morning prayer group right after he got back from the ranch.

Marcus had heard both Mama and Uncle Leigh talking about how it seemed to be helping with everyone's attitudes and how they all interacted. He liked being a part of the reason something good was happening to the family for once. It took a couple months but Marcus was beginning to feel the effects of the prayer meetings. He felt less frustrated and was more easily able to control his fits of anger. The energy was still there, but it was more manageable for him.

*402, 403, 404...*He heard Anna upstairs mumbling his name. Looking over at the mantle he could see the clock showed 3:57 a.m. *She must be having another one of her dreams*, he thought. Sure enough, not a minute later, he could hear her getting up out of her bed and heading to the door. Marcus called out softly in the dark, "Hey, sis."

He could see her stop. "That you, Marcus?"

*433, 434...*he said, "Come sit with me."

Anna made her way down the staircase and sat directly facing Marcus on one of the ottomans. "Don't get many visitors at this hour," he said, smiling at her. She probably couldn't see his face and he felt silly.

She asked, "How long have you been up?"

"Oh, a little over three and a half hours." *455, 456...*

Anna shook her head as she turned on the small lamp next to her. Both of them squinted from the sudden intrusion of light. Anna sat back in the chair and starred at the fireplace for a few moments. Marcus could tell by the fear in her eyes that she was shaken up by whatever her dream was.

Marcus wasn't as close to Anna as he was to Zack and Angie. She had always been a loner, like Sampson, in many ways. It seemed that Anna would rather spend time with Mama or one of the adults than play around with the rest of the kids. Out of all the children she was the one that looked like she could be his blood sister. Her light cocoa complexion looked a lot like his, which was slightly Middle Eastern. She had grown her wavy auburn hair down to the middle of her back, and Mama helped her brush it every night before bed. She had defined cheekbones, just like he did, but a more slender nose.

"Another bad one, huh?" he asked.

She nodded while continuing to look into the fireplace.

"It had to do with me, so cough it up, sis."

"No."

481, 482, stop. Marcus sat staring at his sister, trying to gauge her expressions. It must have been bad, since she wouldn't meet his gaze. "You know if you get it off your chest you'll feel better. Besides, I'm not worried, and you shouldn't be, either. God's in control, no matter what happens in the future. He'll see us through. You need to trust."

Marcus must have said something right, because she hesitantly said, "I was standing off to the side watching from a distance, but not really there. Sampson, Angie and Zack were all scattered in different directions on a large city street. Each of them was lying unconscious or dead. I'm not sure. They weren't moving as far as I could see. Standing in the middle of the street was this creature. It was dark so all I could see was a shadowy outline of its body. It was huge and angry. Something caught my attention as I looked at the far end of the street. You were there, Marcus, but it wasn't you. Something had changed. Your skin and eyes were blood red. Your entire body was somehow—I don't know how to describe it. There was a rage that had come over you and you charged at the creature that was twice your size. It must have seen you because it started running toward you also. I cried out, but you didn't hear me. Just as you two were about to collide I woke up."

All that Marcus could say at first was, "Wow."

Anna looked back into the fireplace. and Marcus wasn't sure what to say. He could tell she was really worried. He finally said, "Works for me. Not sure about that whole red skin thing, but whatever. Should have stayed asleep and watched me kick its butt." *483, 484.* He started doing sit-ups again.

"This isn't a game, Marcus. I'm really scared for everyone."

He tried to give her a reassuring smile. "I know you are. I love you too, Sis. I really don't mind being a part of a strange rendition of David and Goliath. We all know who won."

Anna shook her head again and chuckled at him. He could see she was feeling better, and soon afterwards she started looking tired again. *499, 500...*Marcus stopped and jumped to his feet. Just then he could hear Zack moaning in his sleep upstairs. He cocked his head to hear better. Anna started to ask him what was wrong, but he held up his hand to quiet her.

"Something's up with Zack. I should go check on him. It must be the night for bad dreams."

Anna stood up and pulled Marcus close to her in a hug. "Thank you, Marcus, for listening." With that she kissed him on the cheek and walked to the kitchen to get a drink of water.

He thought, *It's nice to be helpful once in a while, instead of being the problem.* Marcus started for the stairs when he heard the thunderclap in the distance.

While walking upstairs he could hear Zack moaning and tossing in his bed. Then he heard Zack getting out of bed and walking to the window in their bedroom. Something didn't feel right. He opened the door to find his brother staring out their open bedroom window getting wet. Zack jumped and turned around, startled by his presence.

"Sorry, you okay?"

"Yeah. Just hurting a little, is all." Zack turned back to the window. "Another storm. I don't know how much more I can take."

He was about to say something in hopes to encourage Zack when the entire outer wall of their bedroom exploded in a flash of light. Marcus didn't know what hit him as he was hurled backwards through their bedroom doorway and over the upstairs banister. When he finally regained consciousness, he was downstairs in the living room next to the fireplace, lying up against the wall.

Anna's and Mama's screaming filled his pounding head while he fought to focus his eyes. Where he had been standing only moments before was almost entirely engulfed in flames. His bedroom door had been thrown off the hinges and was sitting only a couple feet away from him on fire. As he looked down at his chest, he noticed his hair had been singed and so had his shorts.

As he stood up it was clear that everyone was too panicked to make any decisions. He yelled out, "Everyone outside! Now!" Both Anna and Mama looked at him as Sampson joined everyone from his bedroom.

"Sampson, take them outside and get the pump going. We need to get water on this fire immediately!"

As Sampson grabbed both women, Mama yelled out, "But we need to get Zack and Angie! We can't leave them!"

Marcus said, "I'll get them. Just go!" A support beam came crashing down onto the balcony upstairs.

Sampson ushered the women out the back door while Marcus ran up the stairs to the girl's room, which was closest to the staircase. He didn't stop at the door but instead planted his shoulder with all his weight. The door flew open, revealing that the blast had broken down part of the wall between their bedrooms. Angie had been knocked unconscious and thrown to the floor. She had a big gash on her forehead and was bleeding badly. Marcus didn't have time to check her injuries as he picked her up off the floor and slung her over his shoulder. With grace and speed, he headed down the stairs with Angie while avoiding the fire that was beginning to spread.

Marcus laid her several yards away from the cabin on the wet ground in the rain. He knew the rain would be a big help if they were going to be able to save the cabin. He could see the rest of his family doing as he had told them, pulling out the pump from the shed and connecting the hose down to the lake.

Marcus ran back inside to find the stairs were almost engulfed in flames. He charged through the flames as fast as he could. He could feel several burns on his legs. He ignored the pain, thanks to adrenaline. He took one deep breath before jumping over the fiery support beam in front of the bedroom.

Several more times he burnt himself as he landed inside. He started coughing as he tried to focus his eyes. All of the walls were engulfed in flames except the outer wall, which had a huge hole in it. In the middle of the room was his brother. Zack appeared unconscious but breathing. His entire body was glowing or, to be more precise, the blood pumping through his body was glowing. Marcus could see the streams of red flowing through his brother's chest while orange flames flickered around him. It looked more like lava than blood, but he didn't have time to examine any closer. He needed to get Zack out now!

He grabbed Zack and immediately dropped him back down. His hands were burned from the heat of Zack's skin. The room was beginning to feel like it was swirling. He needed to get Zack out and quick, before he collapsed from the smoke. Marcus pulled up the rug that Zack was lying on and wrapped him in it. It would probably catch fire any second but Marcus had no choice. What he was about to do was going to hurt.

Marcus picked his brother up and put him over his shoulder. The rug immediately caught fire. Marcus screamed at the pain of his flesh burning, but he didn't stop. As fast as he could, he ran toward the hole in the outer wall and leaped.

Thirteen feet below Marcus instinctively tucked and rolled as he let go of his brother. He tumbled several yards before sliding in the mud to a halt. The pain in his left arm where he had been holding his brother was almost unbearable.

Janet and Anna were now standing next to Zack, who had come free of the rug and was lying on his side, glowing.

Marcus yelled out in warning, "Don't touch him!"

Both of them backed away at his warning. Janet looked at Marcus in horror. That's when Marcus looked at his left arm for the first time. Blackened flesh hung down.

Janet tried to examine him, but he pushed her away, saying, "There's no time for that, Mama! We need to get the pump going!"

With that Sampson cranked the manual lever on the old pump to start building up the pressure. Marcus ran over to the hose. He pointed it up at the cabin where the fire was. There was plenty of water coming from the hose, but not enough water pressure to make a difference. If they didn't get the fire under control, they would soon lose everything.

"Faster," Marcus ordered Sampson. *Still not enough pressure.*

Marcus was surprised to see Angie standing only a few feet away.

"We need to get to the roof!" she said.

Before Marcus could say anything, he watched his little sister go over to a nearby tree and climb up. Marcus lost sight of her momentarily. *There she is.* He watched as she leaped off of a nearby limb and landed on the roof. It was very impressive looking, but he didn't have time for admiration. Angie had the right idea. Now they needed to get her the hose. He thought for a second, then yelled for Sampson to stop pumping. When the hose went limp Marcus tied it around his waist and ran over to the pump.

He said to Sampson, "Throw me up to the roof."

Sampson started to argue with him, and Marcus became frustrated. "*Throw me, you big ox!*"

He was only trying to get a rise out of his brother, and it worked.

Sampson scowled at Marcus, grabbed him by the armpits, and hurled him up to the roof. Marcus lost all control and balance as he flew helplessly through the air. He landed hard on the wooden roof, and it knocked the wind out of him. The rain was coming down even harder now, which was good and bad all at the same time. The good part was that it would help with putting out the fire. The bad part was that the roof was very slippery, and Marcus started to slide.

Angie grabbed his right arm to stop him from falling off. Marcus smiled at his sister as she helped him to his feet. He gave her a quick kiss on the cheek to say thank you and untied the hose from around his waist. Angie held it as Marcus made his way over to the part of the roof above the bedrooms. It was smoking but hadn't broken open yet. Shifting all his weight, he kicked down hard on the roof. It didn't take much effort, since the wood was burning on the inside of the house. The flames shot through the new holes in the roof. Marcus continued to kick regardless. They needed a big enough hole to get the water through.

He yelled over to Angie, "Bring over the hose. Sampson! Start pumping!" His brother must have heard him, because water filled the hose again.

Water hit the flames, causing a billowing tower of smoke to rise. It took awhile before they could see they were making an impact. They had a clear view of the balcony and the two bedrooms now.

Marcus could see Zack down below, lying naked on his side in the mud. Mama and Anna knelt on either side, examining him. He watched as the heat radiating from his brother's body created a shell of mist around him. The rain evaporated before it could even touch his skin.

He could hear Mama and Anna trying to get Zack to respond to them. For several minutes there was no reply from Zack, and Marcus feared for his brother's life. If it weren't for the fact he could see the glowing blood running through his brother's body, he wouldn't have even known he was alive. Mama became more panicked the more time passed.

Then Marcus thought he heard a small sound come out of Zack. He wasn't sure at first, but by the reaction of Anna and Mama, it must have come from Zack.

Mama asked, "What, Zack? What did you say?"

Zack spoke again slightly louder. This time Marcus could hear him clearly. His brother said, "Get away."

Marcus watched in hope as Zack's eyes opened. They were glowing, just like the rest of his body, as he said louder, "Get away from me!"

Zack slowly got to his feet. Every movement appeared to be a struggle. He said again, "Get away from me! Further!"

Marcus could see panic and concern in his brother's eyes as both Mama and Anna backed even farther. Zack looked at Mama one more time as if to say, "Good-bye." With that, he crouched down slightly, letting out a cry of pain that hurt Marcus's ears.

Like a rocket he leaped into the air, causing the ground to explode underneath him. Dirt and roots sprayed in every direction as Mama and Anna fell over from the force. Marcus watched his brother flash through the air over the treetops in a blur of light—and then he was gone.

Marcus prayed softly, "God, help him, please."

Twenty

Rebuilding

Leigh had gotten up for prayer that morning, but Marcus was a no-show. A glimpse out his kitchen window told him it was raining.

"I don't blame him. I wouldn't want to come out in this, either," Leigh mumbled.

The phone rang and startled him. He looked up at the clock on the wall. It was almost 4:30. When he answered, an operator's voice asked him, "Sir, I have a collect call from a Zack Renard for Leigh Barrus. Will you accept the charges?"

"You're jokin', right?"

"No, sir. Will you accept the charges?"

"Sure."

"Thank you. You are now connected."

"Uncle Leigh? Is that you?" Zack's voice trembled.

"Is that you, Zack? Where you calling from, son?"

"I don't know. I landed somewhere. I think east, but I'm not sure."

"What do you mean, 'landed'? What happened, boy?"

"Please come get me!" The panic was rising in Zack's voice. "I'm at a payphone and I'm naked, except for a box I found."

"Okay, calm down. I want you to look around. Are there any road signs?"

There was a moment of silence before Zack replied, "Oh yeah! There's one! It says *Route 65*. Oh, and I think I see a sign that says *Conway*. It's hard to tell. There isn't much lighting."

"Conway? Does it say anything else?"

"Nothing. But there is a bus station up the road."

The only Conway he had ever heard of was in Arkansas. "Boy, stay put for a moment. I need to look up something."

Leigh walked over to his computer with the wireless phone and pulled up the Internet. He looked up cities named Conway and couldn't believe his eyes when he saw Route 65 in Arkansas running right into it.

He asked Zack, "You sure, boy, it says Route 65?"

"Yeah. I found the phone book hanging here. I didn't see it before. It's all Arkansas numbers." The boy was almost crying. "Please come quick! I'm hiding in an alleyway."

"Stay put, you hear me? I'll be there as soon as I can. Sit tight."

"Okay."

When Leigh hung up, he frantically finished shaving and got dressed. Just like every day, Blake was out in the barn, already taking care of the animals. Leigh knew something was definitely wrong at the cabin if Zack was in Arkansas.

"Blake," he called out.

"Yup. What's going on?"

"I need you to find time this morning to go up to the cabin. Before you ask why, I just got a call from Zack and he's in Conway, Arkansas."

Blake nodded. "Say no more, Leigh. It's done. I'll have Johnny take over while I'm gone."

With that, Leigh got in his truck and left.

It took nearly six hours for him to get to Conway and find where Zack was. His heart sank when he saw his nephew. Zack was clearly shaken up as Leigh wrapped a blanket around him and walked him to the truck.

On the ride back to the ranch, Zack explained everything.

"I don't know what I'm going to do, Uncle Leigh. Every time there's a storm, something happens to me. It starts off like a tingling sensation, and before I know it I feel like my insides are boiling or burning. I can't really explain it, but it hurts. The only way to get rid of it is to force it out of my body, and that hurts even worse."

Worried for the rest of the family, Leigh sped up their return. "I thought you said you were flying, son?"

"I did, and to be honest, there was something different about the energy in me this time. It felt like something changed in me. The pain wasn't as bad, but the burning inside was stronger than any other time it's happened. I don't know what I'm saying," Zack said, looking troubled.

"That's a good thing, Zack. Your body is building up a tolerance to whatever's happening." Leigh wasn't sure how true that statement was, but it was as good a guess as any at the moment. He knew his nephew needed some encouragement.

It was some time after five in the evening when they arrived at the cabin. Leigh could see the damage as they pulled up. Blake and Sampson were moving the burned wood to the backyard. Leigh could see Janet standing over Marcus at the picnic table out front. As he pulled up, everyone came running out. The looks of relief at seeing Zack were exactly what he expected. The expression on Janet's face almost broke his heart as she opened the passenger-side door.

She held Zack in front of her and examined him. "Are you all right? Are you hurt?"

Leigh called over, "Let the boy be. He's fine. He's had a rough day and, apparently, so did everyone else." He walked to the front of the cabin so he could see more of the damage. He glanced back at Janet, who was still holding Zack around the shoulders. "Okay, gimme the nickel tour and let's see what's what."

Reluctantly letting go of Zack, Janet led him through the cabin and showed him the damage that had been done. Blake joined them as they walked up the staircase, or what was left of it.

At first, Leigh felt devastated as he examined how bad the damage was. He was glad no one was seriously injured. But then he saw Marcus walking through the living room downstairs. His first reaction was horror at the burns up and down the left side of the boy's torso. Marcus wasn't wearing a shirt, and it was evident to Leigh that his nephew must be in tremendous pain. But you'd never know it by the way the boy acted and moved. *The boy will heal*, he told himself, and he shook his head to clear his thoughts.

"As I see it," Leigh said and took a deep breath, "we now have an opportunity to make the changes that needed to be done. So let's take advantage of the situation. We need a bigger room for Sampson. We already talked about that. And we can put another room downstairs if we switch out the living room with the dining room."

At first both Janet and Blake looked at him like he was crazy.

"I'm serious. It'll be a lot of work, but I'll hire more workers at the ranch, and we can rebuild this place better than it was."

There was a long pause before Blake said, "I'll help you, but I don't know who we can get to help that we can trust."

Marcus called out, "The family can help. You can show us how to do stuff."

Janet replied, "I don't remember you being a part of this conversation, young man."

"Sorry, Mama, I just want to help."

"I'm sorry, Marcus." Janet's tone softened. "I'm tired. I didn't mean to snap."

Leigh interjected, "He's right. We don't need anyone else to rebuild. The kids will pick up the skills they need as we go along."

Janet gave him a doubtful look but nodded her approval.

"Good," Leigh said as he turned to look into the boys' bedroom. It was completely charred from ceiling to floor and wall to wall. He examined the large hole in the roof that was letting water in. It was clear that rebuilding was going to take some time. It was hard to see at first, with all the wood and debris lying on the floor. The burn marks radiated from the center of the room.

Janet offered, "Marcus said that Zack was lying in the middle of the room, glowing, when he pulled him out of the cabin."

Leigh could see that Blake understood the same as he did. Zack had started this fire. He was sure the boy didn't do it on purpose, but whatever was going on in Zack's body, they needed to do something about it.

"We need to go shopping, Blake," Leigh said.

"Huh?"

"You know a good scuba gear store nearby?" Leigh turned and smiled at Blake and walked downstairs.

With Blake's help, Leigh was able to come up with a floor plan in just a couple of days. Leigh decided to get rid of the second floor entirely, and build an oversized extension that would become a bedroom and living area for Sampson. He already stood about seven feet tall at six years old, so no one had an idea how big the boy was going to get. His bedroom was going to be one large open space with a barn door going outside, to accommodate the boy's massive width. Leigh planned to have the ceiling going all the way up to the second floor and change the dining area into the living room area so that it would be right next to Sampson's bedroom. He didn't want to isolate Sampson any more than he already was. This way he could be with the family more.

By making all these changes, Leigh was forced to build another bedroom downstairs for the other kids. It was going to be a massive project, but in the long run it was going to be better for everyone. Leigh was forced to hire more workers at the ranch to make up for their absence, but thanks to Anna and Angie, finances were no longer an issue.

At first he wasn't sure how Blake was going to respond to helping out like this, but there didn't seem to be any friction between them. In fact, it seemed to Leigh that Blake was looking forward to spending time with his niece. He wouldn't say it outright, but a connection had grown between them over the last few years, and it showed.

It wasn't long before they started construction on the cabin and everyone pitched in. The children had become so proficient at carpentry that Leigh allowed Marcus and Anna to finish off the new bedrooms downstairs by themselves. The only one who was having trouble was Sampson. His fingers were almost twice the size of either Blake's or Leigh's, making it difficult to use a lot of the tools. To add to the boy's problems, he was on another growing spurt. Leigh felt bad for Sampson. On most days he could see how difficult and painful it was for the boy to walk. The pain was so extreme that Sampson mostly sat outside, watching everyone else work. It was clear to Leigh that he wanted to help, but Sampson just seemed to get in the way when he did.

Saturday afternoon was no different. They had finally finished off the frame of the new wing, and Leigh could see that Sampson felt left out.

He leaned close to Blake and said quietly, "Do me a favor and leave your hammer up on those beams when you take down the ladder."

Blake shot a questioning glance at him.

"For the boy's sake," Leigh added.

"Oh...sorry. Sure thing."

Leigh walked over to the picnic table to poor a cup of water. Sampson sat quietly on a tree stump, only a couple feet away, staring out over the lake. Leigh could see he was in a lot of pain as the boy rubbed his left thigh muscle. Looking back over his shoulder, Leigh could see that Blake had done what he had asked and was removing the ladder.

Clearing his throat first, Leigh called out, "Hey, Blake, do you have my hammer?" Leigh hoped that Blake would understand what he was trying to do.

"You asked me..." Blake said but stopped himself midsentence. "Oh sorry...I think I left it up on the top crossbeam. Let me get the ladder."

"Don't bother." Leigh put a hand on Sampson's shoulder. "Would you do me a favor?" Sampson's expression told Leigh he was more than eager.

"With your reach, could you get my hammer for me?"

"Sure, Uncle Leigh." Sampson didn't hesitate as he forced his bulking frame up off of the tree stump. Leigh could see he was in pain, but the feeling of being useful was more important right now than Sampson's comfort.

Leigh knew the boy had a reach of at least eleven feet and could get the hammer with no problem. He watched as Sampson made his way to the cabin. As he approached the newly constructed frame his left leg gave out. Leigh watched in horror as Sampson stumbled forward into the frame of the new wing. Sampson tried putting out his hands to catch himself from falling but instead of stopping himself, the frame gave way. A loud cracking of several two-by-fours filled the forest, causing everyone to look in Sampson's direction.

Blake jumped out of the way of the falling wood. Leigh hadn't noticed that the whole family had come running outside to see what had happened. They looked on in dismay, along with Leigh, at the sight of Sampson lying on top of the broken frame. The boy turned to see everyone looking at him. This wasn't what Leigh had hoped for.

Sampson was already feeling useless and like an outsider. He wasn't surprised when Sampson awkwardly made his way to his feet and ran into the forest.

"Sampson!" Janet called out to him, but he was gone.

All the rest of the family walked over with Leigh to the fallen frame. He assessed the damage. It had taken them several weeks to build, given all the damage that had been done by the fire. Now it was ruined in a matter of seconds.

"Unbelievable. Stupid ox can't watch where he's going," Marcus complained to no one in particular and walked back to the picnic table.

Leigh examined the damage while the rest of the family talked amongst themselves. Finally he said to everyone, "You know, most of the frame's still together. If we had someone tall and strong we could probably fix this in no time."

Leigh turned toward Marcus to see if the boy had gotten his meaning. He was proud when Marcus turned around and said, "I'll go get the big lug."

Angie added, "You don't know where he went."

"How many big lugs are there running around?" Marcus asked sarcastically.

Angie put her hands on her hips. "I know where he's heading and you don't, so that settles it. I'm going with you."

Marcus shrugged. "Whatever. Come on. Lead the way." He motioned magnanimously toward the woods, and they were off.

As they walked for over twenty minutes through the woods, Marcus was beginning to get annoyed at his little sister. Angie's personality was the total opposite of his. She skipped along the dirt path in front of him, pointing out every aspect of the forest. Often he had to remind her to stay focused. Her constant attempt at conversation—about how beautiful the wildflowers were or how peaceful the forest was—only added to his growing impatience.

He kept reminding himself to be understanding and calm, the way Uncle Leigh had taught him, but it wasn't working. Holding back his frustration, Marcus asked, "Are we close yet?"

Angie continued to skip along in front of him and simply replied, "Yup."

Marcus knew Sampson and Angie had formed a close relationship, like he had done with Zack. They would both come walking back from the woods talking about Scriptures or brainstorming a new way for Sampson to have his hair and beard braided. Marcus laughed to himself as he remembered how his brother looked when she was finished braiding his hair—like a demented Rastafarian. That might have explained why Sampson always let his hair flow wild.

They walked for another quarter mile when Angie finally stopped and pointed down a slope into the distance. "There's his thinking pond."

Marcus's sight was not only clear in the dark, but it had also become stronger for seeing long distances. He could see his brother pacing back and forth next to a big oak tree that slightly hung over a small, semi-stagnant pond. Sampson was clearly upset with himself, and Marcus watched as his brother broke a smaller tree with a swing of his right arm. He knew his brother's hand was going to hurt after that tirade, but he knew it would heal fast. Both his and Angie's burns had healed within days, and it seemed to be a shared ability with all of them. Marcus grimaced as he remembered how bad the pain was from the burns Zack had given him.

Something caught his attention, bringing him back to the present. In the distance, out of Angie's sight but not Marcus's, there were three men with rifles only a couple hundred feet from Sampson. Two of them were maybe in their early twenties, he guessed, and the third man was about Uncle Leigh's age. As he looked closer, he saw they were drinking bottles of beer. A sickening knot built in his stomach.

Sampson punched another small tree down, which caught the men's attention. Marcus watched in dread as the older man's face looked in his brother's direction. He could see the man was scared, and Marcus couldn't blame him. Sampson looked like some wild creature the way he was acting. His long jet-black hair fell well over his shoulders, and his beard and mustache were long enough to reach his chest. Standing just over seven feet tall and over four feet wide, he looked nonhuman. Anyone who didn't know him would be scared, but this man didn't run. Instead, he lifted his rifle, along with the other two men, and fired.

The first shot hit the oak tree behind Sampson, causing him to stop pacing and duck. He didn't see where the shot had come from in time, and the second shot hit him in his right arm. He yelled out in pain as the third shot hit him in the head and sent him crashing to the ground.

Instinctively Marcus attacked. Running down the slope and dodging behind trees, he closed the distance between him and Sampson's attackers. He snapped off a large piece of branch from a dead limb on the forest floor, causing all three men to look his way. The men quickly reloaded their guns and started firing at him. This only helped to enrage Marcus even more. The shots hit several trees as he ran in and out of them, creating a shield of wood.

They didn't have time for another shot; Marcus was too quick. Within seconds he was upon them. The man closest to Marcus was one of the younger ones. Like a pole-vaulter, Marcus used the stick he had grabbed and launched his feet into the chest of the man, sending him sprawling. His rifle went flying several feet away as Marcus turned his attack on the other young man. He ducked and swung the stick hard into the man's feet, interrupting another shot. Sampson's attacker came crashing hard against the ground.

The older man had just finished reloading, and Marcus could see he needed to act fast, or he would get shot. As if it were second nature to him, Marcus grabbed a knife from the young man's belt and hurled it at the older man, stabbing him in his right arm. The man screamed in pain as he dropped the rifle to the ground and grabbed the knife protruding from his arm.

Marcus took his stick and smacked the young man in front of him across the face, sending him to the ground, unconscious. Before his first victim could make it to his feet, Marcus was on top of him and did the same. He turned to face the older man, who was still struggling to pull the knife out of his arm. Marcus didn't wait. Before the man could even react, he leaped and kicked him in the chest, knocking him down. He didn't give the man a chance to move again. Still fueled by adrenaline, he pinned his attacker by putting his right knee into his chest. The man's wide, blood-shot eyes revealed his fear. Marcus yanked the knife out of the man's arm, causing screams to echo throughout the forest.

Firmly he placed the knife against the man's neck. He leaned his face within inches of his captive. "You're lucky I don't kill you for shooting my brother and trying to shoot me."

The man's breath reeked of alcohol. Marcus fought back his desire to vomit. "If I ever catch you up in these woods again, you'll get more than a beating and a few cuts. Understood?"

The man didn't respond.

"*Understood?*"

The man's eyes widened even more as his voice squeaked out, "Yes, yes!"

"Good. This has been a warning."

Marcus's need to get to Sampson outweighed his desire to hurt the man. He slowly pulled the knife away from the man's throat and stood. The man tried to sit up, but Marcus kicked up the stick to his hands and swung it around. The stick broke against the side of the man's head, sending him back to the ground, unconscious.

Marcus cringed slightly at feeling satisfaction for inflicting pain on the man. Violence was something that came too natural to him. That scared him. With the help of Uncle Leigh, he had been able to get a grip on his emotions, but there was always a desire to lose his temper. The feeling nagged at him all the time. He felt like a part of himself was being repressed, and at the same time that feeling was growing as he got older.

He hurried over to be with Angie, who had already gotten to Sampson. It looked bad. There was blood all over the ground and the left topside of Sampson's head had a gaping wound where he had been shot. Angie held his head in her lap as she cried uncontrollably. At least Sampson was breathing. Marcus leaned over his sister to get a better look at the wound. She had brushed back his hair so it was easy to see that it went all the way to his skull. He couldn't find any breakage in the bone, however, which was a good sign.

They both knew they couldn't carry him. Marcus told Angie to stay with Sampson for the moment while he went to do some cleanup. He walked back over to where the men were still lying unconscious on the ground and collected their rifles and a beer bottle. As he headed back to Sampson and Angie, he stopped at the pond to fill one of the beer bottles with water. He walked over to his brother and cleaned the wound on his head. The sensation of the cold water must have helped, because Sampson started to move.

Angie tapped him on the cheek lightly, saying, "Please wake up, Sampson. Can you hear us? Wake up."

Slowly Sampson's eyes opened as he fought to focus them. "Wha...what happened?" Angie chuckled from relief.

Shaking his head, Marcus had to laugh to himself as he answered, "You are one tough nut. Took a bullet to the head and you're still with us."

Sampson started to sit up and the bleeding started again. Marcus admonished, "Whoa. Whoa there, big brother. Lay back down for a minute."

Reluctantly Sampson did as his brother asked. Marcus took off his green T-shirt and ripped it. "We need to wrap you up first, and then we'll head back to the cabin," Angie explained.

Once they had him bandaged, Sampson got to his feet. Neither Marcus nor Angie were much help, but they were there for support. As they made their way back home, Marcus could see the three men were finally starting to move. He knew this was not going to go over big with Mama and Uncle Leigh.

"They did what?" Janet hollered.

"You did what?" Uncle Leigh yelled.

Marcus tried to explain what happened, but he was having a hard time. Each time he would start, the grownups interrupted him. He knew it was because they were just as shocked as he had been at what happened, but he kept losing his train of thought.

Everyone stood around Sampson as he sat on a tree stump outside and Janet cleaned his wounds. The bullet in his arm had gone straight in and out, and the wounds were already beginning to heal. His skull showed no signs of a bullet hole. As far as they could tell, it must have bounced off.

Janet wrapped clean gauze around Sampson's head as she told Marcus, "Go on. Finish."

He had forgotten again where he had left off.

Angie jumped playfully forward. "Okay, let me tell it. Now this is exactly how it happened."

She told of how she ran after him and saw everything. Excitedly she shared how Marcus ran off after the shooters. As the story unfolded, everyone listened intently. Angie wasn't just telling them what she had seen, but she was recreating every sound and word exactly. From the sound of the gunshots all the way to speaking with Marcus's voice, she gave an exact mimic of what happened. Marcus listened in amazement as Angie shared, oblivious to what she was doing.

She finished by saying, "And then we walked back." There was a long silence as his sister examined her audience's faces. "What? Why is everyone staring at me? That's what happened."

Leigh finally interrupted saying, "Okay then. Blake and I have got to get back to the ranch right away, so we'll start tomorrow afternoon to fix the frame." That last part was directed at Sampson as Leigh smiled at the boy.

Janet asked, "Why are you leaving?"

"Oh, sweetheart, trust me. If we don't get back to the ranch now, there's going to be a mess."

A cool breeze made the sunset even more enjoyable for Leigh. He and Blake sat on his front porch in a couple of handmade rocking chairs. The sheriff joined them as they aimlessly passed the time. The shadows from the trees were getting longer as the sun made its way over the hillside. The revving of an engine and the spinning of tires broke the men's moment of tranquility. They watched as a large rusted blue pickup truck raced up Leigh's long driveway and came to a skidding stop in front of the house. None of the men moved as they watched Bradley Cooper and his two boys get out. They were clearly upset. The fact they all had rifles in their hands told Leigh this wasn't a social visit.

Bradley's right arm was wrapped from an apparent injury, and the side of his face sported a large, bruised welt. The boys had similar injuries to their faces. Leigh smirked at the sight. There had been bad blood between Bradley and him for years, going all the way back to high school. Bradley had asked Jenny to the prom in their senior year, but she had turned him down. Leigh didn't know about that until after she'd said yes to him. Why Bradley could never let go of his hurt was beyond Leigh.

At the end of the night of the senior prom, in front of the school, Bradley accused Jenny of going to the prom with Leigh because his family had money. In the fashion of his father, Bradley was drunk and working on a half-empty bottle of whiskey. Alcohol was probably the reason, but Bradley used words Leigh felt should never be spoken, especially not to a woman. Leigh had been brought up to respect women, and this assault on his date was not going to be tolerated. They fought until Bradley was unconscious. Even then, Leigh remembered having to be pulled off Bradley by a couple boys. Bradley had been looking for payback for years. That's probably why he kept going hunting on Leigh's property, some sort of passive retribution.

"What can I do you for, Bradley?" Leigh called out while rocking in his chair casually.

"You know what you can do for me, you no good—" The words flew out of Bradley's mouth like venom.

The sheriff stood up, holding his hand out as he interrupted Bradley. "We ain't going to have none of that!"

Bradley and his sons stopped at the base of the porch stairs. "Sheriff," Bradley pleaded, "he had some crazy boy up in them woods attack us."

"Oh, really?" the sheriff asked. "An' what was you doing up on his property?"

Bradley shook his head. "That ain't the point. He tried to kill us."

The sheriff pulled out the empty beer bottle Leigh had brought back with him and set it on the porch banister. "The way I see it, you an' your boys was drinking an' hunting up on Leigh's property. On top of that, it's not hunting season, Bradley. You're in a heap of trouble this time, an' every word out of your mouth is digging the hole deeper an' deeper."

Jacob, Bradley's oldest son, interjected, "It ain't like that, Sheriff. There was this huge creature up in them woods breaking trees and stuff. We was protecting ourselves."

The sheriff laughed, as did Blake and Leigh. "So what you're saying," the sheriff summed up, "is that a wild boy an' a huge creature attacked you, an' you was just protecting yourselves as you were trespassing on this man's property?"

Leigh could tell that Bradley now understood just how ridiculous the story sounded.

"Now, Bradley"—Leigh stood and leaned against his porch railing. "I don't want to have to press charges, but if you and your boys here don't turn right around and leave my property, I'm not going to be that forgiving."

There was a moment of hesitation in Bradley's eyes. Leigh could see he was weighing his options, but he didn't really have any. Defeated, Bradley turned to his boys. "Come on now. Get in the truck."

Jacob protested, but Bradley smacked him upside the head and said, "Get in the truck, boy! You deaf and stupid?"

Leigh walked to Bradley's truck as they were getting into it. Bradley turned in alarm, and Leigh put up his hands in a peaceful gesture. Once the boys were sitting in the truck and only Bradley could hear him, Leigh said, "I believe you, Bradley, but the problem you're going to have is making everyone else believe. Now you shot someone very dear to me today and caused me a major headache, but for some reason I'm feeling generous."

Bradley listened quietly to what he had to say.

"The property to the east, past the stream that runs north and south, I don't ever use. I'll make a deal with you. You can hunt, fish, run naked for all I care in them woods. But if you cross the stream, I can't protect you or your boys. Let's call this a peace treaty, if you will. You get to hunt on my property without having to look over your shoulder. What do you say?"

Leigh put out his hand in a friendly gesture. Bradley looked at it for a second, then up into Leigh's eyes. He could tell it was killing Bradley that Leigh had gotten the upper hand. Reluctantly he shook Leigh's hand and got into his truck.

After Bradley left, Leigh thanked the sheriff for coming out and helping defuse a potentially volatile situation. Once the sheriff left, Blake asked Leigh what he had said to Bradley. He told him the whole conversation, and Blake was surprised that it seemed to work.

"You know he won't be able to keep his mouth shut for long, right?" Blake asked.

Leigh opened the front door. "I know. But after what Marcus did to him and his boys, I doubt he will be bothering us any time soon."

The two men laughed as they pictured Marcus beating up on the Coopers.

Twenty-one

Transformation

Nine and a half years after the Poughkeepsie murders

"Hold still." The frustration in Mama's voice couldn't be missed.

"Ow!"

"I said, hold still! You kids are going to drive me to go gray."

With one hard pull followed by a loud snap, Mama set Zack's dislocated shoulder back into place.

"Mmm!" Zack grunted as the pain subsided.

Mama handed Zack a large book. "Now study—instead of trying to be some sort of human missile."

"But Mama...," he protested.

"Don't 'but' me, Zachary! I've had enough broken bones and dislocations to fix over the last few years, and I'm tired of it. Your uncle bought all of you these college textbooks to study, and that's what you're going to do, instead of trying to fly."

Marcus had heard the speech several times, and all the kids knew not to fight Mama when she got like this.

Zack surrendered. "Yes, Mama."

She continued spouting as she cleaned up the bloody towels and washcloths they had used to clean up the gash in his arm.

"I know you kids are only nine, but you could be graduating high school, you're so big." She said this to no one in particular. "I got five geniuses, and what do they do with their time? They hurl themselves into the air, expecting what? Gravity stopped working? Dear Lord, give me strength."

Mama finally left the room, leaving Marcus with Angie and Zack sitting alone at the dining room table.

There was a long pause before Angie broke the silence. "I told you to use more finesse. You can't go and blast off like a rocket. You need to build up a magnetic field around you first and control its flow."

"Oh, shut up," Zack said. He went to the living room to sit down with the book Mama had given him.

Angie shook her head and shrugged at her brother's stubbornness. She had grown into a beautiful young woman. Though the smallest of all the children at five feet tall, she was probably the smartest.

"Zack, what are you doing?" Angie yelled at him from behind the couch, using Mama's voice.

Zack jumped up from his seat in fear and turned around to find Angie laughing.

"That ain't funny!" he yelled and threw a pillow at her.

In between laughs she replied, "That's for telling me to shut up."

Marcus couldn't help but laugh with her. Zack's expression was priceless. Marcus was slightly jealous of Zack's looks. He had all the makings of a movie star: six-foot, good build. Both he and Angie had blond hair and blue eyes. What girl wouldn't go crazy over him? *Girl...shoot!* He looked up at the clock on the mantle in panic. "Oh man! I need to be at Blake's in less than an hour. Tell Mama where I went, okay?"

He didn't wait for a reply and headed out the front door. Thankfully, it was a cool spring day as he ran to the ranch, then into town to Blake's house.

Over the last two years Marcus had built a close relationship with both Blake and his daughter, Rachael. It had started when Janet and Blake had discussed allowing the kids to interact with someone outside of the family. Things were beginning to get tough on everyone being stuck in the forest with only the family to relate to, and Blake suggested having Marcus and Zack come to his house to help do some remodeling.

It wasn't long before a friendship grew between the boys and Rachael. Soon after, all of the children had become friends with her, except for Sampson. Blake hadn't told his daughter the history of the family and exposing her to Sampson didn't seem like a good idea just yet.

Uncle Leigh had given Blake a substantial raise for everything that he had been doing not only for the ranch but also for his family. That's what brought Marcus to Blake's house. With the extra money, they were putting in a new deck in the back of the house to go along with the pool Blake had saved up to buy, come the summer of 2016.

Marcus got working on the deck right away once he made it to the house. He had grown into a very large young man. He stood over six feet, three inches, and his physique was impressive. Because of his constant exercising and running over the years, he had built his body into a chiseled, muscular shape that would have put most body builders to shame. It was because of this that Blake had asked him not to take his shirt off when Rachael was home. It was clear that she liked Marcus from the start and made no attempt at hiding it, either. Marcus had learned to respect women and how to be a gentleman from Uncle Leigh. Because of this, Blake trusted him around his daughter.

Rachael was now a senior in high school and was going to be leaving in the summer for college, so there was no time for a relationship anyway. With the skills he had learned rebuilding the cabin, Marcus had become a very skilled carpenter and was on his own as he got started hammering into a two-by-four. He hadn't been working long when he heard a car pull up in front of the house. Marcus knew it was Rachael coming home from school. Her friend Kyrra gave her a ride home every afternoon at the same time. Rachael made her way through the house and out the back door.

"Hi, Marcus." Her smile melted his heart.

She seemed happy today, but there was something about her eyes that made him wonder if something was wrong. He secretly had fallen in love with her and could tell her moods before she knew. There was sadness in her eyes as she pulled her black hair back into a ponytail.

"Hey," he finally was able to squeeze out.

She smiled once again at him. "I'll be here if you need me."

With that she turned and went back inside. He tried not to eavesdrop but could hear everything she was doing. The sound of the refrigerator opening and closing, the snap of the lid from a soda pop can. Soon he could hear her dialing the phone from her bedroom. Marcus knew better than to listen to the conversation, so he nailed down a board in an attempt to focus on something else. It was difficult for him, because Rachael's voice became shaky and quivering as she argued into the phone.

Marcus couldn't help but hear her say, "Fine. No, that's fine. Not a big deal. Okay. Yeah, I'll talk to you later."

Rachael hung up the phone and crying followed. Marcus found himself staring at the house, wanting to go to her side. He tried to focus on working, but the crying didn't stop. Finally he couldn't take it anymore and went inside and knocked on her half-open bedroom door.

"You okay?" he asked gently.

Sniffle, sniffle. She tried to regain her composure as she sat on her bed. "Hey. Yeah, I'm okay. Don't worry about me."

Marcus knew better and took a step into the doorway. "You sure? You don't sound okay."

"Oh, it's nothing really." Rachael tried to make light of her feelings.

He took another step into her room. "No, it's not."

Rachael's emotional wall was broken, and she cried openly again as Marcus grabbed her vanity chair and sat across from her.

"It's your mother, isn't it?" he asked softly.

When the tears flowed even harder, Marcus knew he was right. Rachael looked just like her mother, from the pictures that he had seen of the woman. They both had a slightly round-looking face and full lips. The only thing Marcus could see of Blake in Rachael was her eyes, which were golden brown with speckles.

She mustered a reply through the tears. "She can't have me visit this summer before college. The only two weeks out of the year I spend with her, and she planned her vacation during them. She didn't even ask if I wanted to go with her."

"That's harsh," he replied. Marcus silently prayed to God to give him something useful to say. There was a moment of quiet between them before he said, "All the kids in my family are orphans, and we know what it's like to feel unwanted. I'm not saying your mother doesn't love you. She sounds like she's got her priorities mixed up." It was true for a lot of people, but it didn't seem to comfort Rachael much. He searched for another way to approach the situation.

Marcus thought back to when Mama had explained to all of them how they had come to be with her. The realization that all five of them were nothing more than experiments to be discarded gave life a whole new perspective. This wasn't how Mama had explained it to them, exactly, but it was clear they were never intended to live. They were unwanted, and no matter how much they knew they were loved, it still hurt. Not that any of the children wished to meet the insane man who helped create them, but the emptiness was there nonetheless. Marcus knew what Rachael needed.

"I'm sorry," he said as he got up and sat next to her on the bed. He put his arm around her and pulled her close to him. Rachael wept harder as she put her arms around him and her head on his shoulder. Marcus patted her hair. "I'm sorry, Rachael. I know how much it meant to you, being with your mother."

Marcus was grateful as Rachael calmed down. She pulled away from him and grabbed the box of tissues from her nightstand. As she wiped her eyes, she said, "Thank you for being such a good friend."

She looked up into his face with such love and longing that Marcus's inner alarm went off. Although every part of his physical being wanted to take Rachael back into his arms again and kiss her, his mind told him to run, run away fast. She leaned into him.

"Uh hum," came from the doorway.

Marcus jumped up from the bed at the sight of Blake staring at them with a questioning eyebrow.

"I, I, we were...that is, that Rachael... um...I'm going to go back to work now, okay?" And with that, Marcus slid past Blake to go back outside.

Marcus frantically hammered nails again as he heard Blake ask Rachael, "Want to tell me what that was all about?"

"Oh, Daddy, don't be mad at Marcus. He was just worried about me." Rachael added, "It was Mom again."

Blake replied, "Oh. Now that makes sense."

He could hear Rachael get up from the bed as the springs released. The way her voice echoed off the walls told him that she was probably looking away from Blake. She said, "I'm going to be here through the summer, it appears."

Marcus could hear her cry again. Blake's voice sounded heartbroken when he said, "I'm so sorry, honey."

"Eleven o'clock sharp," Leigh called out as he pulled away in his truck. Marcus, Zack, and Anna waved and excitedly made their way into the woods along the road. It was Friday night, and that meant movie night at Blake's. He didn't care what movie they watched. For Marcus, it meant being with Rachael and after the day that she had, he wanted to be with her for support.

The sun had set about a half hour ago and a cool spring breeze picked up as he followed his two siblings along the dirt path that led to Blake's backyard. Uncle Leigh had insisted they wait until after dark. Marcus knew it was because he didn't want anyone in town seeing them and asking questions. It was just under a mile walk inside of the forest edge to get to Blake's house. He didn't have any trouble seeing in the dark, but for Anna's sake Zack provided them with light emanating from his skin. Marcus had become used to seeing the sight of his brother glowing in the dark, but he knew if someone else saw Zack it would be hard to explain. It had become a problem for Zack when he first started emanating light. They nearly had several more fires at the cabin because of it. Thankfully, Uncle Leigh had come up with the idea of getting Zack a scuba suit to wear. The rubber in the suit that his brother wore under his regular clothes seemed to ground and insulate any heat or electricity.

Anna broke the silence by asking, "Anybody know what we're watching?"

Zack called back from in front, "Insomnia-Ridden Man in Rainy City."

Marcus rolled his eyes at his brother's attempt at humor while Anna replied, "Oh goodie! *Sleepless in Seattle.* I love that old movie!"

"Girly flick," Marcus retorted.

Anna shot him a look and punched him in the arm. "You guys got to pick last week. What was it? Oh yeah. *Fists of Fury.* Boring!"

"What?" Zack shot back. "That is a classic! There's nothing boring about..." He turned around to face them as he got down into a martial arts stance yelling, "Waaaaaaahhhhh!"

Anna shook her head in protest. "Don't start now. We're in a hurry." It was too late.

Marcus had taken up his own fighting stance as he joined Zack in circling each other.

Anna yelled out, "You know I could put an end to this right now!" Marcus ignored her.

He knew she wouldn't dare do that again. The last time she used her powers of influence on them they put green hair dye in her shampoo. He watched his sister back away from them and sit down on a nearby rock. She shot them a disgusted look. "Testosterone play," she always called it, and Marcus loved every minute of it.

He circled to Zack's left side. He knew his brother was right-handed and wanted to try and get an advantage. He was going to need it, since Zack was much faster than he was when it came to hand-to-hand fighting. His brother's reflexes were unbelievably fast. *Enough evaluating.* It was time to attack. Marcus leaped forward with a frontal kick to Zack's chest, but was pushed aside. The match had begun.

Before Marcus could get his footing Zack charged with a flurry of punches and sidekicks to his abdomen. Marcus fought off most of them, but the last kick hit him in the ribs, causing him to hunch.

"Aha!" Zack cried out mockingly.

Something inside Marcus changed. The rush of adrenaline coursed through his veins, causing him physically to raise his game level of fighting. He lowered his head as he waited for Zack to try and hit him again. He didn't have to wait long. His brother once again charged, throwing a punch that nearly hit Marcus across the chin. With accelerated speed and strength he grabbed Zack's arm and pulled him forward, off balance, and threw him to the ground.

Zack hurried to roll over and do a kip up. "You've been practicing," he said with a smile. "This is going to be fun."

His brother threw a flurry of punches nearly impossible to see. Marcus fended them off the best he could, but every now and then one would slip through his defenses in the chest or in the ribs. Zack wasn't as strong as him, but his brother made up for it with accuracy and speed.

Marcus knew he needed to try another approach. He backed up underneath an oak tree and leaped into the air, grabbing one of the lower branches. With one hard pull he used the branch to hurl himself over Zack's head and land behind him. As his brother turned around, caught slightly off guard, Marcus attacked. With a kick to the stomach he hit Zack hard. Marcus hurried to attack now that his brother was on the defensive. He knew he couldn't give his brother even a split second to recuperate.

He threw roundhouse swings and forward high kicks at Zack, who found himself hard-pressed to regain his composure and barely able to fend off the attack. One or two blows landed, causing Zack to back away, but it was enough time for his brother to clear his head. Marcus knew he was in trouble when he threw a punch at Zack and missed. There was no time to defend himself. Zack hit him hard in the stomach then spin-kicked him in the back. He fell forward into another tree as Zack grabbed one of his arms and flipped Marcus to the ground.

Marcus rolled to his back just in time for Zack to step on his chest, which was normally the winning move for their matches.

"Do you yield to the superior warrior?" Zack spoke with an English accent for theatrics' sake. "Or shall I throttle you again?"

This was the usual outcome of their play fighting. Zack was simply faster than Marcus, despite how strong he was. He was about to concede his defeat when Zack pushed things too far. He said, "Since I am the victor, perhaps I should be the one to get the maiden's kiss tonight."

Earlier that day Marcus had told Zack about what happened with Rachael, and now he was making a joke about it.

Something inside Marcus snapped. The barrier he'd built over the years that held back his violent instincts broke down. Rage swelled within him. There was a burning sensation from within his gut that radiated throughout his entire body. He tried to control it, but at the same time there was elation at the rush of letting go. Something primal, something welcomed.

Everything went black.

* **
** *

Marcus woke as Anna tapped him on his cheek and called his name. When he opened his eyes, both his siblings were staring at him with fear.

Marcus sat up. "What's going on?"

Zack nervously laughed. "You don't remember trying to kill me?"

"Huh?"

The smell of burnt hair was overwhelming and caused him to look down at his shirt. There was a hole burnt through it, exposing his singed chest hair.

"What happened to me?" Anxiety was building.

Zack replied, "When you wouldn't stop attacking me, I had to shoot you to save my life. I'm sorry, but—"

"But what? What happened? I don't remember any of this."

Anna spoke softly. "It was hard to see in the dark, but it looked like you were bigger somehow. As if you grew thicker or something. I couldn't really tell exactly, but you wouldn't stop attacking Zack. I tried to make you stop, but nothing I said had an effect on you." She pointed to the hole in the tree that he supposedly made as Zack showed him the bruises and cuts on his body. The bruise on his brother's chest was already becoming black and swollen. Zack winced as he tried to pull his shirt back down over his chest.

Marcus had never been more scared in his life. What had happened to him? Was this another manifestation of how he was created?

"It was like you weren't yourself. You picked up that boulder and were about to crush me with it." Zack pointed in the distance and shined his hand brighter so that Marcus could see the size of it. It was huge. It was nearly three feet high and even wider than it was tall. Only Sampson could have picked that rock up. He couldn't take thinking about it anymore.

"Please don't say anything to Mama or Uncle Leigh until I figure out what is happening. Maybe it's a one-time thing. Please?"

There was a hesitation, but they both finally nodded. Marcus had

156

become the unofficial leader of the children, and he knew they often looked to him for leadership. He was counting on this when he asked them for their silence. He didn't want to worry Mama or Uncle Leigh any more than they already were. Marcus threw away his shirt and wore Zack's zip-up jacket for the night. He didn't want to explain to Rachael how he had burnt his shirt.

"Come on. Let's get to Blake's."

Along the side of the road Bradley Cooper cursed to himself as he pumped the jack under his truck. He had gotten a flat tire again. This was the third time in two weeks, so he was prepared. Bradley held out his flashlight to make sure he had gotten all of the lug nuts back in securely when he heard yelling coming from the woods across the road. He stood up to look. It was too dark to see anything, but the longer he looked, his eyes adjusted. In the direction the noises were coming from he could see faint lights moving around violently in every direction, but they stayed close to each other.

Grunts and moans filled the air as Bradley watched in amazement. He could hear a girl's voice yelling out, and he thought he made out a name, Marcus. He wasn't sure, but the commotion lasted for only a few minutes until a large flash of light lit up the forest and nearly blinded him. It took several seconds for him to get his sight back, but when he did the noise and chaos had ended. Bradley still could see something glowing deep within the woods and decided to follow in his truck.

After following the light he ended up parked in front of Blake Heroux's house. Bradley knew whatever he saw had to be the freaks up in Leigh's woods. Now Blake was friends with them, too. He shook his head in disgust, but he at least had new stories to tell down at the bar. He sped off in a hurry to meet up with his boys as he cursed Leigh to himself.

Twenty-two

New Lead

Beep, *beep, beep* rang out from all of the checkout counters, creating a chaotic chorus. It was the Thursday before Good Friday, and the lines were filled with people from every walk of life. Among them was Michele Townsend, now known as Shelly Renard. She waited patiently, wearing her sunglasses and baseball cap to help cover her appearance. Michele had come home to Newburgh, N.Y. to visit her aunt, whom she hadn't seen in more than nine years.

Against her better judgment, she had talked herself into believing that it had been long enough to have kept her aunt in the dark about her death, or lack thereof. Her Aunt Anna had been a second mother to her after her father had kicked her out of her home at the age of fourteen and never allowed her to come back. She had been disowned by her family because of her teenage pregnancy, and had an abortion without telling her parents. It was a blessing in disguise. For years her father had sexually abused her as a child, and being away from him seemed to help her move on with her life.

Her aunt had been the only solid relationship she had left, and with Easter coming, the compulsion to see her was too great to ignore. Besides, who was going to recognize her? Michele had dyed her hair a strawberry red instead of her natural blond. She had also acquired a dark tan from living in California the last six years. Having grown up in New York state most of her life and having a light-skinned English heritage, anyone would be hard-pressed to recognize her.

The young lady behind the counter swiped the chocolates she was buying for her aunt. *Beep.* "That'll be $4.27."

Michele handed her a five-dollar bill and smiled as she looked up. It was then that she noticed a police officer two aisles over, staring at her. Her pulse sped up as she lowered her head and grabbed the plastic bag full of chocolates.

"Thank you," she said to the clerk. Michele tried to keep calm as she walked toward the exit. Out of the corner of her eye she could see the officer's gaze still on her. Just when she thought she had made it to the exit, a voice rang out.

"Michele? Michele Townsend? It's you, isn't it?" the officer called out as he hurried to catch up to her.

She tried to ignore him and act like she hadn't recognized her own name, but the officer didn't relent. He stepped in front of her with a big smile on his face.

"Michele, it's me. Freddy Delucca. You rememba'," he insisted. "We went out a few times? Years ago. 'Memba, right?"

Michele was caught, but for Janet's and the kids' sake she couldn't admit he was right. Before she could say anything, Freddy pressed the issue.

"Hey, I understand if you don't wanna talk or anything, but you could at least say hi or sumptin'."

She tried to reply in a slightly lower voice than normal. "I'm sorry, but you have me confused with someone else."

Freddy shook his head in argument of the issue. "No way. I'd know that smile anywhere. It melted my heart."

She needed to be more forceful in her denial. Trying to act casual, she reached into her purse and pulled out her C.A. driver's license. "Here's my license, officer. Like I said, you have me confused."

Freddy took the license from her, examining it closely. "I'm very sorry, Ms. Renard. My mistake," he said as Michele took back her I.D.

She simply nodded and headed straight for her rental parked outside. She didn't look back, but felt the officer following her as he walked out to his patrol car. Her heart was racing as she pulled out of the parking lot. Desperately she kept checking her rearview mirror to see if she was being followed. After a minute of driving and no sign of the officer, she relaxed. That had been too close and exactly the reason she never should have come back to Newburgh. Something inside her told her to go back to California, but the desire to see her aunt won the battle.

* **
** *

Nick put away his case files in preparation of his month-long, forced vacation. His commander was making him take the time off due to a degraded work performance. Ever since he'd been shot, Nick had found that his cases had gradually become easier. It was clear he had never fully recovered from the trauma and was even sent to the Bureau's psychiatrist for a while. The strange looks and the way his coworkers treated him with extra care made it clear over the last few years he was losing his edge. He agreed with them. No matter how hard he tried, his performance was sloppy. Failure had become a trademark of his career, and he didn't have anything left in him. The future looked grim now that his job, his reason for existence, was almost over.

All of his team had moved on or been promoted. Allen had been given a team leader position, and Jason moved to another department. Nick was left with three new rookies and given easy assignments to cover the Bureau's interests. He had to admit they were right to do what they had done to him. Nick was still having nightmares sometimes about the day Liz shot him, and there wasn't a day that went by that he didn't think about the sight of Damon being brutally murdered before his eyes. The anger and fear he felt had only driven him to drink more heavily. He wouldn't admit that he was a drunk or had a problem, but Nick knew he wasn't right.

The knocking at Nick's office door brought him back from his self pity. He motioned for the young lady to come in. She handed him a note and said, "This just came in. I saw your name on the case and thought you would want to know also."

Nick read the note. "'Michele Townsend spotted in Newburgh, N.Y. Possible lead.'" He asked the girl as she was leaving, "Who else did you give this to?

"Agent Young."

"Thanks."

He grabbed his jacket and followed the secretary out of his office. As he hurried to the elevator, he caught Allen as he was just about to step onto it.

160

"Yo, Allen, wait up."

Allen held the elevator for Nick, and the two of them headed down to the garage.

"When were you going to tell me about the lead?" Nick asked, catching his breath.

Allen replied, "I thought you had left already for vacation. You're more than welcome to come for a ride, if you'd like. It's probably nothing."

"Are you kidding? I wouldn't miss this for the world."

They pulled up in front of Anna Roberts' apartment several hours later. Nick knew that if Michele was in town it must be to see her aunt. He pointed out the blue Ford parked in front of them. It had the look of a rental, so Allen ran the plates through their computer. Sure enough, it came back having been rented by a Shelly Renard, just like the officer had said.

They both got out of their car and peered into the windows of the rental. The car was still locked, and it didn't look like any personal items were still inside. Nick hoped that this Shelly Renard was Michele Townsend from the case file and still inside with her aunt. Allen knocked on the door and a very nice older woman answered. She was going gray with shoulder-length hair, and her eyes looked a lot like Michele's hospital photo I.D.

She asked, "Can I help you gentlemen?"

Allen showed her his FBI I.D. and asked if she was Anna Roberts, Michele's aunt. When the woman told them that she was, they asked to come in. The woman graciously ushered them both in.

"Would you like something to drink, gentlemen?"

There was something in the woman's eyes that alerted him. Nick asked, "When did she leave, Mrs. Roberts?"

"Well..."

He could tell she was trying to cover her reaction, but it wasn't in her nature. "Look, Mrs. Roberts," Allen jumped in. "If Michele was here, we need to know it right away. There are some very nasty people who may be looking for her, and we're her only protection. Now, for the sake of your niece, when did she leave?"

Tears welled up as she replied in a trembling voice, "She left an hour ago. I don't know where she is. I think she is staying at the Ramada, but I'm not sure."

"It's okay," Nick said to try and calm her. "Just tell us what she said to you. Anything will be helpful."

She sat down in a rocking chair. "I didn't know what to think. My dear little Michele is alive. You can imagine my shock. A lot of what she said is blurry to me, but I remember that she said she was now living in California after moving from Oklahoma."

Allen and Nick shot each other glances when she mentioned Oklahoma. Nick remembered Janet's uncle lived there.

"Do you mind if I have a quick look around your apartment, Mrs. Roberts?" Allen asked.

She nodded in permission.

After not finding Michele or anything else helpful, they excused themselves from her apartment. No Michele meant that either she knew they were coming and ditched the rental car, or something worse. Nick hoped Michele was running, because if she wasn't, then it was more than likely they would never see her again.

Nick looked over to Allen as they were getting into their car and said, "You know I'm on vacation. A trip to Oklahoma sounds like a nice spot to visit."

Allen shook his head. "You're no longer on vacation. I'll call it in. We should be able to get a flight out of Stewart Airport in an hour."

Nick smiled at his old partner. "Yes, sir."

The pounding in Michele's head greeted her as the drugs wore off. Throbbing waves of pain beat within her head as she attempted to open her eyes. She couldn't. Blindfolded. Slowly her memory was coming back to her. She had just left her aunt's apartment and had been getting into her car when someone grabbed her from behind. That was the last she could remember. Michele had had a bad feeling after being spotted by the police officer and berated herself silently for not listening to her gut instincts.

Her senses were now fully aware of her surroundings, even though she couldn't see. She could feel her hands and feet tied with what felt like some kind of hard plastic restraints. In the distance Michele could make out a man and woman talking to each other. She couldn't hear what they were saying. Something about their voices, though, told her she should know who they belonged to. Michele jumped when a voice to the right of her called out, "She's awake."

She could hear footsteps coming toward her; they stopped only a few feet away. A man's voice ordered, "Take the blindfold off."

A rush of light hit Michele's eyes, causing the pain in her head to pound harder. She winced as her eyes slowly focused on what was in front of her.

The man sitting in a chair across from her said, "Welcome, Nurse Townsend. You missed our last staff meeting."

Michele focused to see the man's face clearly. It was Dr. Scharf. What she had feared had happened. He looked different then she last remembered him. His hair was completely white and slicked back. The burn marks along the side of his face and neck were gone, and Michele stared for a moment, not sure if she was seeing clearly or not. The doctor looked like a president of a bank or corporation, wearing a gray three-piece suit with a bright red tie. *He looks quite handsome*, she thought to herself—until he smiled at her. There was something in his eyes that frightened her.

He said, "I've missed you. The good thing is that we have time to catch up on old times. For instance, we can talk about where you've been for the last nine years, or we can talk about where your friend Janet is."

"I don't know…," she started to say.

Tibon stopped her by raising a hand. "Please, please don't insult me. That's only going to cause you more pain than is needed. It's bad enough you attempted to run off with five of my test subjects. What's sad is you probably had feelings for them and then had to watch them die a painful death."

Michele had no idea what he was talking about. He thought the children were dead. She didn't want to show her confusion so she went along by looking sad.

He continued, "Now I need to know where Janet is, or you are going to die a very painful death also."

Michele didn't say anything as they both considered each other. Then Tibon shrugged and nodded to the woman standing next to him. It was Liz Bolan. She pulled a small device from her pocket and approached Michele. With a push of a single button on the top of the device, Liz demonstrated what was in store for her. An electrical bolt flashed between the prongs sticking out.

"Now," Tibon said, "let's try this again. Janet..."

Liz smiled as she stuck the device into Michele's stomach.

Blinding hot pain flashed through Michele, and she screamed.

"Again," Tibon ordered.

Twenty-three

Found

There was no one at the main house, so Nick and Allen headed out back to one of the barns. They questioned a couple of the workers who were feeding the cattle, asking where Leigh Barrus was. They weren't sure, they said, but one suggested Leigh might be up at his getaway spot in the woods. The other one mentioned he spent a lot of time there, but they weren't sure where in the woods it was. Nick noticed the dirt road that led into the hills of the ranch and thanked the workers.

Turning to Allen, Nick asked, "So what do you think?" using his best Midwestern accent.

"I thinks we is going for a little ride up in them yonder hills," Allen replied likewise.

They got back into the car and followed the dirt road. It wasn't long before they found the bush-covered fence, cleverly disguised, along the forest edge. They entered the forest and followed the dirt road. Their gray sedan wasn't meant for the rough terrain they had to travel over. Nick wondered how far the road led and began to get carsick after a half hour of being jarred around. Had they missed another road somewhere along the way? Then he saw smoke in the distance, through the treetops.

The smoke billowed up through the trees maybe a half-mile ahead, and it wasn't long after he could see a cabin. As they parked he noticed there were no other vehicles. If Leigh was here, someone had dropped him off. The trashcans were full of garbage, and the chopping of wood came from the other side of the cabin. Allen slowly walked around the back of the cabin, then turned the corner while Nick followed behind him.

"Hi," came a voice from behind him.

Nick spun and reached for his gun but couldn't move his hand. He looked up to find a tall young man with long black hair and a five o'clock shadow holding a vice grip on his hand and gun.

He said to Nick, "Please, slowly release your grip on the gun." He pointed over his shoulder with his other hand as he continued saying, "My brother here has a big problem with guns, and I don't know what he'll do if you show him yours."

Nick's face went pale as he looked behind the young man. At first he hadn't seen the creature because he was so huge, but as his gaze went upward, memories of the night Damon died flashed through his head. The creature stood well over ten feet tall, but its size was something out of a comic book. His frame was as wide as Nick was tall, probably wider, and the muscles on the arms bulged as if they had been artificially pumped full of air. The creature was wearing a simple self-sewn brown leather animal skin that only covered its massive chest. But even that couldn't conceal the pecs and neck muscles underneath. His pants were made of similar material and hung loosely around his legs. The long beard had several braided stands hanging down and his jet-black hair was pulled back in a long ponytail.

"Sorry about this," the young man said as he released Nick's hand.

Nick looked at him, confused. Then a sudden shock hit him in the back, followed by darkness.

Country music played on an old jukebox in the corner of the bar. The sound of billiards filled the air as the balls made loud noises every now and then. Both of Bradley's boys were playing in the back while he sulked over his fifth beer at the bar. An elderly drunk sat next to him, listening to Bradley's wild stories of creatures that lived up at the Barrus Ranch.

Every eye in the place turned toward the entrance as two men dressed in dark brown suits entered. Bradley watched as they walked up to the counter and the larger of the two men called for the bartender.

"What can I get you folks?" the bartender asked skeptically.

The larger man replied, "We need directions to the Barrus Ranch. The directions we have are sending us in circles."

The bartender smiled. "That's cuz you gots the wrong ones." He pointed to the map the man had set on the bar. "You see here, there's a sign saying make a left. That sign's been wrong for years. You actually got to make a right, and then you'll see signs for it."

The man put a hundred-dollar bill on the bar top and said, "Thank you," then turned to walk away with his associate.

Bradley was too drunk to stop himself. He yelled out to the men, "You looking for them freaks up in his woods?"

This caught their attention, and both men turned around. They walked up to Bradley, and the larger man spoke again. "What freaks?"

"Them freaks that live up in the woods," Bradley insisted. "One of them is as big as a tree and another glows in the dark."

"Really?" the man replied. "I'd like to hear more, if you have the time. Bartender, another beer for my friend here. What's your name?"

"Bradley Cooper."

"Well, Bradley, do you know where in the woods I might find them?"

"Not exactly, but I know who does. He has them come to his house all the time. Give me a pen. I'll give you his name and address."

Consciousness began to come back to Nick as he forced himself to move. His hands and feet were tied to the chair he was sitting on. A pretty young blond was staring into his face only a couple inches away as he opened his eyes. He tried to pull his head away. Her big blue eyes gazed at him intently as his mind raced as to what she was doing or going to do to him.

After several awkward seconds she finally said, "I like this one. He's cute."

When she pulled away, Nick could see his surroundings. Both he and Allen were tied to chairs. He assumed they were inside the cabin. There was a fireplace with several logs burning in it next to a dining table. Sitting at the table was Janet Renard. He recognized her from the photos they had gotten nine years ago from the hospital I.D. Standing next to her was a young woman, possibly in her late teens. She was staring at them both very intently. Something about her gaze was hypnotizing to Nick. He found himself having a hard time taking his eyes off of her. She had long, flowing auburn hair that hung down around her shoulders and a mild, dark complexion, similar to his own. She could have asked anything of him at that moment, and he would have jumped at the opportunity to make her happy.

But Nick's training helped him to look away momentarily and continue to survey his surroundings. Allen sat to the right of him and, standing guard, was a young man with blond hair. He didn't remember seeing him earlier. The one who had grabbed his hand and gun was standing to his left, hovering over him.

Janet said to no one in particular, "I knew this day would come." She looked up at both Nick and Allen now that they were both awake. "Welcome. Before you spout off why you're here or try to give us your story as to how you found us, I want you to sit back and relax. We're not going to hurt you. Anna."

Janet nodded to her, and Anna approached Allen first. She said, "I feel you are hiding something from us, but then again, everyone hides things. I'm not going to embarrass you, but I am going to ask you a few questions."

Nick's gaze was transfixed on Anna. She asked Allen, "Are you from the FBI?" Allen nodded his reply with a childlike expression.

"Are you here to kill us?" Allen shook his head with the same expression. Anna looked troubled for a moment as she stared deeply into Allen's eyes.

After a few seconds she turned her gaze on Nick. "Why are you here?"

He replied, "Janet and Michele are suspects in an ongoing murder investigation. We were following a lead after Michele Townsend showed up in Newburgh. We came looking for her because she disappeared."

Anna broke her gaze with Nick as she turned toward Janet. Concern flickered across her face. "Mama, Aunt Shelly's been taken."

Nick refuted, "I didn't say 'taken,' I said 'disappeared.'"

Now that Anna had broken whatever hold she had over both agents, Nick was able to think clearly.

Without looking back at Nick, she replied, "You didn't have to. You think she was abducted and in trouble."

"How...," Nick began to ask but Marcus interrupted him by waving his finger in front of his face.

Frustration was beginning to overcome Nick, and he found he couldn't keep quiet. Anna and Janet were talking quietly to each other when he blurted out, "What are you people? Do you know who we are? We're the FBI, and holding us is going to make this a lot harder on all of you! Janet, release us at once! This is not helping..."

Nick was jerked in his chair as a large hand wrapped around Nick's waist. Before he could say anything more Nick found he was being lifted off the floor and turned in midair while still tied to the chair. When he stopped moving, he was face to face with the giant. The angry look on the creature's face made Nick speechless with fear.

"That's my mama. If you talk like that again, I'll get mad. Now apologize," the deep rich tone of his voice bellowed.

"Yes, yes, of course!" He wasn't going to antagonize the giant man.

Slowly he was put back down next to Allen.

Nick gathered himself for a moment, then said, "Janet, I am very sorry for my outburst. I don't know what came over me. Please accept my apology."

Janet let out a chuckle. "Accepted." She smiled up at the giant man and said, "Thank you, sweetheart."

The blond girl came out of her hiding from behind Marcus and looked Nick in the face again. "I don't like you anymore," she said to him, then stuck out her tongue.

Anna said in a solemn voice, "The time has come, Mama."

Janet stood up and took her daughter's head into her hands. "I know, dear." Then she kissed Anna on the forehead. Janet turned to face the rest of the family. "I want everyone to get ready for dinner. It's almost dark out, and your uncle will be here in a few hours. We'll discuss this when he gets here. Until then, get moving."

Nick watched everyone go their separate ways as Janet came back from the kitchen with a knife in her hands. Allen hadn't said a thing through the whole ordeal up to this point.

He finally broke his silence when Janet stood before him with a long carving knife. "Whoa! What are you doing?"

Janet slit the rope around both their wrists. For a moment Nick thought that Janet was going to let them go when he remembered that the giant was still standing behind them, eyes fixed on their every move.

Janet cut both of their ropes, then looked up and asked, "Sampson, can you please keep a watch on these two while I start getting dinner ready?"

His deep bass voice replied, "Yes, Mama."

She smiled at Nick. "Isn't he a good boy?" Then she walked away into the kitchen, leaving them with only their hands free. It was going to be a long night.

Nick could see through the window that the sun had nearly set, followed by the sound of a car pulling up to the cabin. Soon Leigh Barrus walked through the front door. His face was apprehensive.

"Whose car is that, and why is it upside down?" He stopped himself when he saw Nick and Allen. "Oh."

"Come on in, Uncle Leigh. We have a situation," Janet said while patting the seat next to her on the couch.

Finally Janet talked to them about what had happened at INYO Industries. She explained where the children had come from and what she and Michele had done at the project with Dr. Scharf. So many things began to make sense to Nick as he listened to her story.

"So, what questions do you have for me?" she asked.

Nick started off the questions by asking, "You're saying that this Dr. Scharf was in charge of the whole operation?"

"Yes. Along with Liz Bolan, who was the supervisor of the project."

Allen shot a knowing glance at Nick. They had suspected for some time that Tibon was behind the murders but hadn't gotten much confirmation until now.

"How much do you know about what they were doing to these kids?" Allen continued with the questions.

Janet shrugged. "Michele and I didn't have a clue what they had done to them. It wasn't until months later that we started having our suspicions. But that's all they are, suspicions. I really don't know what the project was all about."

"We need to contact our local office and make arrangements to have you and the children escorted to one of our safehouses," Allen said.

Nick thought that statement was a bit premature.

"Just like that?" Leigh asked him.

"I sympathize, Mr. Barrus, and I don't mean to be abrupt about this. But if we found you, there's a good chance the killers can, too. We already suspect Miss Townsend's been taken, and if that's the case, then we need to get Janet and the children to a safe location."

Janet and Leigh both nodded. She sounded resigned as she said, "I'll go get the kids packing."

While she went down the hallway Nick asked, "Can we have our cell phones back?"

Marcus must have been listening from the other room, because right away he came in with the phones and handed them back. "Sorry about this, but I think they're broke."

Allen opened up his and tried to turn it on, but nothing happened. The same happened for Nick's phone.

Marcus explained, "When Zack shocked you, I think he fried the circuits."

Allen looked at Nick. "It's late. Maybe we should stay the night and head out first thing in the morning. We can call from the ranch if that's okay with you, Mr. Barrus."

"It's Leigh," he corrected Allen. "And yes, that'd be fine."

Nick wasn't so sure that waiting till morning was a good idea, but Allen kept insisting until he gave in to the plan. The sound of the kids moving around in the other rooms could be heard as they all were busy packing. He had so many more questions to ask, but they would wait. Nick couldn't help but feel redeemed. It was a nice feeling to have after such a long time. Allen went to help Leigh with something outside when the girl, Anna, came into the living room.

Her demeanor was shy and timid when she asked, "Can I talk to you?"

Nick, the only one in the room, answered. "Sure."

Janet's Journal
Saturday, March 26, 2016

This will be my last journal entry for a while, and maybe the very last. Our family has come to a crossroad. I knew this day would come, but it doesn't make it any easier. I have no idea what will happen in the days ahead. The children have grown to young adults and are more than capable of taking care of themselves. Anna tells me that things will work out, but I can't help being a mother. For nine years this forest has been our home. I just hope, whatever happens, we will always be a family. There is one other fear I have, and that's Blake. I don't want to leave him. We were just starting to get close, and now I don't know if I will ever see him again. There's no time to say good-bye, and I hope he won't take it personally. Hopefully I will be able to see him again.

Twenty-four

Betrayal

That night Marcus snuck out his and Zack's door that led to the outside. It was still there from when the bedroom had been Sampson's. The FBI agents had been taking shifts watching the cabin, but he had been able to sneak away easily. The morning light would be up in a few hours, and Marcus wanted to leave a note for both Blake and Rachael. He didn't want to disappear from their lives without letting them know how much he appreciated and cared for them. So with a note in his pocket, Marcus began his trek through the forest at 3:43 a.m. under a dark, cloudy sky. He knew it would take him about an hour to get to Blake's house if he paced himself. He would need the strength to get back so he didn't want to burn off all his energy. The cool April air filled his senses as he made his way through the woods to the backyard of the Heroux house.

He was just about at the edge of the tree line when he saw lights on in the kitchen through the window in the back door. A man wearing all black and what looked like a protective vest stood alone in the yard. A rifle was slung over the man's shoulder and throwing knives were stuck in his belt. At first Marcus thought the man was talking to himself, but then he saw the device in the man's ear. He was on the phone. Marcus listened closely as he ducked behind a tree.

"No, sir. Not yet. I was about to start on the daughter..."

Marcus could hear punches and crying coming from within the kitchen. It was Blake, moaning with each smack of flesh while the man in the backyard finished his conversation.

"Terminate them? You have the coordinates already." The man sounded surprised. "We will be at the rendezvous point within twenty minutes, sir."

Marcus's heart began to pound in his chest as he realized that Blake and Rachael were about to be killed. Just as the man finished pushing the button on the device in his ear, Marcus was upon him. With an instinctive reflex he had run up behind the man and grabbed his head within his hands, snapping his neck. The man dropped to the ground gently as Marcus laid him down. There was only the slight cracking of bone, muffled by the groans coming from Blake.

Marcus stood under the kitchen window where he could hear what was going on inside. He listened to the footsteps and counted five sets. Marcus could hear one of the men ask, "Can we have some fun with the girl while you work him over?"

That was all Marcus could stand. He reached down into the dead man's belt and pulled out the three throwing knives. He knew he didn't have time to be fancy with his approach as he glided up the back steps of the half-finished deck and opened the door. All five men were in the kitchen. The one punching Blake had his back to the door. They all looked up at Marcus. He threw one of the knives into the neck of the man next to Rachael. Marcus could see she had been hit a few times also, which fueled his escalating rage.

The man closest to him tried to turn around and face him, but Marcus was too quick. Like a dance, Marcus grabbed the man around the throat with his left hand and choked him as he used his body as a shield. The others raised their guns as Marcus threw the other two knives into their necks.

Marcus was one knife short as the man to his left was about to fire on him. He hurled the now unconscious man in his arms at his last assailant. The two men fell to the ground as the pistol fired into the kitchen cabinets. Marcus was on top of the man within a second, came down hard with his fist underneath the man's chin, and broke his jaw.

All five attackers were on the floor as Rachael's muffled screams caught Marcus's attention. He ran to her and pulled off the tape they had placed over her mouth. She let out an audible cry at the realization she was being rescued.

Marcus pulled a knife out of the man lying next to her and used it to cut her hands and legs free. She immediately wrapped her arms around Marcus as she trembled uncontrollably. He put his arms around her as he tried to tell her it was all right now. Before he could say anything, she ran over to her father. Blake was bleeding badly from his left cheek and his left eye had been completely swollen shut. Marcus cut him loose, then both of them carried Blake to the sofa and laid him down. He was oblivious to what was going on around him. He had a concussion and needed medical attention.

"Get some ice for his head," Marcus directed her.

She hurried to the kitchen and came back with an ice pack from the freezer and placed it on her father's face.

After a moment Marcus said to her, "It's going to be all right now. Everyone's safe. We should call 911—"

She cried, "No, it's not all right. You don't understand."

Marcus figured she was still hysterical from the ordeal and began repeating himself, saying, "No really! You're fine now. It's over."

She shook her head violently as the tears began to run freely again, "No! You don't understand. They wanted to know where you lived! Daddy wouldn't tell them, and I've never been to your place!"

Marcus understood now why they were going to kill Blake and Rachael. They found out where the cabin was. He hurried into the kitchen again with Rachael following close behind and frantically searched the counter until he found Blake's truck keys. Marcus knew he couldn't make it back in time, but if he drove up the road past the ranch he could cut off several minutes getting back to the cabin.

Rachael said, "Please don't leave."

Marcus turned to her. "I want you to call 911 immediately and the local FBI agency. Here, write these names down."

He handed her a piece of paper and pen from the counter as he told her Nick and Allen's names.

"Tell them that two of their agents are up in the woods of the Barrus Ranch, and they need to come immediately. When I leave, I want you to tie up all of the bodies, even if they are dead. I don't want to take any chances." Marcus went to leave, but Rachael grabbed him by the shoulders and reached up to pull his head down to hers. They kissed.

As they pulled away, Rachael said, "Please be careful."

Marcus didn't know what to say. He knew he needed to leave right away if he was to get to his family in time, yet a big part of him wanted to stay and be with Rachael. He kissed her again, then ran down the hallway and out the front door. Several of the neighbors had their lights on and were standing outside wondering where the gunshot came from. Dogs were barking from every direction as Marcus hopped into Blake's truck and sped off down the road.

The sudden realization of what he had just done hit him while he drove frantically up the road toward the ranch. He had just killed six men without even thinking about what he was doing. It was too much for Marcus to contemplate as he rushed to get back to the cabin.

After a few miles he came to a screeching stop and jumped out of the truck. The shrillness of the sheriff's siren could be heard in the distance, and something else. Marcus could hear overhead a high-pitched whining. It was very faint, but it turned into three separate sounds. He strained his eyes up into the clouds when he saw three large helicopters fly toward the cabin. They must have had some sort of cloak or silencer because he could hardly hear them or see them as they passed. With new urgency Marcus ran at full speed into the forest. He prayed he wasn't too late.

Nick stood a few feet behind Allen as he pointed his gun at his former partner. Allen had his back to him as the two of them stood outside the cabin at a little past 5 a.m. At first Allen was not aware of Nick as he talked into a small device in his hand. Finally, he put the device into his pocket and spun to face Nick with his own gun drawn. The two FBI agents stared each other down until Allen broke the silence.

"Oh, it's just you, partner. Sorry about that," Allen began to lower his weapon. Nick did not.

Nervously, Allen asked, "What's up with you? Put your gun down. It's just me."

Nick shook his head slightly as he replied, "That's not going to happen. Drop your gun. Now!"

He jumped slightly but complied with Nick's demand. "What are you doing, Nick? This makes no sense."

"Shut up! It makes perfect sense now. The young lady inside told me earlier that you were hiding something. Something deceitful, but she didn't know what kind of questions to ask. At first I didn't believe her. *He's my old partner; he wouldn't do something like this,* I told myself. But the more I thought about it, things became clear. I've been watching you all night, hoping she was wrong. How could you? You set me up in that warehouse. You tried to have me killed! I should shoot you where you stand."

Allen's cover was blown, and his face reflected this resignation. "What do you want me to say, Nick? Huh?"

"Nothing. Kick your gun over to me."

Allen did as he was told.

"Who were you talking to? You were telling them where we are, weren't you?"

Allen's mouth curled into a slight smile. "I may have chatted with a few folks."

"Put your hands on your head and get on your knees. Do it!"

Allen once again did exactly as Nick had ordered him, but the smile never left his face. "What are you smiling at?"

With a hint of venom, Allen answered, "For years I gave my life to the Bureau and this country. When the time came for a simple promotion for leading my team, what do they do? They promote you. I had almost twice the seniority and twice the smarts. You were so gullible every step of the way. When they approached me and offered the kind of money they did, it was an easy choice. I have no regrets about what I did—or am going to do. So don't bother with your questions."

Nick couldn't believe what he was hearing. This man he had considered a close friend for years had betrayed him. He wanted to kill Allen, but that wouldn't help him catch Tibon.

"Facedown on the ground," Nick began to order, when something pricked him in the chest. He reached to where the pain was coming from and pulled out what looked like a small dart. Two more hit him, one in the arm and the other in the neck. Nick began to feel dizzy and fell to his knees right in front of Allen, who continued to smile at him.

"Good night, partner."

Everything went black.

***
*** *

Screaming in the distance and the scurrying of several dozen feet along the forest floor up ahead added to Marcus's anxiety. Every tree, rock, or stump he ran past became a blur. A roar that could have only come from Sampson filled the night air. Marcus needed to hurry. The cabin was in sight, and he didn't have time to think. The door to his bedroom was still open, and the dark outline of an intruder became his first target. The sight of two assailants on his brother Zack fueled his building rage.

Before either man could react, Marcus attacked. He was unaware of just how angry he was until he kicked the first attacker in the back. The sound of bone snapping accompanied the thud of the man's body to the floor. The other attacker barely had time to look up. With a swift sidestep Marcus had the man in a chokehold. Not a sound came from his victim. He dropped the unconscious man to the floor.

His brother looked to be asleep. The darts on the floor told him all that he needed to know. There was no time to check on Zack as sounds of more men in the hallway caught his attention. Marcus immediately grabbed the assailant's rifles. They appeared to be some sort of automatic tranquilizer weapons with multiple rounds. Marcus didn't care what kind of gun they were; any help was welcomed. With guns in hand he headed into the hallway. He didn't believe he could become more enraged, but the site of three men tying up Mama, Anna, and Angie in the hallway proved him wrong. One of the men looked up to see Marcus entering the hallway.

Simultaneously they fired at each other. They all had vests on for protection so that meant his aim would need to be on a soft spot in their gear. Marcus dropped one of the men with one shot to the arm. Likewise, he shot the other two attackers, but not before a couple of darts hit him in the stomach. Marcus could feel the drugs trying to take him over as he pulled the darts out. Another dart hit him in the back as he turned to see three men in the living room down the hall.

He violently lifted one of the fallen attackers for a shield and ran down the hallway. Darts hit the limp body in his hands as he hurled it into two of the three shooting at him. Marcus shot the third man in the leg, but not before a couple more darts hit their mark. The first two men were getting to their feet, and Marcus knew he was out of time.

Like a starving lion with wounded prey, he attacked. With a flurry of punches to the body and head another attacker was sent to the floor unconscious. The other man went to grab Marcus, but instincts once again overrode thought as he jerked the man's hand and twisted it. With one quick thrust downward Marcus broke the arm of his attacker across his knee. The horrifying scream did little to stop Marcus. Several times the effects of the tranquilizer tried to overwhelm him, but his body was fighting off the drowsiness. To stop the man from screaming more, Marcus kicked him across the face.

The man's screaming ceased, and Sampson's took over. Again Marcus grabbed two of the tranquilizer guns. Jumping over the furniture, Marcus ran to his brother's bedroom and stopped just inside the barn-door-sized opening. His brother was facedown in the dirt. Again the affects of the drugs kept trying to tire Marcus, but the adrenaline coursing through him never stopped. There were a lot more of the attackers than before. He counted. Ten. The odds were not in his favor. Again he fired the rifles at the men that shot at Sampson. He was able to hit only three before the cartridges ran out of darts. Just as the remaining seven attackers realized their team members had fallen to the ground, Marcus was upon them.

His body crashed into two of the nearest men. Marcus grabbed one of them and rolled onto his back, using the body as a shield against the oncoming darts. The clicking noise of empty cartridges was what he had been hoping to hear as he braced his foot under the man on top of him and kicked him through the air. Two of the other men were caught off guard as their teammate's body crashed into them and knocked them to the ground.

The three remaining men had reloaded and were already firing at Marcus. They filled his chest, arms, and legs with multiple darts. Marcus tried to get to his feet, but the overwhelming drowsiness was beginning to overtake him. He looked up to see the attackers regrouping together. There were six left, but he had no more strength. As more darts hit their mark, he glanced over at his brother lying unconscious only a few feet from him. Blood on Sampson's hands told Marcus his big brother had put up a good fight. He made it to his hands and knees, but he knew he would soon fall victim to the drugs. Again he looked over at Sampson. The realization that there was nothing he could do to save his family was becoming all too real. Visions of his family unconscious and tied up ran through his head as a wave of dizziness and nausea made claim to him. Just as he was about to surrender to the call of sleep, something deep inside of him said, *No. I won't go willingly.*

Again he struggled to move but couldn't. *No*, came his inner voice again. A faint, burning sensation grew from within his gut. It felt familiar, but the tranquilizers in his system made it impossible for him to think clearly. The six attackers surrounded him as he knelt on all fours, staring at the ground. Slowly the burning grew, and Marcus could feel a new surge of adrenaline rising inside him. He shook his head as his pulse raced faster. A powerful flow of energy filled every limb. Even though it was still dark out, he could see the skin on his hand grow dark. He could feel his muscles bulging as his T-shirt ripped slightly at the seams.

The six men backed away from him as he got to his feet. Once again they shot him. This time, however, it didn't seem to have any effect. Rage was all that Marcus felt as the darts dropped out of his body. The pressure from the muscles caused them to fall off and he could feel the holes they had made heal. The six attackers emptied the last of their cartridges into Marcus, but it wasn't enough.

Almost unaware of what he was doing, Marcus attacked his assailants. One by one he broke limbs and ribs with powerful swings of his fists. It was a massacre as bodies were flung around the yard, accompanied by screams of pain and anguish. In less than a minute all six men were either lying dead or dying on the ground. Marcus felt a brief satisfaction as he surveyed his surroundings, but it was short-lived.

From out of the woods several more attackers appeared and fired their weapons at him. At first his body rejected the darts, but there were too many. Dozens of attackers shot at him repeatedly. He screamed in pain and fell to one knee. His strength was fading, and a rush of dizziness hit him hard and darkness finally overtook him.

Twenty-five

Captivity

"Good evening, Miss Renard." The man's voice echoed loudly in Janet's ears, accompanied by a painful throbbing in her head. Slowly she became aware of her surroundings. She was lying on a dark brown leather couch, part of a matching living room set, in the middle of a large office paneled with dark mahogany. Behind her she could see the wooden banister that led to a twin doorway, where two large men stood watch over her. The guns and knives attached to their belts and their military-like appearance didn't help Janet's growing anxiety.

Directly across from her were large floor-to-ceiling windows. It was nighttime, and the lights of what she thought must be a large city reflected off the glass. Positioned right in front of the windows was an old-fashioned oak desk; her old employer, Dr. Scharf, was sitting behind it. He was smiling at her. Janet thought it was his attempt at making her feel comfortable, but it had just the opposite effect.

He gestured for her to come over. "Please, Janet, join me."

Finding she didn't have much of a choice, she did as he asked. Every muscle in her body screamed out in pain as she made her way to the chair across from him. When she sat down Janet noticed that although the desk appeared to be antique on the outside, the top revealed otherwise. At the doctor's fingertips were several control panels and levers along with what looked like a computer screen. The rest of the desktop was filled with tiny holes that gave it the appearance of a pegboard.

"Are you in much pain?" he asked in a gentle tone.

Janet shot him a puzzled look as she adjusted her sitting position to alleviate some of the aching. "What have you done with my family?"

He raised a hand. "In good time, Nurse Renard. I assure you they're safe, for now."

He pressed a button on his desk. "Bring in a glass of water for our guest."

Within seconds the door to the office opened and a young, dark-haired woman brought a glass of water and set it on the desk in front of Janet. The young woman's eyes never looked up or made contact with anyone in the room. She wore what looked like some sort of cream and brown uniform that maybe a chambermaid might wear.

"Leave," he ordered the woman.

She jumped slightly, then swiftly left the room.

"Now," the doctor said, "drink up. The effects of the tranquilizers have nasty side effects: dry mouth, joint and muscle pain. It's a special blend that I made up myself, but it dehydrates the body something fierce."

Janet was reluctant at first, but he was right. She was extremely thirsty, and after talking earlier, her throat felt like it was going to close. She drank greedily from the glass.

"So," Dr. Scharf said, "I need to ask you a few questions, and I will expect you to answer them truthfully and openly. Not like your fellow nurse, Michele."

Her heart cried out in fear for her friend, and thoughts of what he had done to her family immediately crossed her mind. She demanded, "I want to see my family first."

Janet could tell that this annoyed the doctor, but he pressed the touch-screen on his desk and beams of light emanated from the ceiling and desktop to reveal three-dimensional images. She could see all of the children, Uncle Leigh, and even Michele. All except her three sons were in cells with a single cot and toilet. Zack's cell was just like the others, but his left hand and foot were shackled to the wall, giving him just enough room to move a few feet.

Marcus's cell wasn't as accommodating. They had stripped him of all his clothes except for his boxer shorts. He was chained flat against the wall with his arms pulled up over his head. Janet could tell that they had beaten him by the bruises along his ribs and cheeks. He would heal, but she still couldn't stand seeing him like that.

Sampson's cell was huge. They had his arms in a Y position, and they were strapped to some sort of metal restraints. Metal encased his neck and waist, which were attached to metal girders into the walls of his cell. His hands and feet were completely encased in the metal, making it impossible for him to move any part of his body.

Fighting back her tears, Janet asked, "What do you want from us?"

He smiled once again. "That is exactly what I wanted to hear from you. To answer that question, I must ask you one in return. First, I must qualify it, so you understand my query."

Once again, the doctor pressed a button on his desk. The images of the family disappeared and were replaced with three separate images side by side. They were videos of the family's abduction. The first one was of Zack releasing a blast of energy at two of the attackers. The second was of Sampson breaking down the door to the cabin and the fight that followed. The last one was of Marcus disabling and killing several of their attackers. Each one of the videos played in a loop as Janet watched in horror.

Dr. Scharf was chuckling to himself as he watched Marcus's video. "I have dedicated most of my adult life striving to make this day happen, and here it is. Watch this part when they think he is just about to succumb to the tranquilizer." Janet watched Marcus's video.

He said, "Wait for it…wait…there! That's a thing of beauty!"

Janet was horrified as she watched her son transform into a dark hulking figure, then attack the men around him.

"Isn't it remarkable? I call it the Berserker Phase. It's a trigger within him that releases an overload of adrenaline, filling every muscle in his body. For a short time he is as strong as his larger brother. Amazing! My boy!"

This last part was said with such pride. Janet felt a twinge of jealousy when he used that expression. Marcus was *her* boy, not his.

"I didn't mean to take anything away from what you have done, my dear. In fact, I am so very grateful to you."

Janet watched as the doctor reached for something behind his desk and then, with one push with his hand, Dr. Scharf stood up. He held a golden cane with his right hand as he walked around his desk and leaned on it in front of her. She was shocked. The last time she saw him he had burn marks up and down the left side of his face and was in a wheelchair.

He laughed openly at her. "What? Surprised? You have five of my test subjects living with you for nine years, seeing just some of the things they are capable of, and you think I was going to let them have all the fun? I don't think so, Miss Renard."

The images continued to run behind his back as he motioned his left hand toward them. "You see these videos?"

She nodded.

"Can you tell me how this footage is even possible?"

Janet had been confused about a lot of what he was saying, but this question made no sense to her.

He further explained, "You see, for all practical purposes, these children shouldn't exist."

This didn't seem to make any more sense to her, but she tried to explain by saying, "Well, Michele and I overheard that you were going to kill the babies and us, so—"

"Oh, please." He waved his hand at her to stop. "Maybe I shouldn't expect an RN to understand my question, so I will spell it out for you. They should be dead!"

Still she didn't know what he was talking about.

He leaned toward her and yelled, "What did you do to them?"

With more strength than she thought he would have, the doctor grabbed her by the throat and began to choke her. He said, "I placed a genetic marker in their DNA. At the age of three the marker was supposed to take effect and cause every organ in their bodies to shut down. That is, unless they received a specialized treatment, which only I can provide. Now, what did you do to them to counteract my marker?"

He paused for a second, then added, "I want to make myself perfectly clear. There are two avenues you may pursue. The first is to tell me what you did, and I spare each of them a horrifying death. In the second I am forced to run DNA tests and figure it out for myself. The second choice ends with that horrifying death. Just so you know, my men have no morals. Anything goes. In any case, I will not lie to you. I am going to kill you, regardless of what you decide. You caused me grief, along with that friend of yours. It's just a matter of how quick

184

and painful it'll end. Guards, take her to her cell. Let her think it over."

"Yes, Tibon," came a reply from one of the guards.

The doctor turned and sat in his chair. He looked out the windows at the lights of the city as the guards came over and grabbed Janet from her seat.

She pleaded, "I don't know what you want from me. We didn't do anything. You're insane!"

Tibon ignored her.

Janet cried for a long time at the realization and seriousness of what was about to happen to her and her family. She was helpless. Nothing she could say or do would answer Tibon's question, and even if she knew the answer, it wouldn't change the fact that he was going to kill her and the family.

After several hours of crying, exhaustion began to take its toll. Janet had no idea what time it was, but it must have been in the early morning hours before she lay down on the cot. Silently she stared at the ceiling until a small still voice inside her asked, *What would Uncle Leigh do?*

Janet contemplated this question for only a few seconds before the answer came to her. She had come to the end of herself and rolled off the cot onto the floor. Kneeling, Janet began to pray. She cried out, "Lord, forgive me for not coming to you sooner. I have been so angry and bitter at you. I realize that we have our own decisions to make and we live in a messed-up world. I'm sorry for blaming you. I don't know if we'll be alive tomorrow, but I'm putting our lives into your hands. Let your will be done."

Three-dimensional images of the entire family in their respective cells flashed above Tibon's desktop, along with Agent Nick Catlin. He thought about every possible answer to his questions, none of which were adequate. To see a nurse raise five of his test subjects successfully when he had spent years trying to create one viable subject to no avail disturbed him. In addition, she was able to somehow counteract the safeguard he had built in.

He whispered, "How on earth are they alive?"

The upside was that he had five viable subjects now who would advance his research by years. Also, his financial backers would now be able to see videos of what they were going to be purchasing. That would fund his research indefinitely. But he couldn't get past his one question. Hours passed as he searched for insight.

Eventually each of his captives woke from their drug-induced sleep. He became increasingly disturbed as he watched each of the children fall to their knees and begin what seemed to be praying. He wasn't sure why, but he became annoyed and turned them off. The thought came to him that perhaps this was what had saved their lives, but he dismissed it. There was no God. He had made these children, and the reason they were alive must be because of something he had overlooked or Janet had done to them. Once again he pulled up his computer screen and began to go through his research notes from the project nine years ago. There had to be something he missed.

Anna found it difficult to sleep after praying. Between the pain in her joints and muscles and the anxiety of not knowing what happened to her family, sleep was impossible. Instead she closely examined her cell. It had four white walls, a door with no handle, a cot, and toilet. There was something about the room that didn't feel right, but she couldn't place what it was. The only other thing in the room that she was able to spot was a small hole over the doorway that wasn't even an inch round. She looked more intently. It must be a camera of some sort. It made sense that her captors were watching every move she made.

Soon after this discovery two guards and a lab technician came into her room. As the technician drew blood from her, Anna seized the opportunity to escape.

She said to the guards, "Give me your weapons."

They both began to laugh at her. Anna tried again to order them, but they both just shook their heads at her. She was struck with the realization that she had lost her gift of persuasion. That's what was different. She sat quietly for a minute and closed her eyes. It was difficult at first, but then she heard it. A high-pitched noise was emanating from the walls of her cell. Somehow it was interfering with her abilities.

Fear crept in, and she felt overly exposed. She was still wearing the red pajamas from the night before, and not having any way to protect herself and knowing she was being watched just added to this feeling. She crossed her arms around herself and curled up into a ball with her knees to her chest. Knowing she wasn't going to be able to sleep, she leaned up against the wall and prayed again. Anna could feel the presence of God's voice speak to her. It wasn't an external voice she heard, but rather a whisper she could hear when she listened. God's words spoke to her, and all at once a peace came over her body and mind. Within seconds she was lying down on the cot and asleep....

When she awoke again it was to the sound of her cell door opening. She sat up immediately to see a guard at her door and a woman walking toward her with a tray. On it was a cup of water and a slice of plain toast. She set it next to Anna on the cot, never raising her eyes. The woman looked to be in her late twenties, maybe early thirties. She wore a tan and brown uniform with a matching scarf over her head. Anna could see that the woman had long black hair pulled back in a ponytail. It reminded her of Sampson and Marcus's hair.

God spoke again to her and she knew what to do.

Her voice was scratchy, but Anna managed to say to the woman, "Your sister is safe. God wanted me to tell you."

The woman's eyes shot up to meet Anna's. The shocked look told Anna the woman understood her.

The guard yelled, "Come on, already! What's the holdup? No talking!"

The woman lowered her eyes once again and retreated, leaving the tray behind. As the door closed, Anna grabbed the water immediately and began to drink. She hadn't realized how thirsty and hungry she was. While Anna ate she wondered what God had in store for her. Several hours passed with only one visit, and that was to draw blood again. There was no sign of the woman Anna had seen earlier. Anna wondered if she would see her again.

Allen sat in a conference room by himself. Several video monitors were affixed along the dark mahogany paneled walls, accompanied by several abstract paintings. He was sitting back in one of the large plush chairs that encircled the large oval table in the middle of the room. Allen knew Tibon would want an update from him, but first he better check in with the Bureau. He pulled out his cell phone.

"This is Agent Allen Young. Please place me through to—"

Before he could finish his sentence he had been put on hold.

When someone picked up again the voice rang out, "And just where are *you?*" It was Allen's department supervisor, Mr. Chadwick.

Allen stuttered, "I…I'm…not sure I understand, sir."

"I just got off the phone with our office out of Oklahoma," Chadwick retorted, "and they have six dead bodies, a ranch hand that was nearly beaten to death, and a young woman claiming that her boyfriend said for her to call us. She said you and Nick were in trouble! Now, where are you?"

Allen mouthed the word *boyfriend* as he attempted to piece together what he was hearing. He tried to think up an excuse as he replied, "I don't know where Nick is, sir. I just got off my flight. I'm heading back to the office. Nick wasn't with me. I thought he was on vacation."

"I want you in my office as soon as you walk in this building. We are tracking Nick's position now, and he seems to be somewhere in New York City. We're trying to pinpoint his exact location, but we're having trouble."

Allen didn't hear anything else after he heard they were tracking Nick. He cut his supervisor off. "Sir, may I ask how you are tracking him?"

By the sound of the response his supervisor was only more aggravated by his question. "You never mind that! Get here—now! There's work to be done." The phone abruptly hung up.

Allen jumped out of his seat, exited the room, and walked directly into Tibon's office. Allen could see him sitting behind the desk examining something intently.

"We've got a problem," he declared.

Tibon shot him an expression of annoyance. "What problem?"

Allen took a deep breath. "The FBI know where we are, and I'd wager they'll be here in an hour, maybe two at the most."

Tibon pushed the intercom on his desk. "Immediate evacuation. Lower level subjects to be evacuated to alternate site C, followed by essential personnel only. Kill the rest in the testing bay."

When he was finished he grabbed his cane and walked over to Allen. "I'm going to let you live for the moment. You had better show me you're worth it."

He pressed a button on his cane head and spoke into it. "Liz, I want you to oversee the thirteenth floor personally. No one gets in or out, understood?"

"Understood," came from the cane.

Without warning Tibon grabbed Allen by the throat, lifting him into the air, then pushed him up against the paneled wall. Allen grabbed at Tibon's hand, trying to get free, as he struggled to breathe. "Now listen closely. I want you to bring me Janet and her uncle, then get my helicopter on the roof. Think you can handle that?"

Allen nodded. Tibon released him, dropping him to the floor. He quickly got to his feet and left to do as he was told.

Finally it came. The door to Anna's cell opened, revealing the woman she had talked to earlier. Anna handed the woman her tray as she set down another tray to replace it.

The woman again kept her eyes down but whispered, "Tell him down floor."

Anna hadn't noticed until that moment that the humming inside her cell had stopped. "Get down on the ground against the wall."

The guard did just as she ordered him to.

Anna was beginning to get up when the woman pulled out a gun from underneath her uniform and pointed it at her.

Anna froze as the woman asked, "How know sister? Hurry. Only have minute."

189

Anna had known this question would come up. "You both have a locket from your mother that only you and your sister know about. Your mother gave it to you before she died. Just know your sister is safe, and if you help me, we can find her together."

The woman hesitated for a second, then put the gun away. Anna let out a sigh of relief. The woman grabbed a uniform from out of her apron and tossed it onto the cot.

She said, "Put on." Anna swiftly put on the uniform as the woman closed the cell door slightly, so no one could see them.

Anna asked, "What's your name?"

Still watching the hallway she replied, "Tavita." She pointed up at the place where the camera was. "Soon back. Hurry!"

Something about the woman's name—Anna struggled to remember where she had heard that name before. There was no time for that now. She needed to focus on getting her family.

Anna said, "Pleased to meet you, Tavita." She ordered the guard onto the cot and under the covers. Anna took his pistol and cracked him across the skull. She took the covers and put them over his head to hide from the cameras, then followed Tavita out of the cell. As they stepped into the hallway a voice came over the PA system.

"We will begin immediate evacuation of the building. All personnel, report to your designated stations."

Anna nervously asked, "What's that all about?" She could see Tavita was just as confused. "Do you know where my family is?"

Tavita nodded and led her down a hallway as several personnel walked past them. Anna prayed they would get to her family in time.

Twenty-six

Influence

The restraints around Angie's wrists dug into her skin as she fought against the two guards escorting her down the busy hallway. Flashing red lights added to the already chaotic scene, but it told her that something big was happening. Each of the guards had a communicating device in their ear, and the balding one was talking to someone through it.

"We're transporting test subject Block 4D to the transport now. We should be there in less than a minute."

Angie knew this could be her only chance of escape. They must not think of her as a threat because they only had her hands restrained. If they were really worried about her they would have tranquilized her again. They went down an elevator, and just as the guard had said, they arrived at a loading dock within a minute. There was a ramp leading up into the back of a tractor-trailer where three more guards were waiting. Angie assessed the situation like Marcus had taught her. They were all dressed in dark gray uniforms with pistols at their sides. Angie could tell they had some sort of vest underneath their uniforms. This was not going to be easy.

Two of the guards stood at either side of the ramp while the third one stood inside the back of the truck. She could see seats and several electronic devices set up. It was clear several people were going to be transported comfortably for extended traveling. Angie knew that if she allowed herself to be strapped inside the truck, there would be no hope of escape.

She waited for the right moment to make her move, and it came almost immediately. The ramp was too narrow for her and the two guards to be at either side of her so they pushed her in front of them.

Angie walked up the ramp where the other guard was waiting to take her. She pulled back slightly to make him reach out for her. It was now or never.

Before any of the five guards could react, she grabbed the guard's arm that was reaching out and pulled him toward her. At the same time she leaped into the air and kicked both guards' faces that stood behind her for leverage. The two guards fell off of the ramp to the hard concrete below. Angie used her momentum to flip over the guard whose hand she currently was holding and wrapped her restraints around his neck. With all her weight she pulled back on the guard's neck, sending him to his knees gasping for air.

The two other guards on the landing floor reached for their pistols. Angie released the gasping guard and pulled out his pistol. Before her attackers could get off a single shot, Angie shot them in their arms and legs. She was surprised that what she shot them with was not a bullet, but rather the tranquilizer darts. She rapidly shot the other guards to send them into a deep sleep while she figured out what to do next.

Angie grabbed one of the guard's communication devices and put it into her ear.

A voice rang out from the device saying, "All guards head to the security wing for the transport of the three male subjects."

Her brothers. She needed to get to them before it was too late.

Angie surveyed her surroundings until she spotted a small ventilation vent over the entranceway to the loading dock. Just to the right of the vent was a security camera, and it was pointed directly at her. Running over to the doorway again she jumped up to the railing and leaped up to the vent. Her small fingers managed to make it through the slots of the vent as she yanked it off and fell back to the floor. Once again she jumped up onto the railing and into the shaft, disappearing from sight.

Tibon looked out his office windows while Janet and Leigh sat across from his desk. Janet could see that Uncle Leigh had been beaten. His right eye was partly swollen shut, and his bottom lip had a noticeable cut that appeared infected. She figured Tibon probably tried to get answers from him when she couldn't give them.

The silence in the room only added to Janet's feeling of dread. Why was he just staring out the window? Was he doing this on purpose to add to their discomfort? She was going to say something when Tibon turned around.

He looked intently at her. "Have you decided?"

Janet took a deep breath. "Yes." She paused to gather her thoughts.

Before she could continue, Tibon nodded to one of the guards standing next to Uncle Leigh. The guard immediately punched him in the stomach. If it weren't for his hands tied behind the back of the chair, Uncle Leigh would have fallen to the floor. He began to cough as he tried to catch his breath.

"All right! The answer to your question is: I have no clue! Sorry, but that's the truth." Janet had thought about lying to Tibon, but that wasn't going to help the situation. He was going to kill them no matter what she said.

Tibon leaned forward on his desk. "You are going to suffer along with your family, I promise you. Now I'll give you one last time to—"

Leigh interrupted him. "I…I'll tell you, but I don't think you're going to like it."

Tibon considered Leigh in surprise as he sat back down in his chair. "I'm all ears, Mr. Barrus."

Janet thought Uncle Leigh looked stronger as he said to Tibon, "God."

Tibon scoffed.

"No, I'm serious," Leigh refuted. "I know we didn't do anything to those children other than love them and point them toward God. Did it ever occur to you that maybe something bigger than you could be the reason they're alive? No, I guess it didn't. You're so busy trying to play God that you've totally missed the big picture. We're no scientists, so there's only one other possibility. God."

There was a long silence between them before Tibon sat forward. "That was truly inspiring. I actually have goosebumps on my arms. Oh, sorry, that's because it's cold in here. Spare me your super religious, overzealous sermons."

Janet could see Tibon was angry as he stood up.

"The only reason they are alive right now is a flaw in their genetic code, which I will correct shortly. Mr. Barrus, I am god for all intents and purposes. I gave them life, and I'll take it away when I feel like it. Just as I'm going to do to both of you."

"Sir?" a voice echoed out of the intercom in the desk.

Annoyed, he pushed the button on the desk. "What?"

"Both female subjects have escaped. We have security searching the building already."

All expression left Tibon's face. "Keep me informed. Lock down Security Sector D. They'll want to free their brothers. Have all nonassigned security waiting there for them."

"Yes, Tibon," came the reply.

He snapped his fingers at one of the guards. "I want you to go down to the lab. Bring back the case they should have ready for me. Looks like things could get messy. Move it!"

Anna looked down from the walkway they were on to see dozens of young women and some men being huddled up against a wall. The room looked like it could have been a gymnasium at one time, judging by its size. On the far left wall were what looked like several hundred medical baskets, used in hospitals for infants. An uneasy feeling began to creep up on Anna. She wanted to know what all the baskets were for, but she didn't have time.

She scanned the group of people until she spotted Agent Nick and Aunt Shelly. Her heart skipped a beat when the ten guards with rifles lined up across the room from the group. Tavita told her that several of the staff were to be killed off, and by the looks of things it was about to happen. Anna made her way down the staircase to the floor below, only to be stopped by a guard.

"Hey," barked the strong voice. "Where are you going?"

He stepped in front of the two women and pointed his rifle at them. Anna hadn't come up with a plan yet, but Tavita stepped in front of her.

"We were sent by Tibon to..." Tavita couldn't think of anything else to say.

Anna followed her lead. "We're sent by Tibon to get the prisoners."

The guard shot her a look of disbelief and started to raise his rifle higher. Anna released her will on him. "You will bring me five of those guards immediately."

He looked confused for a second, then turned away from them and went over to the ten guards who were lining up like a firing squad. Anna watched as the guard brought five of them back with him.

One of them asked, "What's going on here?"

Anna had never tested her abilities to see how many people she could influence at once, but she had no choice. She said to all of them, "We've been sent by Tibon, and you'll obey whatever I tell you to do."

All six guards nodded as she ordered the same guard to bring back two more. She didn't want to try all eleven until she was sure it would work. After a few seconds he brought two more back. Anna said again, "By orders from Tibon, you'll do whatever I tell you to do."

One of the two new guards asked, "Who are you?"

She had her answer. She pointed at the one guard and said, "Seize him immediately!"

The guards immediately grabbed the one guard. They were very efficient and had him on the floor knocked out within seconds and handcuffed. Unfortunately this scuffle attracted the attention of the other three guards. All three turned and began to walk over toward Anna and the other guards.

Tavita spoke softly to Anna. "Trouble."

"What do you think you're doing?" said one of the guards. Anna thought he must be the one in charge because of the red stripes on his right shoulder.

Again the man bellowed out, "I want answers now! Who are these women?"

She ordered the guards, "Shoot them!" then tackled Tavita and sent them both sliding under the staircase.

Shots began firing, and women's and men's screams echoed throughout the large room. It seemed like an eternity to Anna, but the shooting finally stopped. The screams continued as she opened her eyes to find all the guards on the ground. All except one. The leader was slowly getting to his feet as he held his left arm close to his side. He had been shot, but not fatally. Her eyes went wide as the guard picked up his rifle and looked directly at her and Tavita.

They had both made it through the shootout without being hurt, but that was all going to change in a moment. If the guard fired on them from as far away as he was, there was nothing she could do. It was too far a distance to use her influence. As the guard began to raise the rifle in their direction Nick came up from behind him and punched the back of the guard's neck. He fell, unconscious, to the ground. Nick searched through the man's pockets and found the keys.

Anna ran over to Nick and gave him a hug.

"Good to see you, too," he said with a slight smirk. As he unlocked his handcuffs, he said, "Thanks. It didn't look good there for a moment."

Anna replied, "We still need to get to the rest of the family."

"We need to get your brothers free. We're going to need all the help we can get." He tossed the keys over to the crowd of people standing around, unsure of what they should be doing.

From out of the crowd Aunt Shelly made her way toward Anna.

"Oh, sweetheart," Aunt Shelly said as she stood staring at her. Anna began crying and wrapped her arms around her aunt, who still had her hands bound.

The two of them cried as Anna said, "I've missed you so much."

Nick interrupted the reunion. "Sorry, ladies, but there's no time for this right now."

Anna pulled away and wiped her eyes with her pajama sleeve. "He's right. Tavita, do you know a way out of this building?"

"Yes."

"Good," Anna began. "You need to take these people out of the building before more guards come. Can you do that?"

Tavita nodded and started directing everyone toward one of the exits.

Nick turned to Michele. "You too. Don't argue, but I need Anna to come with me. Her gifts are going to come in quite handy."

Anna added, "He's right, Aunt Shelly. You need to go with Tavita. Nick's with the FBI; we can handle this. Go."

With one last hug Michele began to follow the crowd while Nick checked the guards for weapons. He grabbed two rifles and several cartridge reloads. He also took one of the guard's ear communicators. As he put the device in he tossed one of the rifles at Anna. She grabbed it out of reflex.

She must have looked awkward to him because he said, "Look, Anna, I need you to understand that you may need to shoot someone. Are you going to be able to do that?"

Violence wasn't something she felt comfortable with. Inflicting pain on another had not been a thought that had crossed her mind—until a day ago. Anna looked down at the rifle and pulled out the cartridge to check for bullets, then reloaded it.

"Let's go," she replied.

He said to her, "We need to see if we can somehow shut the power off in this building. We would have a better chance if they can't see us with all these cameras."

Anna had passed a room earlier that looked like a power room and told Nick to follow her. The two of them headed back up the stairs without seeing anyone else. The hallways were quiet in the lower section of the building as Anna navigated them back through several of the hallways. Finally, she found what she was looking for. Shots were fired, and Anna's instincts took over.

She dived back around the corner as several bullets imbedded themselves in the wall behind her. Nick immediately began shooting as Anna tried to gather her wits. Shots were being fired from the hallway they needed. Anna could see the door to the power room.

Anna put her hand on Nick's shoulder and said, "Stop." He reluctantly did as she asked and she waited for the shots to die down.

She yelled out, "We give up. I'm coming around the corner with my hands up. Don't shoot. I'm unarmed."

Nick's eyes told her he wasn't happy with what she was doing, but she pushed her rifle into his hands before he could stop her. Slowly she turned the corner to be met by three guards with their rifles pointing at her.

One of them called out, "You too! Drop your weapon and come out with your hands over your head!"

Anna didn't hear him, but Nick mumbled something. She was sure she didn't want to know what he said. They both walked slowly forward toward the guards as told. When the guards were satisfied that there were no tricks involved, they moved in and pushed them up against the walls to be handcuffed.

Anna grunted, then ordered, "Take your hands off of us."

The guards did as she said.

"Now call in that you have killed both of us."

One of the three began doing as she said. She could tell he was getting an earful, but she continued, saying, "Now open this door. We have some talking to do."

Nick smiled at her as the guards followed her every command.

Twenty-seven

Escape

With all the commotion in the halls, Angie found it easy to find one of the workers' dressing rooms and change into one of their uniforms. She covered her head with one of the workers' hats and cautiously stepped out into the busy halls. She had no idea which way she needed to go to get to her brothers, so she decided the best thing to do was ask someone.

Angie gauged the looks of several workers before picking a very young man. She asked him where they were keeping the other prisoners, using the excuse that she was new. It was clear he was in a hurry, so there was no questioning the request. He gave her the directions and scurried away.

She was surprised at the lack of security in the halls. The only personnel in sight were running back and forth with equipment with such intensity that no one even noticed her. Two floors and several hallways later, Angie had made her way to Security Section D. She watched from a distance while two guards stood at the entranceway. A couple of workers approached the entrance and showed their badges before being allowed to enter. She needed one of those badges. Examining her surroundings once again, she noticed several security cameras up on the ceiling. The entranceway was at least twenty feet high and it looked like the hallway beyond was just as large. There was no way she was going to get past the security guards without being detected. The entire security staff would be on her before she got two steps down the hallway.

She could try and backtrack. Maybe if she found a quiet hallway she could get up into the ventilation again, but she would only be able to guess which direction she would need to go. Angie had no idea which way the vents went and she could end up lost or waste valuable time. No, she needed to get in to her brothers now, before it was too late. Just then all the lights in the hallway began to flicker before turning off for a brief moment. Immediately the secondary lighting system came on. It was now or never. Taking a leap of faith she hoped some of the security systems had been disabled.

After a deep breath she approached the two guards while keeping one hand in her pocket on the tranquilizer pistol. She tried to see if they would let her pass, but they both put out their hands to stop her.

"I.D., now!" one of them barked at her.

She backed up a couple steps and forced a smile. "I'm so sorry, gentlemen. I don't know what I was thinking. Here, will this do?"

Angie pulled out the pistol and shot both guards. They had no time to react; they simply fell to the floor. Angie took a quick look around. No one saw her—she hoped.

The hallway was huge, and for a moment she asked herself why. Then she felt stupid. It would need to be in order to transport something very large. Hopefully that large something was her brother. She hurried to the end of the hallway where the corridor turned to the left. Stopping at the corner, Angie looked around it to find a dozen guards, all heavily armed. They had several large carts and one that was big enough to transport Sampson. There was one large metal door that was open, where five guards stood holding what looked to be more tranquilizer rifles. Angie wasn't sure what they were waiting for, but she needed to do something soon.

There was no hope of success, but she had to try. Taking one step into the hallway, she pulled out the two pistols she had with her. Before she could take a shot someone grabbed her from behind. She screamed, which caused all the guards in the hallway to look in her direction. Someone large and strong had wrapped their arms around her as she continued to scream in desperation.

"Now, little lady, let's not make this difficult, on you, that is," a man's voice spoke into her ear.

"*Aaaahhhh!*" she screamed again while trying to kick him.

The guards in the hallway laughed at the sight of her struggling. Angie found herself violently slammed to the floor. Her breath was knocked out of her as she let out one last cry. She fought to catch her breath as the guard's heavy body lay hard against her back.

"*Noooooooo!*" A deep loud rumbling voice vibrated the walls and floors around her. The floor shook, followed by a loud explosion. Metallic clanging echoed throughout the hallway. Angie watched the guards attempt to stay on their feet as the horrifying noises continued. The guard that had been holding her down lost his grip and fell off her. Each of the guards in front of the open metal door tried to raise their rifles at whatever was inside. She didn't see a single shot fired when a steel girder came flying out of the doorway. Several guards were hit.

Sampson came charging out of the doorway. He had what looked to be metal orbs around his hands and he began smashing them down onto the floor, hitting more of the guards in the process. After several tries they fell off his fists, but Sampson didn't stop his attack. Some of the guards tried to stop him, but her brother pushed them aside like annoying flies. One of the guards got off a shot that hit Sampson, but it wasn't enough to subdue him. He finally saw her lying at the end of the hall and began charging towards her.

She looked next to her, and the guard who had grabbed her lay frozen in terror. The man finally came to his senses and tried to run. Too late. Sampson hurled the man down the hallway—followed by a loud thud.

He picked up Angie in his arms and held her close. For a moment Angie thought everything was going to be all right as she said, "Thank you, big brother. I love you too."

Without warning everything began to shake again. Sampson was able to stay on his feet as a large metal door flew off its hinges and smashed along the far wall down the hallway. It looked to be adjacent to where Sampson had been.

Angie looked in horror as a huge creature emerged. It stood three or four feet taller than Sampson, even though it was hunched over. The top of its head was scarred and mostly bald, except for a few patches of short gray hair. The creature's left eye was missing, and it looked like the socket had been broken several times without healing properly. Its left shoulder was enormous, and it made the creature lopsided as it looked down the hallway at them. The muscles were gnarled up and down its left arm, which almost dragged along the floor.

It looked enraged as a scream of insanity echoed along the hallway. Without warning or provocation, the creature charged at them with surprising speed. Sampson tossed Angie around the corner, out of harm's way. When she turned to look, the creature tackled Sampson. Another thunderous breaking of metal rocked the hallway as the two behemoths broke through the floor. Angie leapt to her feet to look through the hole to see what was happening. She could see another hole in the floor below where the two of them must have fallen through. The distant noises of a struggle were all she could hear.

Zack was jerked off his cot onto the floor. The entire cell vibrated like an earthquake, and he watched in fear as the walls cracked. Horrifying screams could be heard outside his cell. He could hear distant screams coming from the hallway. His first instinct was to send a burst of energy and break open his cell door, but he was still chained to the floor. There was something about them that drained his energy. Every time he tried to build up an electrical charge he could feel his strength leave his body.

When the trembling stopped, he sat back onto the cot. What was that? Was someone coming for him? No one came. Another loud rumbling, followed by an even more horrifying scream, added to his anxiety.

The cell shook again and the walls cracked more. He tried to stabilize himself on the cot, but the vibrations were too much and once again he found himself on the floor as the cot broke off the wall. Another horrifying scream came from the hallway followed by another loud explosion. When it was all done Zack went to stand up again, only this time his chains were hanging loose. Immediately he began to build up an electrical charge in his body, which wasn't interrupted. With as much energy as he could gather, Zack released a burst of electricity at his cell door and broke it open.

With renewed strength he stepped into the hallway and surveyed his surroundings. There were several guards' lifeless bodies lying scattered along the hallway floor. Also, a large, bent metal door lay only yards away from his cell. Something had caused this mess, and Zack didn't want to stick around to find out what. He was still in his boxer shorts, so he began taking the jacket off of the nearest guard. He was getting dressed when a loud bang came from behind him down the hall.

He turned to see Marcus standing naked. His brother's breathing was rapid, and he had a look of insanity in his eyes. Marcus arched his back and screamed a horrifying cry of anger. Zack watched as his brother's skin began to darken into crimson red, but it faded quickly. Within seconds Marcus's color was normal, and Zack could see his breathing begin to slow down. Zack rushed over to his brother and took off his jacket. When Marcus became aware of his surroundings, he immediately covered himself with his hands.

"Thanks," he said to Zack as he tied the jacket around his waist.

Zack could tell his brother wasn't completely all right yet. "Good to see you alive."

The anger in Marcus's eyes told him that his brother was fighting off one of his testosterone-induced rages.

Marcus replied, "Same here. I'm sorry you had to see that."

He waved his hand to dismiss the need for apology as a strong, foul odor assaulted Zack's senses.

With one hand over his nose Zack asked, "What's that smell?"

If looks could kill, Zack would have been dead by the one on his brother's face.

Frustrated, Marcus asked, "Did you have a toilet in your cell?"

Zack was taken aback by the question and replied, "Yeah."

Sarcastically, Marcus replied, "Good for you. Some of us have been chained to a wall for almost two days with only a nightly hosing down to freshen us up."

"Sorry," was all Zack could say.

"Let's get out of here. First I need some clothes."

Zack pointed to the guards' bodies down the hallway. "Let's go get you some pants."

They both took clothes off of the guards lying in the hallway and got dressed.

"Marcus, Zack! Oh, thank God you're alive!" Zack was surprised to hear Angie's voice.

He looked down the hallway to see his sister running toward them. "Sampson's been attacked! You've got to help him!"

"By who?" Zack asked.

"I'll tell you on the way," was all she said.

The three of them hurried through the hallway as Angie explained what happened with the guards and creature. A few faint tremors could be felt as they looked into the hole. The jump was too far. They would need to find another way down.

"What?" Tibon screamed at the head of security who stood across from his desk.

The guard lowered his head in fear. "They've all escaped, sir. Including subject BH31."

"I want every available guard and worker to find them in the next fifteen minutes, or I will have you all killed! Is that understood?"

The man replied, "I'm sorry, sir, but that's not possible. The remaining security were killed or injured in the escape, and I'm afraid that most of the subjects are in the streets as we speak."

Tibon pulled out a pistol from behind his desk and shot the man in the head. Janet screamed as his body fell next to her.

"Understood," Tibon coldly replied as another guard entered his office with the case he had asked for. "It's about time. As of this second, you are promoted. I want this building on lockdown within two minutes. Do you understand me? I don't care if everyone has evacuated or not."

The guard looked at the body of his former boss lying at his feet. "Right away, Tibon!"

The new head of security left the office in a hurry as Tibon pushed the button on his cane. "Agent Allen, where are my helicopters?"

"They'll be here in under fifteen minutes," came the reply.

"Meet us on the roof with my personal guards when they arrive."

"Yes, Tibon."

* **
** *

The crowds had gathered along the sidewalks, keeping several yards away, as they watched the two giants fight in the middle of the street. Several cars and trucks had been crushed, and traffic had come to a standstill. Screams could be heard coming from the crowd every now and then as Sampson and the creature pounded each other. It was a close struggle, but the creature was too strong, even for Sampson. Marcus could see the creature choking the life out of his brother in the center of the intersection.

He said to Zack, "Find something and charge up! I'll get it off of Sampson! Go!"

With that Marcus was off. He ran straight for the creature, who was oblivious to his approach. He built up his speed and leapt off of a nearby taxi's hood. With all his strength, Marcus landed his left foot in the back of the creature's head. It felt like he hit a rock as he bounced off. He hit the pavement and rolled into the grill of a tractor-trailer.

Marcus was trying to shake the dizziness from his head when he saw the creature's fists coming down at him. Instinctively he rolled out of the way as the asphalt exploded. He jumped onto a light pole and swung around to kick the creature again in the head. This time it swatted its hand at him and sent him flying through the air. Marcus landed hard against a brick building and blacked out for a second.

As he opened his eyes, the creature was right on top of him. It was about to bring its fists down. He knew it was too late to move, but a burst of electricity hit the creature before it could hit him. The creature fell over onto its side. Marcus could see Zack standing in the middle of the intersection. Quicker than he had expected, though, the creature got to its feet and began to charge at Zack. Marcus watched as Zack frantically released electrical blasts. The impact of the blasts only slowed it down slightly. With each blast the creature appeared more enraged as it closed in on Zack.

His brother stood helplessly in harm's way as he released more bursts of energy. Marcus knew he needed to do something. Grabbing the nearest weapon he could find, Marcus charged after the creature.

He wasn't going to be able to close the gap between them, but the manhole cover he picked up was going to have to do the trick. Just as the creature was about to collide with Zack he hurled the manhole cover at the creature's head. A sickening thud echoed as the creature landed hard on its face. Before the creature could get to its feet, Marcus had picked up the manhole cover again and jumped onto its back. Violently he beat the creature with the metal cover. The monster screamed out in pain, but that didn't last long. It rolled with surprising speed and flung its arm back at Marcus. The impact with the building made Marcus dizzy. Unconsciousness tried to overtake him. Dazed, he watched Zack.

His brother ran over to one of the crushed cars and opened up the hood. The creature looked in Zack's direction and got to its feet once again. Grabbing the battery, Zack absorbed its electricity. The creature was almost upon him when he turned and released another bolt of energy. This time his brother hit the creature in the dead center of its chest and knocked it down. He could see that Zack was rejuvenated as he began to approach the creature. It tried to sit up, but Zack shot another blast that hit the creature in the face. This time its head smacked against the pavement hard from the force of Zack's blow.

It cried out in agony while trying to get to its feet. Zack shot it again, and the creature tumbled onto its side. Marcus noticed that at least a dozen police officers had gathered about fifty feet from the creature. They pointed their pistols and rifles as they waited to see if Zack's last blow would immobilize it. Several seconds passed. The creature lay on the sidewalk, motionless. The police had begun to move forward when it pounded the street, causing a large explosion of asphalt and dirt.

A cloud of debris filled the air. For a second Marcus could no longer see the creature. That was all it took for it to leap to its feet once again. The police opened fire on the creature, sending it into a rage. It grabbed the nearest car and hurled it into the police officers. They tried to get out of the way, but most of them were struck. Zack began blasting the creature once again, but there was little effect. Marcus forced himself to his feet and once again joined the fight. He picked up a tire iron as he ran past one of the open trunks of a wrecked car.

The creature was bleeding from the gunshots as it approached Zack. It was about to hit his brother when Marcus smashed the tire iron into the creature's shin. It screamed out in pain as it fell forward onto the street. It tried to get up, but Marcus swung the tire iron again into the creature's jaw. The sickening thud and bone cracking echoed off of the buildings. Finally, the creature stopped moving as it lay on its face in the middle of the street.

Marcus waited to see if the fight was truly over. A strange sound filled the air as a crescendo of applause erupted from the crowds. Marcus looked around, and for the first time, noticed several camera crews and media gathered at a distance. Thousands of people lined the streets as police and fire vehicles made their way to the scene.

He was trying to make sense of what he was seeing when he was violently struck from behind and forced into a nearby street sign. Marcus shook off the headache he was feeling from the impact just in time to see Sampson. His brother had grabbed the creature from behind and put it into a chokehold. Its eye bulged as Sampson squeezed. The creature was somehow able to get to its feet with Sampson on its back and ran backwards into the nearest building. Sampson's body hit with the brick building, but he didn't let go. Again the creature stepped forward, then back again with all its strength to crush Sampson into the wall.

Marcus could see that his brother was losing his grip; within seconds the creature had loosened itself. It spun and grabbed Sampson by the throat, trying to finish what it started earlier. Out of nowhere Marcus watched as Angie leapt onto the creature's head and poked it in the eye.

"Leave him alone!" she screamed out.

It was enough to get the creature to let go of Sampson, but only for a second. It jerked its head, sending Angie through the air. She landed hard onto the street. It looked like she tried to roll with the landing but lost control. His sister smashed into the bumper of a taxi and lay still. The creature turned once again to Sampson. Sometime during Marcus's last blackout Zack had been hurt and was lying unconscious a few feet away from him and Angie and Sampson. His family was being killed before his eyes. He was supposed to protect them. They looked to him.

The internal burning surged forward like a dam bursting.

"No!" he yelled across the street at the creature.

It turned around and faced him. Marcus attacked. Within just a couple steps he had begun to become the dark creature. His skin grew a dark crimson as his muscles pumped with an overload of adrenaline. The two combatants charged at each other. Just as they were about to collide, Marcus rolled underneath the creature's legs, causing it to stumble forward. He ran to the sidewalk and ripped out the nearest light post, sending sparks shooting in every direction. As the creature turned to face Marcus it was met with a violent blow to the head. Several times the lamppost came crashing down onto the creature.

With a sudden halt the creature grabbed the post and pulled it from Marcus's grip. It then hurled the post into the nearby crowd. Men and women screamed as it came crashing toward them. Once again the creature charged. Marcus could feel his muscles pulsating with power, and it was growing with each passing heartbeat. The creature tried to grab him. Marcus propelled himself over the creature. He was moving so fast that it was instinct alone that dictated his attack. Holding both fists together, he pounded the creature's neck. Both of them fell hard to the asphalt. Marcus didn't hesitate. He got onto the creature's back and began to beat its upper spine. The fury and rage rose to new levels of insanity with every blow. The cracking of bones and the creature's screams of pain filled the streets.

Even after the creature stopped moving Marcus continued his assault. It was the sight of blood on his hands that made him stop. He stared with horror at his hands. Only seconds before, visions of his family being hurt ran through his head. Now all he could see was a monster—only the monster was him. His breathing slowed and the adrenaline gradually subsided. He could feel his muscles going back to their normal size. He slid off the creature, and for the first time saw the police who had gathered behind a barricade. Several red laser sites were pointed at his chest and the creature.

With both hands Marcus pushed the creature onto its side so that he could see if it was still alive. It was breathing, but nothing else. If the creature was anything like he was, then there was a chance it would heal. A faint guttural voice interrupted the waves of emotions that were trying to overwhelm him.

"Kill me," the creature said.

It could speak.

"No. We can help you," Marcus offered as he leaned down to look into the creature's one good eye.

The blow to the back of the creature's neck must have affected it somehow. The insanity was gone as the creature once again said, "Kill me. Kill me, please."

Marcus felt pity for the creature. He could tell it had been tortured and experimented on for years. It wasn't his fault he was this way, and Marcus wanted to help him.

"No. You'll heal, right? We can help you. Please let us help you."

The creature began to move. Marcus could hear several police officers getting restless behind the barricade.

"Stay down," Marcus pleaded. This creature could have been him, given different circumstances and events. He could be this creature's brother, for all he knew. Marcus wasn't about to let it be killed.

Again the creature tried to get up, and several guns were cocked. Marcus pleaded again but the creature wasn't listening. Slowly and painfully it stood up as Marcus turned to the police and yelled out, "Don't shoot!"

The creature used whatever strength it had left and pushed Marcus to the sidewalk next to an unconscious Sampson.

"No!" Marcus yelled out as he watched the creature stumble toward the police. Simultaneously they fired. Round after round of shots were fired as the behemoth fell forward just a couple yards away from the barricade. Marcus could see the creature take one last breath before it stopped moving. He was sure it was dead. Marcus slumped down next to his brother Sampson, who was just regaining consciousness. All the violence and death hit him at once.

Twenty-eight

Flight

The private elevator made its way to the thirteenth floor. Anna was upset that they had to change their plans since talking with the guards they had captured. Nick turned off the main power, but one of the guards told them that the backup generators would kick in right away. Nothing would shut down for very long, if at all. After interrogating the guards further she found out they had another problem, far more pressing than finding her family. The guards revealed that the thirteenth floor was armed with pumps that were set to distribute enough deadly toxins in the air to kill most of the population of New York City. One of them overheard that Tibon planned on releasing the chemicals once he left for their secondary site.

At first Anna fought with Nick about their course of action. She desperately wanted to find her family, but Nick was right. Saving millions of people from being killed was more important than her family. Nick had changed into one of the guard's uniforms in hopes of blending in, and it worked. They made it to the elevators easily, almost too easy. This made Anna nervous as they ascended in the elevator.

When the door opened there was no one in the hallway. The guard had said to follow the hall to the right, which led to an open, undeveloped section of the building. That's where the pumps had been installed. Nick turned the corner and stopped. Anna could see a woman with long black hair and dark eyes standing before them. She could feel something evil radiating from the woman. Anna had never met the woman, but she sensed that Nick knew who she was.

He pointed his rifle and the woman did likewise. Nick pushed Anna back around the corner as bullets began to fly past them.

The two sides shot several rounds until both of their rifles were emptied. Nick began to reload, but before he could fire another shot Liz attacked. With a large blade she tried to stab Nick. Instinctively he lifted the rifle to block her, but Liz grabbed the strap to the gun and yanked it out of Nick's hands. The gun slid down the hall. He grabbed the hand that held the knife. Anna was surprised at how strong the woman was. Nick was having a hard time defending himself. He stood about six feet tall, but this woman wasn't even her height.

The blade was only inches from Nick's throat when Anna said, "Put down the knife."

The woman ignored her. Anna panicked and grabbed her hand to try and help Nick. It was enough. Nick lifted his knee into Liz's ribs, forcing her to back away, but not for long. With a crazed look in her eyes she backhanded Anna, sending her to the floor. Nick tried to grab Liz but was met with a swipe of the blade. It cut through his arm, and Anna could see he was in pain as he backed away. The woman continued her attack with a demonic smile.

She slashed at Nick over and over until she finally cut him across his stomach. She was fast, almost too fast. The hallway was coming to an end, and Nick had nowhere to go. He tried opening the door, but it was locked. Anna could see there was a security lock that required a handprint to open. The guards never mentioned that, but she hadn't asked. Anna was unsure what to do until she saw Nick's rifle only a few feet away. The woman had Nick pinned, and he wasn't going to last much longer. Reluctantly she pulled the trigger on the rifle and sent a single shot into the back of the woman. Anna watched as the woman dropped.

Nick walked over to her as she trembled at what she had done.

"Thank you," he said as he grabbed the rifle from her. "Are you all right?"

She nodded, unable to speak. Anna watched as Nick pulled the woman's body over to the secured door and placed her hand on the device. The door opened, and Anna helped him pull her lifeless body inside.

"Who is she?" Anna asked.

"I believe her name is Liz Bolan." Anna remembered that name from stories Mama had told her years ago.

She closed the door behind them in hopes that no one would come looking. Anna surveyed the room with Nick. The room was huge. It encompassed the equivalent of one fourth of the floor. The windows were the only things that had been finished. Building equipment and metal rods lay in piles as well as Sheetrock and wood. Metal cabinets and office chairs were randomly dispersed along with several metal dumpsters throughout the room. It was a mess.

Nick began to describe to Anna what one of the pumps would possibly look like before they started searching. It wasn't long before Nick found one of the pumps and was able to figure out how to disable it. He showed her what he had done, and then they continued searching the room. The pumps were strategically placed every fifteen feet along the windows. Anna was on her fifth pump when she heard Nick grunt.

She stood up and called over to him, "You all right?"

There was no reply, and she couldn't see him. Anna was getting a very bad feeling as she picked up the screwdriver she had found and held it like a knife.

Again she called out, "Nick, you there?"

She froze as Liz stepped out from behind one of the girders with the rifle in her hands. Shots fired and blew out the window behind her. The glass shattered as a rush of cool wind blew glass shards out of the building. Bullets shattered another window as Anna dove behind a nearby dumpster. The bullets ricocheted off the dumpster by her head and she screamed.

Liz called out, "There's nowhere to run, little lady, and your abilities have no effect on me, so why don't you just come on out from behind there and die with some dignity?"

Anna trembled as the wind blew in from the open window. She could hear the noise of alarms and traffic from outside as she tried to decide what to do. The gentle voice of God spoke to her, and she tried to quiet herself to listen.

It said, *"Don't move."*

The four siblings sat in a secured area only a few yards from the building. The FBI had arrived, and one of Nick's coworkers had been placed in charge of seeing to their needs and taking their statements. The streets were a circus of police and fireman trying to coordinate their efforts to get into the building. Zack heard one of them say the building was locked down, and they couldn't get in. He figured that was probably why the large wrecking crane had been brought in.

Medics attended to their wounds as they all watched the scene around the building from a distance. Zack was sure they were all feeling the same way. They wanted to break into the building and find the rest of their family, but the FBI and police wouldn't allow it. Several times reporters and camera crews tried to break past the blockade that had been put up to shield them from the crowds. It had only been a few minutes when the sound of gunshots came from the building. Two of the windows burst open, followed by more gunshots. What startled Zack the most was the scream that he heard.

Apparently Marcus heard it more clearly because he turned toward Zack and said, "Anna's in trouble! You need to get up there now!"

Zack didn't know what to say at first. How was he supposed to… then it hit him. Marcus wanted him to fly.

He protested, "I can't. I've tried. You know that."

Marcus grabbed Zack by the jacket and pulled him face to face. "I don't care! You will fly, and you will fly now! *Is that understood?*"

Zack knew his brother was right. He had to succeed if Anna was in trouble. Marcus ran over to the nearest police officer and grabbed his taser stick. Marcus tossed it to him as three officers tackled his brother. Marcus didn't put up a fight as he watched from the ground. Zack turned on the stick and began shocking himself. He could feel the energy filling him until the stick was drained completely. He kicked off the shoes that one of the officers had given him before running toward the building. He gathered all of his strength and channeled it through his bare feet as he began to approach the building. Angie's voice ran through his thoughts as he remembered her saying, *"If you can control the magnetic current that surrounds your body, you can direct your flight."*

He ran that thought through his head and focused. He released everything he had in him and exploded upward into the air. The force of the blow created a hole in the street as he soared up toward the window. Fighting to control his balance, he pressed out an energy shield around his body. For a brief moment he thought he was going to lose control, but failure wasn't an option. He continued to surge upward toward the broken window, and for a split second he smiled. He was flying.

Anna could hear footsteps approaching as she leaned against the dumpster. She jumped when Liz stepped into sight.

With a smile, her assailant said sadistically, "Time to die."

Just then a loud explosion came from outside. Liz turned her attention out the window.

A light flashed before Anna's eyes and blinded her. It took a few seconds, but her vision finally cleared. She stood up, anxious to see what had happened. Sprawled out on the floor was Zack. He was moaning as he attempted to get to his feet. Anna let out a cry of disgust when she saw what had happened to her attacker. Liz had been impaled on a metal rod.

Anna ran over to Zack and grabbed him into a big hug. She wasn't sure what specifically she was crying about as she held tightly to her brother—the relief that he was alive, the fact he just saved her life, or the guilt she felt from being relieved her assailant was dying.

Zack patted her hair. "It's okay now. Calm down. You're all right."

At the sight of Nick walking toward her, Anna let go of her brother and ran to give him a hug. She had thought he was dead. When she turned around, Zack's eyebrow went up in disapproval.

With a gentle shove, Nick pushed Anna off of him. "We still need to disable these pumps."

Anna showed Zack what they were doing as she filled him in on Tibon's plan. In just a couple minutes all the pumps were disarmed.

"Now we need to get to the roof," Nick insisted.

Anna stared at him blankly. She wasn't following his logic.

Nick explained, "The only way Tibon is getting out of this building is through the air, and that means the roof. By the sounds coming from outside, the building is surrounded. Tibon only has one other option, and we need to get there now!"

They ran for the door when Nick stopped in front of Liz. He aimed the rifle at her head.

Anna turned back around to see Nick. "Don't. Don't be like her. Walk away and leave her in the hands of God."

He looked at Anna. She could see the anger and fear he was experiencing at that moment. Her heart went out to him as he put down the rifle and began to follow them again out the door.

Twenty-nine

Sacrifice

Marcus watched from the ground as Zack shot up into the evening sky, then disappeared through the broken window. He smiled as the police began to cuff him. The FBI agent in charge of them came over and told the police to release him. He thanked the agent for understanding and was immediately distracted by a familiar sound coming from overhead. At first he couldn't remember where he had heard it before. He concentrated to sift through all the noises around him. There were several police and news helicopters circling the building, making it difficult to distinguish the sound.

Finally he was able to hear the sound more clearly, and it hit him. It was the sound of the three helicopters from the cabin. Only this time he could make out five distinct sounds. Alarmed, he looked up just in time to see a missile hit one of the police helicopters overhead. A loud explosion filled the sky as burning debris fell down upon the crowds below.

Panic struck. All screamed and ran for cover. The debris from the helicopter came crashing down on top of a fire truck. Immediately the two vehicles exploded, sending fiery shards of metal in every direction. Utter chaos ensued as police and firemen scrambled to move the crowds back. Medical personnel rushed to take care of the injured, while Marcus and his siblings were forgotten momentarily.

Marcus watched missiles flying overhead. The night lit up like fireworks as several more helicopters exploded in the sky. Burning debris rained down in every direction. They were now in the middle of a war zone.

Running over to Sampson, Marcus yelled, "We need to get to the roof! Helicopters are coming and they are probably going to escape if we don't get up there."

Sampson methodically scratched his chin, as he always did when thinking.

After a few seconds Marcus impatiently yelled, "Come on already!"

Without even flinching at his rudeness, Sampson asked, "How fast can you run?"

"How is that important?" he replied out of frustration.

"Little brother," Sampson began saying slowly, "it is very important. This building has thirty floors, given the width of this street, not to mention the velocity of the wind at such heights, all come into consideration. I will need you to be able to run at least forty-seven miles per hour or faster in order to get you to the roof. That is, of course, if you are capable of doing what I believe you are."

Marcus looked at Sampson. "I think I know what you're getting at, and I'm not sure how fast I can run. I don't know if I can go forty-seven."

"Well, like you said to Zack, you must."

Resigned to the fact that Sampson was right, Marcus tried to find enough room to run. Sampson ran toward the building, dodging falling debris. The only break they had gotten was the fact the crowds had backed away. Marcus was able to get a fairly clear path to run to Sampson. He waited for his brother to give him the go ahead. Sampson finally nodded to Marcus, who was several yards away in the middle of the street.

Marcus didn't hesitate as he started his sprint. He gained momentum and thought he might actually get to the speed Sampson was asking. A piece of propeller fell out of the sky and landed in his path. Marcus adjusted and ran around the piece of metal, but it slowed him down slightly. He needed to gain speed and fast if he was going to make it through this idea of Sampson's alive. With all that he had in him, Marcus accelerated toward Sampson.

Just as he was about to collide into his brother he placed his right foot into his brother's large hands and was catapulted up the side of the building. Marcus used the momentum to leap off of the building back toward the other side of the street. He bounded upward between the two buildings as he climbed higher and higher. He began to lose momentum just as he made his last leap. He feared it wasn't enough as he reached out to grab the edge of the roof.

Desperately his hand dug into the roof ledge. He had barely made it. Marcus glanced down as he dangled by his one hand. He pulled himself up over the roof edge and onto the tarred surface. He took a deep breath as he thanked God for giving him the strength to make it. Marcus leapt to his feet and began to cross the roof. There was an entranceway that sat in the middle, which made it easy for Marcus to hide behind. On the far side of the roof was the landing pad, and a helicopter had already landed, along with trouble.

Agent Allen and four guards, dressed like the ones from the cabin, stood watch by the helicopter with rifles in hand. A light went off in Marcus's head: Allen wasn't on their side. It didn't matter now, because he knew on his best day he couldn't take on that many men with bullets. They were too far away. They would see him coming way before he could ever lay a finger on one of them.

Just then he could see two more guards walking toward the helicopter with Mama and Uncle Leigh in front of them. Following behind them was a man in a business suit carrying a silver metal case. Marcus had never seen him before, but he guessed it was probably Dr. Scharf. He had heard the FBI agent call him Tibon, but whatever his name was, Marcus knew he was the one in charge. Finally an idea came to him, but he needed to be quick.

Nick found the stairs to the roof and the three of them made their way upward. He stopped and motioned for them to be quiet. Several figures were just in front of them and walking through the door to the roof.

"Someone just went onto the roof," he informed them and then motioned them to come forward. Slowly he pulled open the door. He could see Janet and Leigh being escorted by two guards and a man bringing up the rear. Probably Tibon. Nick knew they didn't have time to think of a strategy, so he moved instinctively.

Before anyone could react Nick was able to place the point of his rifle the base of Tibon's head.

All of the guards pointed their rifles at Nick as he yelled out, "Drop your weapons! Now, or he dies!"

Allen shot back, "You're not going to shoot him! Drop your rifle, and perhaps you'll live through this, Nick!"

"That's not going to happen, Allen! Tell your boys to drop their guns, or I swear I'll blow his head off!"

Allen grabbed Janet from one of the guards and put his pistol to her head. She cried as he yelled out, "Nick, you'll drop your weapon, or I'll end her right now!"

This wasn't going the way he had hoped. Nick didn't want to get anyone killed. He hurried to run through his options. Something behind Allen caught his eye and interrupted his train of thought. Marcus's head peeping over the roof's edge. Nick jerked Tibon's head upward in hopes that he didn't see the boy. Thankfully, everyone else had their eyes on Nick and didn't see him.

Now, kid, ran through his head as he hoped Marcus understood what was at stake. The noise from the helicopter would mask any noise the kid would make, giving him perfect cover. As if Marcus had read his mind, he leapt from the roof ledge behind Allen and the guards. Marcus grabbed two of the guards simultaneously by their collars and threw them off the roof, while at the same time grabbing one of their rifles.

Nick was impressed at the speed and agility Marcus had. Within a fraction of the time it would have taken him, Marcus had the rifle pointed between Allen's shoulder blades. The other two guards in black turned abruptly on Marcus but didn't do anything.

"Drop the gun from my mother's head now!" Marcus demanded. "All of you drop your guns and release my family!"

That a boy.

"Drop your weapons!" Allen ordered and released Janet.

"Mama, Uncle Leigh, go stand by Agent Nick," Marcus directed.

Nick now had the entire family, minus Angie and Sampson, with him. Zack and Anna hugged Janet and Leigh as Nick kicked Tibon in the back of the shin, sending him to his knees.

"Zack, toss those rifles to the street below."

Zack did as Nick asked. There was something unnerving about

Tibon not saying a word through the whole ordeal. Nick kicked the case out of Tibon's hands. He didn't know what was in the case, but better safe than foolish. Nick caught Tibon looking up at Allen, but it was too late.

Allen had caught the message and turned on Marcus with surprising speed. Marcus had been looking at Nick when Allen knocked the rifle out of his hands. The two guards closest to him joined Allen as they attacked Marcus. All three men threw punches and sidekicks at him as he moved away. The guards were exceptionally quick. It was clear to Nick that these guards were anything but ordinary.

At the same time Allen made his move, so did Tibon. Before Nick could react he was flipped over. Tibon leapt to his feet with the rifle that had been in Nick's hands only moments before. He pointed the gun at Nick. Zack shot a burst of electricity that broke the gun. Two of the guards immediately tackled Zack.

With surprising speed Tibon grabbed the metal case and headed for the helicopter. Before Nick could get to his feet, Leigh grabbed Tibon. Tibon pushed him aside effortlessly. Nick watched as Tibon jumped into the helicopter, only to be met by Allen, who had broken off the fight with Marcus. Allen swung, Nick ducked. Nick kicked Allen in the stomach, followed by a hard fist to the back of his neck. Allen fell to his knees. Nick kicked his old partner across the face. Allen lay unconscious.

Nick ran over to Zack, who was still struggling with the two guards on the ground. With a grab to one of the guard's jackets, Nick lifted the man to his feet and ushered him over the edge of the roof. Now that both of his hands were free, Zack punched the other guard in the throat. He kicked the gasping man off of him. Nick pointed over to Marcus. Zack was on it. He let out two bursts of energy at Marcus's attackers.

Both men fell down and Nick could see a disappointment in Marcus's expression.

"I would of had them." Marcus complained.

The two brothers smiled at each other as the family grouped together. They all watched as Tibon's helicopter pulled away from the building.

"Zack, can you hit them?" Nick asked.

Zack let out another blast of energy and just missed the helicopter. Again he tried, but the farther Tibon got away, the harder it was to aim.

From within the helicopter Tibon flung open the case he was holding. Inside was a transmitter to activate the pumps. He flipped the switches as he picked up a headset sitting on the seat next to him.

He spoke into the microphone. "Do we have a confirmation of the dispersal?"

A voice replied, "Nothing yet, sir."

Again he flipped the switches in the case.

He asked again, "Do we have confirmation?"

"Negative, sir."

Tibon screamed out of frustration, then said, "Empty your missiles into the building."

"Affirmative," came the reply.

He looked down into the case where the five vials of blood had been placed inside of the foam casing. At least he had what he would need to start over. They were all going to pay.

The family looked on in horror as one of the helicopters fired missiles at them. Zack hurried to the edge of the roof. The boy began to glow. Nick could feel the hairs on his arms and neck tingle from the electricity in the air. Making a jerking motion with his hands, Zack started releasing several blasts of energy from his hands. Explosions bombarded the night as Zack hit his targets. Nick was amazed at how accurate he was. The helicopter that Tibon was in fired more missiles toward the building. It would only take one—miss. It came. One of the missiles made it past Zack's defenses.

"Get down," Nick yelled. Everyone fell to the roof top.

The hissing through the night air grew louder until it reached its crescendo. A deafening explosion rocked the building. The roof shook underneath everyone, and smoke billowed up from the side of the building.

"Move! Now! Everyone get up *now!*" The urgency in Nick's voice got everyone moving. "Inside! We need to get out of this building and fast!"

Marcus helped everyone up to their feet and toward the door. Nick looked around the rooftop for Allen, but he was gone. He didn't have time to look for his old partner and cursed under his breath. The family made their way to where the elevator was. Nick knew they didn't have time to take the stairs. Marcus pushed the button frantically. When the door opened, all exhaled in relief.

Sampson watched as his brother bounded up the side of the buildings. He let out a large sigh when Marcus had made it to the roof. Enough time had been wasted standing around waiting for someone else to rescue his family.

He walked over to Angie, who had been watching from a distance, and said, "Are you ready, little sis?"

Angie smiled at her brother. "I'm ready for anything. What do you got in mind?"

"Getting our family," he replied.

Clapping her hands, Angie said, "Oh goodie! Lead the way, big boy."

"Stay here a minute."

He made his way through the debris toward the wrecking crane. The FBI hadn't had a chance yet to use it because of the attack. Sampson reached up to the arm of the crane and tipped over the vehicle so he could reach the large wrecking ball. With one jerk from his left hand the chain snapped and Sampson began tugging the ball toward the middle of the street. After he planted his feet, Sampson lifted the ball and slowly spun it over his head. Gradually the spinning became faster and faster until finally Sampson released the ball straight at the building.

The impact created a loud thunderous explosion, causing bricks and metal to fill the air. When everything settled there was a large hole in the side of the building, more than big enough for him to step through. Angie followed Sampson into the building. The hole opened into one of the loading docks, and Sampson quickly pointed to a ventilation shaft overhead.

Angie put out her arms as if to say, "Carry me."

Sampson pulled the vent face off and lifted his little sister to the opening. She kissed him on the cheek then jumped up into the vent and disappeared. Sampson knew he couldn't be as tactful with his approach and found the nearest doorway inside. All of them were locked. He hunched over and put his shoulder into the door. They easily broke open and revealed several workers standing inside.

"Everyone outside!"

They all began to run past him in fear for their lives. Sampson guessed there had to be a good hundred or so as they ran out of the building. He could see outside that the police were escorting the people out of harm's way. Once there was room, Sampson began moving into the hallway. He purposefully went to the other side of the building so as to not hurt Angie. The ceiling was right at his head, and Sampson was often forced to duck down to avoid hitting signs or lights. He found one of the stairwells, but as he examined it, he realized it would be a tight fit for him to make his way up through the building with any speed. No, he needed to move—and move quickly.

He hunched down as far as he could, and then leapt up through the ceiling. Plaster and metal fell all around him as he crawled to the next floor. Again he punched through the ceiling with a powerful leap and continued his way up each floor, calling out for his family. He was interrupted as a deafening explosion knocked him backwards off his feet. At the end of the hall he could see a large fiery hole in the side of the building. With renewed purpose Sampson began making his way up through the floors as smoke filled the halls.

Marcus watched the numbers go down on the elevator floor display. It seemed like an eternity, and he was growing impatient. The smell of smoke made its way through the ventilation of the elevator and grew stronger with each passing floor. Without warning the elevator shook as another explosion rocked the building. Anna and Janet let out short screams of panic as they fought to keep their balance. It sounded different then the missile did earlier, but it still couldn't be good.

Another explosion went off, and the elevator stopped abruptly as everyone grabbed each other trying to stay on their feet. The floor display had gone blank and Marcus began to push every button he could see. Nothing was working. They were stuck.

Anna panicked. "What're we going to do?"

Nick tried to reassure everyone, saying, "We're going to be fine. We can get out the ceiling door. Marcus or Zack, can you reach up and pop it open?"

Marcus put out his hands to boost Zack up. Zack propped open the door and made his way to the top of the elevator. Smoke had filled the elevator shaft and was making it more difficult to breathe. Marcus jumped up through the hole and landed next to Zack.

He asked, "Can you give us some light?"

Zack obliged as his skin began to glow and lit up the shaft. Marcus used his sight to see if he could find the nearest door. He could see the doorway above them and tried to find something to grab onto to get to it. As he attempted to climb up the shaft walls he noticed that everything was covered in grease. Marcus couldn't keep a grip on anything, and the wires were just as greasy as everything else. Another explosion went off inside the building, and the doorway that Marcus was trying to reach lit up briefly—it was on fire. Even if they could get to the elevator doors, it wouldn't do them any good now.

Nick called up to them. "Any luck?"

Zack replied, "Not yet. Looks like a fire has broken out in the building and is blocking our only exit."

There was a moment of silence before Marcus heard someone. He strained his ears to hear who it was.

"Mama! Uncle Leigh! Anyone!" Angie's voice rang out from above.

Marcus yelled, "Angie, we're in the elevator. Angie!"

Zack joined in as the two of them cried out together. After a couple minutes of trying, Marcus thought she hadn't heard them, but then a crack of light filled the shaft above. It came from a couple floors up. Angie's head popped through the opening.

"Stay right there! Don't go anywhere!"

Zack laughed as his sister's head disappeared out of view. Marcus fought off the desire to say something sarcastic, but Uncle Leigh had warned him to break that habit. A couple more seconds passed when Angie reappeared with a long rope. She dropped it down, but it only reached to the floor above.

Marcus called up to her, "That's not enough rope!"

She replied, "It'll have to do!"

He watched as his little sister dangled upside down on the rope with her foot wrapped around it. Slowly she lowed herself down to the end of the rope. They were amazed as Angie tied the end of the rope around her ankle then dropped upside down to reach for them.

"Marcus, you'll have to be the go-between and climb me."

"Get the rest of the family up here one at a time," Marcus ordered Zack.

With one strong leap, Marcus grabbed Angie's hands and dangled. He didn't know if his little sister could hold him and someone else, but they were about to find out.

Janet was the first one up as Zack lifted her to reach Marcus's foot. She grabbed on with all her strength as Marcus began to climb up Angie's body. He knew he was hurting her, but she didn't make a sound. Once they made it all the way to the top of the rope Marcus helped his mother through the open doorway. Again he climbed down and did the same with Anna.

Once Anna was safe Marcus climbed down again. As Zack began to help Leigh out of the elevator another explosion shook the building. Leigh fell back down inside the elevator with Nick as the snapping of wires filled the shaft. One of the wires that had been attached to the elevator came crashing down. Marcus grabbed the rope and pushed Angie out of the way just in time. Zack jumped down into the elevator as the cable crashed down where he had been standing.

The snapping of more cables forced Marcus to make a decision. It was the only option he had. Marcus climbed back up the rope and began pulling Angie. Janet began protesting, but he knew if he didn't get Angie out, she would be killed. Angie screamed in protest as he pulled her through the doorway just in time to see another one of the cables pass by her head.

Another crash could be heard below where the others were still trapped. Angie began beating on Marcus. She yelled, "Why'd you do that? They're still down there!"

He grabbed her firmly by the shoulders. "I made a choice! And it was the right one! We need to find another way to get to them."

The four of them gasped in horror as the last of the cables broke. The cries of three men filled the shaft as the elevator plummeted.

Janet cried out, "No! *God, no!*"

Marcus was just as shocked and upset as everyone else, but he knew they didn't have the time to grieve. He forced the three women to move as he prodded them down the hallway toward the stairs. They were on the tenth floor, and he hoped the fire hadn't spread to the stairway yet.

Sampson had made it to the sixth floor when an explosion rocked the ceiling above him. Tiles and lighting fell down as he continued his search for the family. The building was huge and finding them would require clear thinking. Sampson began to put himself in his family's place. If he was on the roof and the building began to explode, how would he try and make it out the fastest way? The elevators would be his first and best chance, if they were working.

He followed the signs to the elevators. When he finally found them, another explosion sent more of the ceiling falling down on him. With no time to waste Sampson put his shoulder into the doors of the elevator and broke the wall open. He nearly fell down the shaft as he grabbed the wall to steady himself. As he peered up the shaft he could see one of the elevators a couple floors up. It wasn't moving, but he could faintly hear voices coming from it.

He tried to call up, but no one responded. Angie's screams were all he needed to hear. Sampson was about to yell out again when the sound of something breaking interrupted him. Before he could say a word, the elevator plummeted directly toward him. Instinctively, Sampson kicked his foot through the other side of the shaft and braced himself underneath it.

The impact of the elevator was stronger than Sampson was prepared for. His feet began to slide down the sides of the shaft as he fought to stop his downward slide. The walls were slick, making it impossible for him to slow down. There was no time to think as panic overcame Sampson. With all his strength he pushed out with his feet, breaking through the shaft walls. He screamed in pain as the soles of his feet were being ripped off and only his bones made contact with the metal sides.

Slowly he came to a stop and the voices of the men inside could be heard. Sampson let it rest on his shoulders and he punched another hole into the shaft wall.

He yelled to whoever was inside the elevator to move away from the doors. Sampson took his pointing finger and punched a small hole in the floor. With a little work he was able to bend the metal open large enough for a normal-sized person to fit through. The first face he met was Zack's.

He said, "You have no idea how good it is to see you right now."

Sampson tried to smile at him, but the weight of the elevator was becoming a burden. He helped the three men climb down into his hand and through the hole in the shaft wall. Once they were all safe Sampson needed to get free himself. He lifted the elevator over his head and told the men to step far away from the hole. With all his strength Sampson pushed the elevator back up several floors. Before it began to fall again he pushed off one side of the shaft and crashed through the wall once more. He looked back just in time to see the elevator fly past where he had been only a second before.

All three men thanked Sampson as he lay in the hallway. He knew his feet were in bad shape, and the pain was almost unbearable.

Uncle Leigh asked, "Are you going to be able to walk? You're bleeding pretty bad."

"We do what we must," was all he could say.

A voice came from down the hallway. It was Marcus and the rest of the family.

They all came running and embraced each other as they cried from the shock of seeing them alive. Everyone joined together to help him get to his feet as he fought through the pain.

Marcus pointed down one of the hallways. "I think that's the exit."

Everyone ran down the hallway to find that he was right. The doors Sampson had broken earlier still hung on the hinges and several police and medical units were waiting outside. Sampson waited for everyone to get through the doors and make their way out the gaping hole in the side of the building. His family climbed over bricks and girders as some of the firemen spotted them and came to help. Marcus stayed with him as they took up the rear. Sampson appreciated his brother trying to help him walk. There wasn't much anyone could do for him, but the gesture was appreciated.

He and Marcus had almost made it through the outer hole when another explosion went off. Sampson looked up to see the ceiling of the loading dock begin to fall. He instinctively grabbed the large steel beam over his head, which was keeping everything from falling down upon them. It took every ounce of strength he had left to hold the beam up. He wasn't going to be able to hold it much longer, and Marcus still needed to get out of harm's reach.

Marcus began to scream for help, but Sampson yelled out, "Go!"

The pain in his brother's eyes broke Sampson's heart.

Marcus yelled at him, "I'm not leaving you! Help! Someone, get a crane or something! *Now!*"

Marcus was becoming hysterical and refused to leave. The rest of the family had stopped to look back at what the commotion was and Sampson knew there was no other option. Sampson watched as Mama began to run toward the building. He was thankful the police held her back.

Marcus tried to find some sort of metal poles, anything, to help support the beam long enough to give him enough time to get out of the way, but it was futile.

Marcus was in tears when Sampson said, "I can't hold this much longer! You need to go!"

A slight shift in the beam caused Sampson to slump down a little further.

Marcus looked up at his brother. "I love you. I can't leave you."

Sampson managed a slight smirk for his brother's sake. "I know. No

228

greater love, Brother. Now *go!*"

Marcus began running away from the building and grabbed the rest of the family. Sampson tried to hold up the beam as long as possible as he watched the family get farther and farther away.

Finally it was too much, and he let go.

Marcus watched as Sampson disappeared in a pile of steel and rubble. Mama, Angie, and Anna all let out screams of anguish as the police and firemen forced them to run away. Everyone sprinted as the sound of the building collapsing screamed at them from behind.

When they finally made it to a safe distance, everyone stopped to catch their breath. Marcus looked around to make sure everyone from the family had made it safely. Angie was crying in Zack's arms as they grieved the loss of Sampson together. Uncle Leigh and Anna stood over Mama as they tried to console her. Marcus watched as she knelt in the middle of the street, overcome with anguish. He had never seen Mama like this before. The pain and longing for her son made her impossible to console. Mama's voice cried out over and over for Sampson, knowing she would never be answered.

It was overwhelming for Marcus. He felt responsible for Sampson; he had always felt responsible for the family. He had failed them. Watching the pain he had caused by not saving his brother blanketed him like a dark shadow of guilt. If he had killed Tibon on the roof, none of them would be suffering like this. It was becoming too much for Marcus to bear. The compulsion to run started to rise.

At that moment Anna looked up with tear-filled eyes and locked glances with him. She shook her head as if she knew what he was thinking. "Don't do this to yourself, Marcus," she murmured. "Please don't leave us."

But it was too late. He heard her, but he didn't stop. Within seconds he was gone.

Thirty

Aftermath

The fresh air was a nice change from the stale rooms Nick had been forced to stay at over the last couple weeks. Spring was ending, and the warmth of summer was making its presence known. The sporadic clouds overhead made way to a strong breeze as he watched Anna try to keep her long auburn hair out of her eyes. It was the first chance for any of the family to see the light of day, and it was Nick's job to escort each of them through the courtyard. Guards surrounded the acre of land in every direction as snipers and gun turrets stood high overhead.

The government wasn't going to take any chances with the family, despite the fact they had saved millions of lives. Time was running out. Nick felt responsible for them being treated like terrorists and experimented on. He wasn't going to stand by silently.

"So, how have your dreams been lately?" he asked Anna casually.

While looking up in the sky she replied, "Not bad. I'm finding it a little easier each day, but it's difficult."

She exchanged a knowing glance with him. Once they reached the center of the yard he cautiously turned on a jamming device in his pocket.

"Act normal, and don't look at me directly. They're monitoring everything we say, and I only have a few minutes before they realize something's interfering with their microphones." Anna looked up once again into the sky and kept walking as if he hadn't said anything out of the ordinary. *Good girl.* She was following right along, like he thought she would.

"I'm sorry for what's going on here. I don't have a say in the matter. Just know I haven't told them about you."

"Why, thank you." Her eyes never left the tower on the north end of the yard.

"They haven't found Marcus yet…" He wasn't sure if he should tell her everything, but the guilt he was feeling demanded he give the girl some good news. "Before you make plans for your escape, you'll want to check out the secure medical facility down on level twelve first. I believe you may not want to leave him behind. You know who I'm talking about?"

A slight smirk curled at the side of her mouth, but her eyes never looked at him. "I know, but thank you again. Will you be joining us?"

He had already been contemplating this next question. His career and life with the FBI was over as far as he was concerned, but being a fugitive on the run didn't sound like a pleasant alternative, either.

"I'm not sure," he answered.

She turned and looked him in the eyes. With a big smile she said, "I am."

About the Author

DANIEL L. CARTER, born and raised in New York State, has always enjoyed Sci-Fi and Fantasy stories. Some of his favorite authors include Robert Aspirin and Stephen R. Donaldson.

Having acted in plays, such as *Diary of Anne Frank* and *Damn Yankees,* Daniel soon turned to writing skits and short plays, as well as directing. After studying at Elim Bible Institute and Hudson Valley Bible School, the desire to blend fantasy and faith drove him to begin a journey on finding a story that would do just that.

The Unwanted, Book One in *The Unwanted Trilogy,* opens up a new world of Science Fiction and Fantasy that will appeal to many ages. Daniel is currently working on Book Two, *Children of Anak.* He and his wife, Margo, reside in Western New York.

To email the author: **dlc@theunwantedtrilogy.com**

www.theunwantedtrilogy.com
www.oaktara.com

Breinigsville, PA USA
15 August 2010
243628BV00001B/4/P